THE VAMPIRE AND THE TATTOOIST

E. BROOM

THE VAMPIRE AND THE TATTOOIST

Gavin Stone is a mess after having killed an evil witch to save his wolf shifter friend, Ian. He desperately wants comfort from his as-yet unclaimed mate, Hunter Marsden, but Hunter has no idea Gavin is a vampire.

Hunter Marsden is a tattooist and head over heels in love with Gavin. But he's concerned. Whenever he goes out with Gavin, it seems someone is always following them. When a strange letter appears on his kitchen worktop threatening his life, Hunter has no idea what to do.

Pulled into a world he never knew existed; will Hunter survive?

With the help of Gavin's family of vampires, the local witches' coven, and the local wolf pack, can they keep both Gavin and Hunter safe while uncovering more of the secret underground network?

CHAPTER 1

*G*avin was sitting in his room crying. His brothers were there holding him. Bruno was laying on his legs, offering comfort. But what comfort could they bring? He had just killed someone and ripped their throat out. All he saw when he closed his eyes was the dead witch on the ground and blood *everywhere*.

Gavin had killed the man to stop him from murdering the wolf shifter Ian, but even so, that was the first person he'd ever killed, and he never wanted to do it again. Sure, he was a vampire and could be fierce when he needed to be, but killing someone wasn't something he'd ever thought he'd have to do.

There was a knock on the door, and before anyone could say anything, in walked the human female Annie, his coven leader's mate's mother who now lived with them. She'd adopted everyone when she moved in, and truth be told, everyone had fallen in love with her. Annie was carrying a plate of biscuits.

She waved Raz out of the way and sat on the side of Gavin's bed, putting the plate down beside them, and picked up his hand. "Now then, sweetie, I've made you your favourite biscuits. I know at the moment nothing can cheer you up, but biscuits always help. I also came to see if you wanted a hug. When Davy's upset, he always needs a hug."

Gavin nodded, took his hand back, and signed to her.

"I got some of that, but not the last bit. Something about being scared?" Annie said.

Gavin nodded.

"Mum, Gavin's asked if you're scared of him now," Dave said gently.

Annie looked shocked. "And why would I be scared of you, young man? You killed that nasty man to save a friend. I would have done the same thing if I'd been there. Oh, I don't mean ripping his throat out, as that's a bit messy, but I would have found something to stab him with."

Gavin gave her a strange look.

"Don't look at me like that. I would kill if I needed to. Sure, I'd be a mess afterwards, but to keep those I loved safe, I would kill a stone," Annie told him. "You, Gavin, are not a horrible person. You're one of the sweetest people I have ever met. If you need to cry, throw things, or hug everyone to start feeling better, then you do just that."

Gavin threw himself into her arms, his head resting on her chest as his shoulders started shaking again and he silently cried all over her.

Annie rocked backwards and forwards, rubbing his back and muttering nonsense words. She didn't hurry him, she didn't complain he was getting her wet, she just hugged him like a mother.

While Gavin was with Annie, Mathis stood up and moved away from the bed before he grabbed his phone and sent a message to Gabriel, his mate, checking on him. He wasn't expecting a reply straight back, but at least Gabe would know he was thinking about him.

"Father, Cairo, Troy, Kevin, and Ian are with Gabriel as he informs the coven what's been happening and takes his place as coven leader and head of the Southern Witches," David told him quietly, walking into the room.

Mathis smiled at him. "Thanks. I know I should be there, but..."

David touched his shoulder. "He knows. Do you really think he would want you there when Gavin needs you?"

"I know, but I still feel guilty."

"He understands," Dave assured him, coming to stand next to David.

Mathis knew that his mate would. Gabriel was the most accepting mate and loved Gavin like a brother. "I wonder if it would be worth ringing his tattooist and asking him to come round," Mathis pondered, thinking aloud.

Gavin must have heard him, as he pulled out of Annie's arms and started signing to him.

"Slow down, Gav. I'm missing some words."

"He said not to call Hunter. He can never know what Gavin's done. He'd be disgusted and want nothing more to do with him," Dave translated. "Hunter's not like that," Dave said to Gavin. "You don't need to tell him what happened, but you could tell him you're sad and let him try and cheer you up," Dave suggested.

Gavin shook his head no and signed again.

"I can't face him yet. I feel so guilty. Mathis, Raz, he wants to know if you're disappointed in him. He wants to know that you still love him," Dave translated.

Mathis moved back to the bed and sat down, pulling Gavin back into his arms and hugging him. Raz came over and hugged the both of them.

"We're not disappointed, Gav. We're so proud of you for protecting our friend. Of course, we still love you," Raz told him.

"Gavin, why would I be disappointed in you or stop loving you when I did much worse — and to our father? I thought you would fear me and never want to come near me again, but not even half an hour later, you were asleep in my arms, trusting me as you always had. Like Raz, I am so proud of you, baby brother. You defended your friend. Do I wish I had killed him instead of you? Yes, but only because I've killed before and you never have. But never think that any of us are disappointed in you."

Gavin hugged his brothers hard.

"Oh, I know! I've just had the best idea," Annie said, smiling at him. "Gavin, tonight, Thomaz and I will cook all of your favourite foods and have an 'I killed my first-person party.' How does that sound? It's against the law to be sad at your own party. I wonder if I have time to send Willard out for decorations. Lots of red, I think, for blood and some fake fangs." She patted his leg, ignoring his shocked look. "Leave it all to me, sweetie. This will be so much fun. My first kill party," she said while standing up. "Don't forget to eat your biscuits, sweetie." And with that, Annie was gone.

Everyone was still for a moment before Dave burst out laughing. "God, I love my mum."

"I still say humans are weird," Raz said, shaking his head. "Anyway, Gav, you can't be sad. Remember, you need to design a new game, Vampires versus Witches," Raz told him.

Gavin nodded, smiled, and signed.

"That will be so much fun. I like Sean and Kaydan and can't wait to work with them on it," Dave translated for them.

"I see strong bonds of friendships forming with a few of the other witches," David said.

"Me, too," Raz said. He picked up the plate of biscuits, holding them out to Gavin. "Want one?"

CHAPTER 2

*H*unter was sat in the studio's kitchen, drawing in his sketchbook. He had a few minutes to kill before his next appointment arrived and was thinking up designs for Gavin. He sighed. Gavin was the most perfect man he'd ever met. Okay, so their first meeting wasn't the best.

Hunter had found some art books to read at the local library and, like always, had sat on the floor by the stacks to read them. Gavin, also looking at the art books, hadn't seen his legs and tripped over them, falling to the floor. Hunter had been mortified, helped Gavin sit up, and then spoke to him. Gavin had signed his reply, but not understanding sign language, they'd chatted with Gavin writing messages on his phone.

They laughed and talked and looked at art books. The only slight blip was when he thought Gavin had a boyfriend, but it turned out the man looking for Gavin was his brother.

After he got home that evening, he'd jumped online and looked for sign language courses. He joined one, and every spare moment he had, he learned to sign. It wasn't as hard as he thought it would be. It was remembering to do the facial expressions, as well, that sometimes stumped him. Luckily, Gavin wasn't deaf, but Hunter still needed to learn them, as Gavin might still use them. It would also be beneficial to know sign language as it would help when he had deaf or mute clients.

But for now, he needed to start getting ready for his next client. This was just a consultation. He was talking to a young woman who lost her breasts due to cancer. She wanted a large tattoo over her chest and was coming in today to discuss ideas, designs, and placements.

He grabbed his work sketch pad and walked back to his room. He picked up his photo album and pencils and made sure everything was ready, then went out to the reception area to await her arrival.

"All ready?" Taha, his business partner and best friend, asked while smiling at him.

"Yep. How's your day looking?"

"Busy. I'm glad we opened this place."

"Me, too," Hunter replied.

He'd met Taha at college, and they'd bonded over their love of art and tattoos. It only made sense that once they finished college, they went travelling to hone their skills and then came back and opened their tattoo shop, calling it Area 51, as they were also both Syfy nerds. They'd been open for a good few years now and were just getting busier and busier.

"Shell is also slammed today. He's already with his first client," Taha told him. "Luke's out getting cakes."

Hunter frowned. "It's not his birthday today, is it?"

Taha laughed. "Nope, he declared today cake day."

"Nothing wrong with that. I hope he brings back something nice."

Taha looked shocked for a moment. "Dude, it's cake."

"It is, but no carrot cake or beetroot cake. Vegetables don't belong in a cake."

"Yeah, okay, I'll give you that one."

Just then, the door opened and the bell above it jingled, and a young man and woman walked in, the woman looking nervous. That gave them a hint of who she might be.

"Danni Sargent?" Hunter asked.

She gave a nervous smile. "Yes."

"Welcome to Area 51. I'm Hunter. Are you ready to come through, or do you need a minute?"

"No, I'm ready now. I don't know why I'm this nervous. I know we're just talking today."

"It's understandable to be nervous. Shall we go through, and we can talk?" Hunter asked.

Danni nodded. "Yes, please. Can my husband come with me?"

"He can," Hunter said, noting the relieved look on both their faces. He led them into his private room, closing the door behind them.

The room was nice and big. There was a table and chairs off to one side, a leather couch along one wall, and a side with a sink. In the middle of the room was his tattoo chair and station with his tattoo gun. There were no colours out as they weren't needed. He led them to the table, and they sat down. "Can I get either of you a drink?"

Danni shook her head. "Not for me, thanks."

"I'm good, thanks," her husband said.

"I'm Hunter Marsden," he says while holding his hand out.

"Mark Sargent," the husband said, shaking it.

Hunter pulls his sketchbook closer. "Shall we start?"

Danni nodded and took a breath. "As I told you on the phone, I've had both my breasts removed due to cancer three years ago."

"How are you doing now?" Hunter asked her gently.

Danni smiled. "I'm in remission, thank goodness. No more chemotherapy," she said, grabbing Mark's hand. "As you can imagine, it was a horrible time, but fingers crossed, that's over now." The smile fell from her face. "But now I'm left with a bare chest covered in scars. Which is actually depressing."

"Not to me. It's a sign that you survived," her husband said, looking at her. "But I can see how unhappy you are, which is why we're here."

"Do you know what you want done?" Hunter asked.

Danni shook her head. "No, I was hoping you could help with that."

"I can," Hunter said, pulling the photo album closer. He opens the album and turned it towards the Sargent's. "These are pictures of some of the tattoos I've done on other women." Hunter pointed to the first one. "This lady wanted me to tattoo a full breast on her with the 3D effect, so it looked like a real breast. This one, however," he said while pointing to another, "is a leaf design imitating the breast, and this one is completely different." It was a large butterfly design spanning the whole of the chest.

Danni was looking at the picture Hunter pointed out.

"There are more on the next page if you want to see them."

Danni shook her head. "I don't need to see anymore. I like this one." She pointed to the leaf design and then looked at Mark. "What do you think? You're the one who will be looking at them."

Mark smiled. "I love that design. If that's the kind you want, go for it."

Danni nodded. "Hunter, I would like something like this, but with different leaves. Is that possible?"

"It is," Hunter said, grabbing his pad and opening it on a

fresh page. He sketched for a few minutes and then turned it to show them.

"Oh," Danni said on a long breath. "Hunter, that's perfect."

"Okay, let me just transfer this onto some tracing paper and then I'll get you to take your top off and lie on the couch so I can check the placement and the size, and I can get it drawn up properly."

As Hunter transferred the design, Danni walked to the couch, took her top off, and laid down, with Mark standing beside her.

When he was ready, Hunter came over. "Right, let's check the sizing. Mark, do you want to grab the mirror off the side and hold it in front of Danni so she can see what the design looks like."

As Mark got the mirror, Hunter laid the design on Danni's chest, so it covered her scar and created an amazing curve.

"What do you think?" Hunter asked.

"It looks good. Mark?"

"It looks perfect."

"If I flip it over," Hunter said, turning the drawing and placing it on the other side, "this is what this side will look like."

"Doubly perfect," Danni said.

"Agreed."

"Good. What about the size? Do I need to make it bigger or smaller?"

"No, it's perfect just as it is," Danni told him. "That size covers the surgery scars."

Looking, Hunter saw some smaller burn scars from her treatment. "Do you want me to draw some leaves to cover up the burn scars?"

"Maybe something like fallen leaves," Danni suggested.

"I'll draw some designs and show them to you when we

start the main tattoo," Hunter told her. "Because of the scarring, some of the lines won't be perfect, but we can fix all that with shading."

Danni nodded. "I understand."

"You can put your top back on. While you're doing that, we can discuss colours. Do you want it to be coloured or monochrome?"

Danni looked at Mark. "You decide," he told his wife.

"Monochrome please."

"No problem. We can go and book your sessions in and get started. It's going to take a couple of sessions to do the tattoos. The outline itself will take roughly three to four hours. How are you with pain?"

"Not too bad, but I'm not sure how I'll cope for four hours."

"We can go as slow as you need and stop whenever you need breaks. Plus, I'll need to stop from time to time, as well," Hunter told her.

"Thanks," Danni said, standing up now fully dressed.

"How much will the tattoo cost?" Mark asked Hunter.

"Nothing."

Danni's mouth dropped open. "What?"

"Your tattoo is free," Hunter told them.

"I don't understand."

"I don't charge for tattoos to cover up cancer scars," Hunter told them with a smile.

"Can I hug you, then?" Danni asked, her eyes welling up.

Hunter laughed. "You can." He opened his arms and Danni walked into them.

"Thank you so much, Hunter."

"You're welcome. Now let's go and book in your sessions, shall we?"

Hunter smiled as he watched the Sargent's leave. They still couldn't believe Hunter wasn't charging them. But as

THE VAMPIRE AND THE TATTOOIST

Hunter said, he never charged cancer sufferers. In his opinion, they'd been through enough and deserved a break. If he could bring just one bit of joy back to their lives, and make them feel just a little better, then that was all the payment he needed.

He grabbed his phone, frowning when he didn't see a message from Gavin. True, the man could get lost in his work, but he still managed to text Hunter at least a couple of times a day. He shot a message off to him.

Hey Gav. Hope you're having a good day. I feel like Italian tonight, want to come?

It had taken him a while to coax Gavin out. Gavin readily admitted that he was pretty much a hermit, so Hunter was making it his mission to take him out. He thought once or twice that he caught someone following Gavin, but he couldn't be sure. *I mean, why would someone be following him?*

Looking at the reception desk, Hunter saw the box of cakes. Opening it, he smiled when he saw a lemon muffin. He snagged it before anyone else could and walked off to the kitchen to make himself a drink and hope that Gavin messaged him back.

CHAPTER 3

*E*veryone was still in Gavin's room when his phone pinged with a message. Gavin knew straight away it was Hunter. Everyone else who would have texted him was already with him.

Raz smiled at him and nudged his shoulder. "Is that your man texting you?"

Gavin sighed and everyone laughed.

"He is so your man and you know it," Dave replied. "What does he want?"

Gavin pulled a face at him and signed.

"I fully admit I'm nosey. Now open your message and see what he wants," Dave said happily.

Gavin shrugged, but a smile was tugging at his lips. He grabbed his phone and opened the message. He read it, his eyes filling with tears again.

"What? What's wrong?" Mathis asked, practically snatching the phone out of Gavin's hand and looking at the message, ready to run over there and punch the guy in the face if needed.

"What did he say?" David asked, growling.

Mathis looked up. "He invited Gav to dinner at the local Italian restaurant."

"If you don't like Italian, Hunter won't mind you changing restaurants," Dave told him.

Gavin wiped his eyes and then signed.

"You're seriously throwing over dinner with Hunter for the party my mum is organising for you?" Dave asked in shock.

Gavin nodded and signed.

"We understand, Gav. If you need to be surrounded by family today, then that's what we'll do," Mathis said. "Maybe tell him you're not feeling so good, and you'd take a rain check on the date."

Gavin bit his lip and then nodded. If he said he wasn't feeling well, then that should give him a couple of days before Hunter asked him again.

He held his hand out for his phone and shot a message off to Hunter.

That sounds nice, but I'm not feeling well today. Can we rain-check until I feel better?

Once sent, he set his phone down and looked at Mathis before signing.

"Gabriel understands. He knows you need me," Mathis replied.

Gavin signed again.

"I'm not leaving. You need me."

Gavin rolled his eyes and signed again.

Mathis shook his head. "I didn't understand all of that."

"Gavin said that Gabriel needs your support, as well. He's just announced he is the coven leader and leader of the southern witches. He'll want you there. I really don't mind," Dave translated for him.

"You could always go for a little bit, then come back for the party," Raz suggested.

Gavin nodded.

"Okay, let me go and message him, but I'll be back for your party," Mathis said, pulling Gavin into a hug.

Gavin patted his back and let Mathis go.

Mathis looked at Raz, who nodded. He knew what Mathis was asking: look after our brother and call if you need me.

Mathis looked at David, who nodded, as well.

"Thanks," he said to everyone, then walked out, closing the door behind him. He pulled his phone out as he went and rang Gabe, who picked up on the first ring.

"Hey, Vampie," Gabe said. "How's Gavin?"

"Sad but coping. Annie's throwing him a 'I killed my first person' party tonight. She's sent Willard out to get red balloons and fake fangs, and she and Thomaz are cooking all his favourite foods."

Gabe laughed. "Gotta love Annie."

"Yep. Open a portal, little witch."

Gabe gasped. "No, you need to be there for Gavin."

Mathis smiled. "I have been, and now I've been kicked out so I can spend time with you. Open a portal, little witch."

A moment later a portal opened, and Mathis saw Gabe there smiling at him.

Mathis hung up the phone and walked through it towards him. As soon as he was close enough, he pulled Gabe into his arms and kissed him, the portal closing behind him.

HUNTER CHECKED his phone and smiled when he saw he had a reply from Gavin. He opened the message, and his smile dropped off his face when he read it. Poor Gavin. He wondered what he could do. Chicken soup was supposed to be good when one was feeling rough. He should find a takeaway that delivered and send him some. Yes, he would do that. He went online and found a local restaurant that did chicken soup and delivery.

Hunter shook his head. He didn't have Gavin's address. He couldn't ask Gavin for it, as that would spoil the surprise. Maybe Dave would know where Gavin lived. Well, he could hope, anyway.

He sent Dave a message. Now all he had to do was hope Dave knew.

DAVE AND GAVIN were playing with Bruno when Dave's phone dinged. He pulled his phone out to read his message, smiling when he saw who it was from. He opened the message and read.

Hey, Dave. Do you have Gavin's address? He's feeling under the weather, and I want to send him some chicken soup to help him get better.

Dave grinned and shot back a message with the address, saying how nice that was of him. He put his phone away, still grinning.

Gavin looked at him and then signed.

Dave laughed. "I'm not being weird. I'm just happy."

"You're always weird," Raz said helpfully from his seat.

"I still prefer unique," Dave replied.

Bruno barked.

"Thank you, Bruno. Nice to see you agree with me."

Raz just laughed and shook his head.

CHAPTER 4

*H*unter smiled as he hit the order button. *Done.* Now all he had to do was wait for the soup to be delivered. He didn't like the thought of Gavin not feeling well. He wanted to go and check on him, and he would, just maybe not today.

He was pulled from his thoughts when Shell popped his head round the door. "Matt's here."

Hunter smiled and got up. "Thanks, Shell."

He walked into the reception area and saw Matt, a long-time friend and client. "Back again?" he said as they gave each other bro hugs.

"You know it," Matt said, grinning.

"Come on through. I've got everything ready for you," Hunter said, leading him into his room.

As Matt entered, he pulled off his t-shirt and sat down on the tattooing chair. Matt noticed that the picture he'd sent over was sitting next to the ink colours and tattooing machine.

Hunter washed his hands, then pulled on a pair of blue gloves before sitting on his stool next to Matt. "So, just checking, you still want this design and for me to freehand it?"

"Yep, perfect," Matt said.

"How's the family?" Hunter asked as he wiped over Matt's skin with an antibacterial wipe.

Matt sighed happily. "The family is great. Jay and Abby are expecting twins. They announced it at dinner last night."

"Congratulations, I'll send them something," Hunter said, grabbing his machine and dipping it in the black ink.

"The whole family is over the moon. It's been hard for them. They had their hopes dashed so many times that this was the last time they were going to try IVF. The toll it was taking on them was horrible. They waited to tell us until Abby was four months along, but she's started showing already."

Hunter grinned and briefly looked up. "I see a lot of spoiling for Jay and Abby."

Matt laughed. "And the twins once they're born. I might even get their names tattooed on me."

Hunter looked at him for a moment. "We could do a nice design, but won't that be weird having your nieces' or nephews' names on you?"

Matt looked thoughtful, something which Hunter was glad about. He went back to inking up Matt's skin and let him think about it while the machine gently buzzed.

"You might be right. I'll wait and see," Matt paused before saying, "Mum said she saw you out at dinner with a cute guy the other day, her words, not mine."

Hunter felt himself smile. "Gavin. It's early days, but I have high hopes that we can build something amazing together."

Hunter had known Matt and his family since play school, and even though they went in different directions after school, they remained good friends.

"That's great, Hunter. You need someone special in your life. Tell me about him."

So as Hunter worked, he told Matt all about Gavin, about how they met, what he did, and how amazing he thought Gavin was.

"So you're learning sign language so he doesn't need to write everything out all the time?"

Hunter nodded. "Yeah, plus it will help if we ever get any deaf or mute customers in."

"You'll have to send me some links so I can learn, as well."

Hunter looked at him in surprise.

"What? When I meet him, I want to know what he's saying."

"I'll bring him to the bar soon so you can meet him," Hunter promised.

Just then, Hunter's phone pinged.

"Do you need to get that?" Matt asked.

Hunter shook his head. "Nope, that should just be a notification of a delivery to Gavin. I messaged him earlier asking if he fancied Italian tonight, but he's not feeling great, so I sent him some chicken soup."

"You old romantic, you. I hope your Gavin feels better soon."

"Me, too."

CHAPTER 5

Annie, Thomaz, and Willard had been busy. Willard had brought all the red balloons he could find, as well as red streamers, and had made the sign that he and Stefan were just hanging up.

"I don't think I had a 'I killed my first-person party,'" Stefan said, looking around the ballroom at all the decorations.

"I bet you weren't as upset as Gavin though, were you?"

Stefan shook his head. "No, the first person I killed was attacking a woman and her daughter. I felt no remorse for killing him. If I remember rightly, I went home, changed, and then went to the local tavern with my friends."

"So you did have a party then," Willard points out.

Stefan laughed. "You're right, I did. Did you ever imagine, even in your wildest dreams, you'd ever be throwing this type of party for a vampire?"

Willard laughed. "I can honestly say it never even crossed my mind. But then, neither did staying in a vampire coven."

"Don't you mean living?"

Willard sighed. "I know we joke with Davy about leaving,

but this is his home. He can't be wanting his parents living with him. The same as I'm sure at some point you'll need to go back to the palace."

"Between you and me, it's much more fun here. Seeing how happy David and your Dave are, and Giovanni and Seth, and all the events that have happened since we arrived… yeah, much more fun than a boring palace."

"I vote we stay here then until the boys kick us out," Willard said with a massive grin.

"I think that would be wise; otherwise, can you imagine what Annie or Louise would do if we even suggested leaving?"

"Especially if it's before they've been and played with the wolf cubs," Willard said. "I might even go with them."

"I might, as well. I think it's time I met the wolf king."

"How come you've never met him before?" Willard asked curiously while taking a step back and looking at the banner to make sure it was straight.

"Until your Dave came along, different paranormal groups didn't really mix. Our sons have done a lot in changing that."

"Our boys are smart cookies," Willard said, grinning.

"They really are."

The front doorbell rang.

"I'll get it," David shouted out as he was walking down the stairs.

He opened the door and was shocked to see a food courier standing there.

"Hi, I have a delivery for Gavin Stone," the smiling driver said. "It's all been paid for," he said, handing the bag over to David.

"Oh, thank you," David said, taking the bag and shutting the door. He was halfway up the stairs when he realised he should probably have tipped the driver. Oh well, it was too late now. The smells coming from the bag were amazing, and he wondered who had sent food to Gavin.

He knocked on Gavin's door and walked in, laughing when he saw Dave and Gavin playing catch with Bruno.

"Gavin, you have a delivery," David said, holding out the bag to him.

Gavin jumped up and took the bag, looking inside with confusion written on his face. He plopped down on his bed and pulled out the container and a spoon. He looked for a note, but there wasn't one. He looked at the others.

"Okay, so there's obviously no note in that bag. Hunter messaged me earlier, concerned that you weren't feeling well, so he ordered you some chicken soup," Dave told him. "He hoped that the chicken soup would make you feel better."

"Damn, I'm going to have to like the guy now," Raz said begrudgingly.

Gavin smiled and nodded, opening the container and sniffing before crossing his legs on the bed and eating the soup.

Dave looked at Raz. "I told you Hunter was a decent person. He'll treat Gavin right."

"I guess," Raz grumped out.

Gavin happily ignored them, eating the hot chicken soup that tasted amazing and was so thoughtful. He knew he wasn't sick, but the soup was making him feel better, anyway.

CHAPTER 6

Mathis was sitting in what was now Gabriel's office. Kaydan, Sean, Kevin, Ian, Cairo, and Troy were with them, Stefan having left earlier.

"How did the coven take the news?" Mathis asked him.

"There were a few disgruntled looks, but on the whole, everyone was shocked at first and then fine with us looking into them," he paused. "I've sealed Leonard's room, plus Kay's room is sealed, as are the lemming's, so only I can get in there at the moment."

"What do you want us to do?" Ian asked.

"Nothing for tonight. We should all go to Gavin's party. He needs all the friends he can get at the moment."

"Are you sure, little witch?" Mathis asked him. "Will you not be needed here?"

"I really don't care. Gavin needs us. The coven can do without me for one night."

"And us," Kaydan said. "Gavin's our friend, as well."

"Plus, we've never been to a kill party before. This will be fun," Sean said, grinning.

"In that case, let's all head back to the coven now," Gabriel said, standing up.

"Can you send us to our cars first?" Kevin asked.

Gabriel nodded and swirled his hand, opening a portal.

"See you all soon," Ian said, walking through the portal, Kevin, Cairo, and Troy following behind him. Once they were all through, Gabriel closed the portal before opening a new one to the vampire coven.

The four of them walked through and came out in the vampires' kitchen.

"It smells amazing in here," Kayden said, taking a sniff.

"Hot sausage rolls just out of the oven. You can have one each, but *only one*," Annie told them. "The rest are for the party."

"Thanks, Annie," Sean said, grabbing two and handing one to Kayden before Gabriel and Mathis took one each.

Annie wiped her hands and rushed around the kitchen island, pulling Gabriel into a hug. "Are you alright?"

Gabriel hugged her back and smiled. "I am for the moment, but I'm surrounded by friends who will be helping me."

Annie pulled back. "That you are. I should be throwing you a party, as well as a congratulations."

Gabriel shook his head. "No, Gavin's need is greater than mine."

"Silly boy, we'll just have your celebration another day. Now Gavin is still in his room."

"Then we'll go and see him. Thanks, Annie," Kayden said.

The others thanked her, as well, before Mathis led them upstairs to his brother's room, munching on the sausage rolls as they went.

Mathis knocked on the door, and without waiting for a reply from anyone inside, opened the door and walked in, Gabriel, Sean, and Kayden following.

Gavin was just putting down his empty soup bowl when his brother and the others walked in. He jumped up and pulled Gabriel into a hug.

Gabriel hugged him back. "We've come for your kill party," he said as he pulled back, grinning.

Gavin gave a silent laugh before pulling Sean and Kayden into hugs.

He released them and then looked at Gabriel and started signing.

Gabriel gave a rude snort. "Gavin, you're my friend and my brother. You are much more important than my coven, and there is nowhere I would rather be than here with you tonight, helping you celebrate your first kill. And no, I never thought I would say anything like that or even attend a kill party."

Everyone laughed.

"Mum decided on the party to try and cheer Gav up. She sent Dad out for a lot of red decorations because, you're not allowed to cry at your own party," Dave told them, grinning.

"I love your mum. Do you think she'll adopt me for real?" Sean asked him.

"I don't see why not. I mean, she's adopted the vamps and Kevin and Ian. Pretty sure she's adopted Troy, as well," Dave replied.

"Why were you eating soup when Annie and Thomaz are downstairs cooking up a storm?" Mathis asked Gavin, changing the subject.

He was surprised when Gavin blushed.

"His tattooist sent him chicken soup, hoping it would make him feel better," Raz replied before Gavin could say anything.

"Damn, I'm going to have to like him now," Mathis said begrudgingly.

Raz laughed. "I said the same thing."

THE VAMPIRE AND THE TATTOOIST

Gavin got a sad look in his eyes and started signing.

"Gav, stop," Mathis said, gently stopping his hands from signing. "He's not too good for you. Stop that line of thinking right now."

"Yeah, Gavin, listen to your brother. We've only recently met, like, *very* recently, and neither me nor Sean thinks any differently of you now that you've killed someone," Kayden told him, touching his arm.

"He's right. You're our friend and nothing will change that. And your man, the man who sent you chicken soup to help you feel better, won't change his mind about you, either," Sean added.

Gavin sighed and leaned into Mathis.

"I know it will take time for you to come to terms with what happened, but all of us are here for you," a voice said from the doorway.

Everyone looked round and saw Ian and Kevin standing just inside the bedroom.

Kevin strode forward and pulled Gavin into his arms, hugging him. "You saved my best friend and second. I make this promise to you. I will help you with whatever I can to help you process what you went through or any situation you get into in the future."

Gavin hugged him back before signing his thanks. Just as he finished, Ian pulled him into a hug.

"I owe you a debt, so many debts. If you ever need my help, call me. I can't thank you enough for saving my life. Your quick thinking saved both of us and stopped an evil man. I don't think any less of you for having to kill someone to save my life. But, if we are ever in that situation again, let me kill the bad guy. I have a tough reputation to keep."

Kevin snorted. "Yeah, he's such a badarse he's ignoring calls from our king."

Ian turned to look at Kevin and scowled. "So are you. But

that's fine; the next time he calls I'll answer, and when he asks what's been going on, I'll tell him *everything*."

"Hey now, there's no need to do that," Kevin protested while the others laughed.

"It's only fair, babe," Creed said, walking into the room.

"Betrayed by my own mate and best friend," Kevin said, shaking his head sadly.

"There, there," Creed said, patting his arm. "Annie said to tell you everything is ready for the party and to come down when you want."

CHAPTER 7

*E*veryone left the room to go downstairs and wait for Gavin. He wasn't sure having a kill party was really the best thing to make him feel better, but knowing he'd hurt Annie's feelings if he didn't go, he walked to the mirror to make sure he looked presentable and to wipe off any tear tracks he had. He was more than thankful that vampires didn't cry tears of blood. That was just nasty. Sure, everyone knew he'd cried his eyes out, but no one needed to see the evidence.

He was just about to leave when he remembered that he hadn't thanked Hunter for the soup. He grabbed his phone and sent him a message.

Thank you for the soup. It tasted amazing and was really thoughtful.

He closed his messages and shoved his phone into his pocket, and with Bruno at his side, left the bedroom and walked downstairs to the ballroom.

The ballroom doors were open, and he saw everyone in there waiting for him. From what he could see, the room was decorated within an inch of its life with red balloons, red streamers, what looked like red teardrops cut out of cards, and a big banner.

He plastered on a smile and walked into the room. Everyone clapped when they saw him, and then David, Dave, Stefan, Louise, Gio, and Seth stepped forward.

"Gavin, we know that you've found it hard to deal with taking a life. You are the gentlest, sweetest person I think we all know," David said. "But we are thankful you were with Ian when the witch tried to kill him, and none of us think differently of you. To us, you are still the gentlest, sweetest person we know."

"We have all, in some way or another, celebrated our first kill. Indeed, it was Willard who pointed out to me that I went drinking with friends after my first kill, which was my celebration. But a party surrounded by friends and family is a much better alternative," Stefan said.

"But know we are all here for you, even if it's just to sit with you when the feelings get too much or to hold you when you need a cry. Whatever we can do to help you process, we will," Seth concluded.

Gavin gave a wobbly smile and signed, and Dave came forward and translated.

"Gavin says, 'Thank you for your support and for coming to my party and thank you for turning a horrible experience into a party everyone can share in. It's true that killing that horrible man was hard, but I would do it again if it meant saving a friend.'"

"Well said," Gabriel said, smiling at Gavin.

"Now that the talking part's over with, let's eat," Seth said, grinning madly.

"That's my darling, Seth, keeping it real," Gio said, laughing and grabbing his mate's hand, pulling him into his arms and kissing him.

"All right you two, break it up," David said to them, shaking his head.

Gavin walked around his family and friends, keeping a wide smile on his face even if he didn't feel it inside. He was touched that everyone had started learning sign language so they could understand him. He only needed his phone a few times when he used words that people didn't know. And no one was treating him any differently.

Escaping from the vampire he was talking to, he headed for Gabriel and his friends just as Mathis, Raz, and Thiago appeared carrying plates of food.

Gavin grinned when he saw Thiago and hugged him.

"Sorry I'm late," Thiago said to him.

Gavin shook his head and signed that he didn't mind, as this party was a spur-of-the-moment thing. Then he pinched a sausage roll off the plate, making them all laugh.

"Your family are all so welcoming and friendly," Sean said. "I honestly never thought I would see the day when vampires and witches became friends."

"Or witches, vampires, and wolves," Gabriel put in.

"Or demons," Mathis said, smiling at Thiago.

"Who's that man there?" Sean asked, pointing over to a group who were laughing and chatting. "He doesn't seem like a wolf, and he doesn't look like a vampire."

Mathis laughed. "That's Troy. He's a cat shifter."

"A house cat?" Kayden asked in surprise.

"Yep," Raz said with a loud laugh.

"I am *not* a house cat," Troy shouted over to them incredulously.

"Does anyone have a ball of wool?" David called out. "Looks like the kitty needs a bit of fun."

Gabriel held his hand out and a ball of wool appeared. "Here you go, kitty. Have fun," he said, throwing the ball at Troy.

"I hate you all so much," Troy muttered, catching it.

"Scared a ball of wool will fell you?" David asked, laughing.

Troy grinned. "Not in the slightest, old bean. Not like the little scratch that did, in fact, fell *you*. How long were you out for, vamp?"

Chuckles were heard around the room as the smile fell off David's face and he growled, much to Troy's amusement.

"No killing the kitty," Dave reminded him, patting his arm.

"I don't need to. I'm sure one of our new witch friends could do something unspeakable to him if I ask nicely."

"Well, would you look at the time? I'm sure there is something horrific going on at our coven that needs Gabe's attention," Sean said quickly.

Gabriel laughed, then sobered and sighed. "Yeah, there probably is. But it can wait until morning, and no, the kitty is safe from us witches."

Troy laughed. "Bad luck, old bean. Maybe tomorrow."

CHAPTER 8

*H*unter had finished working on Matt's tattoo, and after tidying and cleaning his room and not being able to spend the evening with Gavin, he joined Taha, Luke, and Shelby at Matt's bar.

Hunter loved coming here. No matter what day of the week one came, the place was always busy. The only food served here came in packets, and there was no dance floor. Instead, the back of the room had two pool tables and a dartboard.

There was the main bar area with tables scattered about and a jukebox. If you wanted somewhere quiet, there was a snug area with fewer tables and chairs that was always a lot quieter.

This evening, however, the friends were in the back at one of the pool tables.

"So how come you're not out with your mystery man tonight?" Taha asked him.

"Gavin isn't well today. I sent him some chicken soup to help him feel better, and anyway, he's not my mystery man. He'll be in the studio soon as I'm designing a tattoo for him."

"Taha mentioned that you met him at the library," Shell said before leaning over the table and taking his shot.

Hunter nodded, taking a drink from his bottle. "Yeah, I was sitting on the floor in the stacks as I do, and he was engrossed in looking at the books and didn't see my legs. He tripped over them and fell in front of me." Hunter smiled at the memory and shook his head. "My dream man literally tripped over my legs."

"And fell into your lap?" Luke asked, smiling.

Hunter laughed. "Not quite, but nearly. That's why I'm learning sign language, so I can understand him when he talks, and he doesn't have to write everything down."

"Is he deaf?" Taha asked.

"No," Hunter said with a shake of his head. "Mute."

"It would be worth us learning sign language, as well, so we can chat with your man and understand deaf or mute customers. I can't believe none of us had thought about that before," Shell said, sounding put out.

"I can send you the links to the place I'm learning from if you want," Hunter offered.

The friends all said yes, before Taha took his shot. He stood up and looked at Hunter. "But something's wrong. What is it?"

Hunter sighed. "I don't know. A few times when we've been out, I swear someone was following us."

"Why would anyone do that? What does your Gavin do for a living? Is it dangerous?" Taha asked.

Hunter shook his head. "No, he's a computer game designer."

"Is he good?" Luke asked.

"Really good. Two of his games are Vampire Academy and Atlantis Attack."

Shell's mouth fell open. "I love those games. Your man has some skill."

Hunter smiled. "He really does."

"But that still doesn't explain why anyone would be following him," Taha said. "Have you mentioned it to Gavin?"

"No," Hunter said. "The first time it happened I wasn't sure. But the second time, I didn't want to scare him."

"Are you sure they were following Gavin and not you?" Shell asked, leaning against the pool table and taking his shot.

"I've not felt someone watching me when I'm on my own, only when I'm out with Gavin. He told me he's pretty much a hermit, and it took me a while to coax him out for dinner and coffee shop dates, so I can't see that he would have made any enemies."

"How about someone in the gaming world jealous of his success?" Taha questioned.

"Would people stoop that low?" Luke asked.

"Stranger things have happened. Tell you what, when your man is better, invite him here. We'll let you walk with him, and we'll follow a few minutes behind to keep an eye on you both and see if someone is following him," Taha suggested.

"What if you find there is?" Hunter asked.

Taha smirked. "Then they'll find out what a martial arts expert can do."

Hunter laughed and held up his bottle. "Thanks."

"Game going well, then?" Matt asked laughingly as he carried over more drinks for them.

"Just putting the world to rights," Luke said, grabbing a new drink. "Thanks."

"Did Hunt tell you someone could be following his man?" Taha asked.

Matt glared at Hunter. "No, he seemed to have forgotten that part. What the hell, Hunt?"

"I don't know for sure. We've come up with a plan to see

if someone is following him. I'll bring him here and the guys will follow behind and see what happens."

Matt nodded. "Good. If he is being followed, we'll protect him. He might not know it yet, but he's got us now as his protectors."

"Operation Protect Hunter's Man is a go," Luke said, holding his bottle up. Everyone grabbed their drinks and clicked, sealing the pact.

∼

THE PARTY WENT on a long time; everyone was having fun, and no one wanted to leave. From somewhere unknown, Dave pulled out some party games: Twister, Connect 4, and giant Jenga.

"I would pay big money to see your father playing twister," Kevin said to David and Gio sometime later.

The brothers laughed.

"Me, too, but alas, I don't think that will ever happen," David said.

"Not like Seth, Dave, and Ian. Look at them," Gio said, grinning over at the players.

Seth, Dave, and Ian were cracking up as Dave was trying to reach the red with his right leg. He fell in the process and landed on top of Ian, who collapsed on top of Seth, the three of them laughing like loons.

"I think we should go and rescue our mates," David said, laughing while walking in their direction.

"Ian can rescue himself," Kevin said as he followed them.

David and Gio helped their mates up and taking pity on him, Kevin helped Ian.

"Why don't we have parties like this?" Ian asked Kevin.

"Because we don't have parties, you know, being fierce mercenaries and all," Kevin replied.

"Are you saying we're not fierce?" Seth asked him with a laugh.

"You are, but your Dave is keeping it real," Ian said.

"I really am," Dave said with a giant smile that turned into a yawn.

"And very tired," David pointed out.

Dave leant against him. "I really am. Do you think anyone would mind if I went off to bed?"

"Nope. I'm going to look for Creed and drag him off to bed," Kevin said grinning. "See you all tomorrow," And with that he walked off looking for his mate.

"I'm heading off, as well," Ian said. "See you at breakfast."

"Ian, if you want to bring anything to make the room you're staying in feel like yours, help yourself," David said to him.

Ian grinned. "Thanks, vamp. I might just do that." And with that, he walked off.

~

Gavin had slipped away from the party. Everyone was having fun and laughing, more so when Dave produced the games. Gavin tried to have fun, he really did, and he would lose himself in the party, but then remembered why they were having it in the first place and his happiness would fade.

Now he was sitting outside in the garden. Fairy lights were dotted around, giving a soft glow to the patio area. Gavin was sat in one of the patio chairs, his feet pulled up and his head resting on his knees. He looked towards the back of the garden where the woods were. But he didn't see the woods, all he saw was the dead witch.

He heard a noise behind him and wiped his eyes before looking up to find Sean and Kayden standing by the table.

Kayden was carrying a plate overloaded with biscuits, and Sean carried three drinks.

Gavin smiled at them and nodded to the chairs.

"Thanks," Kayden said, sitting down next to Gavin and putting the plate of biscuits down.

Sean passed out the drinks before sitting down on Gavin's other side and childishly leaning across Gavin to grab a biscuit.

Gavin gave a silent laugh and took a biscuit.

"You missed the fun. Dave, Seth, and Ian were playing twister and landed in a tangled heap, and David, Gio, and Kevin had to rescue them," Kayden said, laughing at the memory.

"Look," Sean said, grabbing his phone. "I took sneaky photos." He opened the pictures up and showed them to Gavin.

Gavin laughed silently before signing.

Kayden translated for Sean. "The coven house is so much more fun since Dave arrived and made friends with the wolves."

"I can understand that. Dave is awesome, and the wolves... I'm not sure what I expected them to be like, but fun-loving wasn't it." Sean sighed. "Truthfully, I'm glad Gabe made friends with them. We are so in over our heads with all the crap we found out. We knew Roberto and Kay were mad, but Elder Leonard was a surprise. I mean, how could we not know how evil he was?"

"Because he was good at hiding it," Gabe said, walking over to join them. "Can I join you?"

Gavin nodded and signed.

"I know I could have just sat down, but that would have been rude," he replied while sitting. "The party is winding down, and I couldn't find any biscuits."

Gavin pushed the plate closer to him before signing.

Gabe laughed and looked at Sean. "You took pictures?"

"Oh yeah, look," he said, passing his phone over.

Gabe burst out laughing. "If ever we need to blackmail one of them, we can use those." He looked at Sean and Kayden. "I'm staying here tonight. Do you want me to send you home?"

"No, Dave told us earlier we can crash in the same room we had last time. We can relax here and not worry about anything until we get home tomorrow," Kayden said.

"Plus, after breakfast tomorrow, we can talk Vampire versus Witches," Sean said, smiling at Gavin.

Gavin nodded and signed.

"Gavin said he can't wait to start it. He was bored with the one he was working on," Kayden translated.

"This one will be epic," Sean said, grinning, picking up his drink, and holding it out to clink it with the others.

CHAPTER 9

Hunter got home after closing time. He'd had fun with his friends but missed Gavin. He hadn't known the guy long but found he was already missing him when he wasn't around, which was strange as he'd never felt that way before in any of his previous relationships. There was just something special about Gavin.

Hunter shook his head. That was an understatement. Hunter was under no illusions that he wasn't completely in love with the guy. He knew it was late and Gavin might be sleeping, but he grabbed his phone and sent a message, not expecting a reply until morning, but knowing that he had to message to let Gavin know he was thinking about him and hoping he felt better.

He walked into his kitchen, flicked on the light switch, and headed to the sink to grab a drink when something on the counter caught his eye. He looked at it in confusion. Nothing had been there when he'd left that morning.

Hunter reached out and picked the piece of paper up and read what was on there.

THE VAMPIRE AND THE TATTOOIST

You will die for what he did. He killed the Master. We will kill you.

Hunter read the note twice, confused. What master and who killed him and why was someone now after him? Also, how had whoever wrote this got in?

He walked around the whole house to find all the doors and windows were locked, which added to his confusion. He wasn't sure he wanted to spend the night there without changing all his locks, so he grabbed his phone and called Taha.

"Hey, what's up?"

"Someone broke in, but I can't see how they did it. Can I come and crash at yours tonight until I get the locks changed?"

"You know it. Are the police on their way?"

"No, I'll explain everything when I get to yours," he said, shoving the note into his pocket. "Be there in a bit."

"I'll put the kettle on."

"Thanks," he said, hanging up and running to his room to throw some clothes and stuff into a bag before thumping down the stairs. He left the house, locking up behind him, and jumping into his car, drove the short distance to Taha's place. Hunter usually walked there as he only lived a street over, but with that weird note, he was taking no chances.

Moments later, he parked outside of Taha's and grabbed his bag, got out of the car, and walked to the front door. He didn't have to knock as Taha was standing in the doorway waiting for him.

"Come in and tell me everything. Coffee is on the table."

Hunter walked in and sighed, dropping his bag by the stairs. "Thanks for this."

"Always," he said, walking into the lounge. "Have a pew and tell me everything. You said your house was broken into, but you didn't call the police."

Hunter sat on the sofa and leant forward his arms on his knees. "It was strange. Nothing was taken as far as I could see, no doors, windows, or locks broken, but I found this on my kitchen worktop." He pulled out the paper and passed it to Taha.

Taha took the paper and read it. "What the *hell?* Any idea what this means?"

Hunter shook his head. "Not a clue."

"Hunt, maybe those men were following you and not Gavin."

"But why would they only follow me when I was with Gavin? And Gavin, I need to keep him safe. I'm suddenly glad that he's sick at the moment," he said, running his hands over his face. No matter what, he had to keep Gavin safe.

"Wait, before you start panicking, what if whoever left this message left it in the wrong house?"

Hunter looked up. "Fingers crossed."

"I'll protect you and Gavin," Taha promised. "Plus, I know a guy. If for some reason this is too much for me, I'll call him. He'll help."

"You sound sure of that."

"I completely am. I trust this guy. Plus, you know him: Troy Nettles. You've met him a time or two."

Hunter nodded. "Yeah, I remember him. Works away a lot and has a serious 'come near me and I'll kill you' vibe."

Taha laughed. "Yep, that's him. I might message him, anyway. If he's away, he'll need time to come back."

"What if this really is nothing, just the wrong house?"

"Then we'll know for sure. But Hunt, better safe than sorry."

"Yeah, okay, but wait until tomorrow to call him."

~

GAVIN WAS up in his room. The party had finally wound down and everyone had gone to bed. He was sitting in his chair, he didn't want to sleep, afraid that if he did, he would relive killing the witch.

He had always found the best way to deal with his issues was to write about them, getting all the emotions out and onto paper.

He grabbed a notebook and a pen, glancing at his phone as he got them. How had he not noticed he had a message from Hunter? He smiled to himself as he clicked it open.

Hope you're feeling better. Sleep well, and I'll message you tomorrow. I miss you! X

Gavin gave a small smile. He missed Hunter as well, so much. He wished Hunter knew he was a vampire and was here now, holding him, chasing his fears and nightmares away. But Gavin hadn't been strong enough to tell him. Too scared that Hunter would run away and want nothing more to do with him.

He clicked on the message and hit reply.

I miss you, too, Hunter, so much. Something horrible happened, and I really need you. Can you come?

But before he could send the message, he shook his head, closed the window, and put his phone down. He sat there thinking for a moment, and before he knew it, he'd fallen asleep.

He was standing in White Ladies as he watched Gabriel get hit in the chest with some kind of witch ball and go flying backwards. Faster than a human could track, Mathis killed Kay, sliced his head right off.

Being outside, the smell of blood wasn't that strong, but was there. He felt Ian latch onto his arm.

"Breathe through it, Gav," the wolf said to him, not letting go of his arm. "Don't let it control you."

Gavin took a breath, then another. He was just turning to look at Ian when he felt a disturbance in the air behind him, and before he could move to look, he was being pulled backwards.

He was shocked when he found himself in a room with Ian.

"What the hell?" Ian exclaimed, dropping Gavin's arm as the portal closed and a man stood there.

"This is just perfect," the man said with a laugh. "I got myself a wolf and a vampire."

"What do you want, and who the hell are you?" Ian demanded.

"I am Leonard Banning, and I am a witch, obviously."

Gavin gave a quiet snort. Another nutter from Gabriel's pack.

Leonard looked at him. "Well, vampire, do you have nothing to say?"

"Gavin doesn't talk," Ian said.

Leonard looked angry. "Then he is nothing," he said, dismissing him. He looked away and, quickly raising his wand, shot a witch ball at Ian.

Ian groaned and clutched his stomach.

"I'm now going to kill the two of you. Gabriel will, of course, be blamed, and his budding alliance with the vampires and wolves will fall apart as both sides try and kill him."

Quick as a flash, Ian shifted into his wolf, but Leonard shot another witch ball at him.

Gavin knew he had to do something and shifted into his vampire form and pounced on the witch.

Leonard was so startled that he dropped his wand and screamed, but Gavin didn't care. This witch was hurting his friend and causing his new brother problems, so going on instinct, he bit into Leonard's neck and ripped a chunk out.

Realising what he had done, Gavin dropped the body, staring in horror down at the bloody mess.

He felt his brothers and others come into the room before his knees gave out and he collapsed onto the floor. He felt his brothers rush to his side and hug him as he cried silent tears.

But suddenly, his brothers drew back, horrified looks on their faces. He looked up as they stood up and moved away.

Mathis looked down at him. "You're evil, Gavin. You've shamed the family. You are no longer our brother."

Suddenly, Hunter was standing there, a look of fear and revulsion on his face. "You are nothing *to me. How could I be mated to an evil creature like you?"*

Gavin silently cried out. It couldn't be true! his beloved brothers no longer wanted him, and Hunter thought he was evil. No, it couldn't be true.

He woke up, his mouth open in a silent scream, tears streaming down his face. It was a dream, only a dream. His brothers still loved him — indeed, the whole pack did — and Hunter still liked him for now. He brushed his hands over his face, wiping away his tears. He didn't want to be alone. He needed his brothers, but they had mates and would be busy with them, but he needed company. He got up from his chair and left his room, walking downstairs to the kitchen. He crept in so as not to wake Bruno and got himself a drink before going to sit next to Bruno's crate.

Bruno lifted his head and looked at him, so Gavin opened the crate and let Bruno out. Bruno walked over to him and licked his face before settling himself down on Gavin, falling asleep on his lap. Gavin stroked him until he fell into a dreamless sleep.

CHAPTER 10

Thomaz walked into the kitchen early the next morning, looking towards Bruno as he always did, where he saw Gavin asleep on the floor with Bruno lying over him. He walked over to them and knelt down. Bruno lifted his head and gazed at Thomaz. Thomaz rubbed his head. "You're a good boy. Are you looking after Gavin?"

Gavin came awake and saw Thomaz next to him. He moved and Bruno got off him, then Thomaz helped him sit up.

Gavin signed, "Thank you and sorry."

"There is nothing to be sorry for. Did you have bad dreams?"

Gavin nodded. "Mathis, Raz, and Hunter turned against me and called me evil."

"Spell the last word for me. I got everything else but not the last one," Thomaz said.

Gavin spelt, "E," "V," "I," "L."

"Oh, Gav, they'll never think that of you, and neither will your Hunter. Your dreams are just messing with you," he said, pulling the young vampire into his arms.

Gavin rested against Thomaz for a moment before pulling away and smiling at him.

"Okay, I need to let Bruno out and you need to go have a shower before your brothers realise you slept down here last night."

Gavin nodded and signed, "Thank you."

"Always, little brother. You know if you have another bad dream and your brothers are busy, come into my room and I'll sit with you. Hell, you can even sleep in my room if you need to. As much as Bruno is the best therapy, sleeping down here isn't very comfy."

Gavin signed, "Thank you," again and sent him a happy smile.

Thomaz helped him up and watched as he left the kitchen. The smile fell from Thomaz's face. He would need to talk to Mathis and Raz later and give them the head's up. Before that, though, he had to let Bruno out. He looked at the lovable lab. "You're a good boy, Bruno. I'm thinking this house needs more dogs, though. What do you think?"

Bruno smiled as only a dog could and barked his agreement, then happily walked out with Thomaz.

∽

HUNTER WOKE up the next morning, for a moment not knowing where he was until he remembered he was in Taha's spare room. He lay there thinking. How had someone broken into his house and not left a trace? Who had left the message? Was it really left in the wrong house? He had no answer to any of these questions.

He wasn't sure what he thought about Taha contacting his friend Troy, but if something was going on, he was sure Troy could find out what it was and how to stop it. Knowing he wouldn't get any answers lying in bed, he got up and grabbed his washing stuff from his bag, then walked into the en-suite to get ready for his day. Half an hour later, he stepped into the kitchen and smiled as he saw Taha standing by the cooker, making breakfast.

"Aw, honey, you cooked," Hunter said with a laugh.

Taha turned and smiled. "Yep, today is a proper breakfast day. The coffee pot is full, so pour two mugs and I'll plate all this up."

"You'll make a lovely wife one day, Ta," Hunter said while getting some mugs out and filling them up with the magic bean liquid.

"So will you, Hunt. When you marry your Gavin, are you wearing a white dress?"

Hunter laughed. "I am, a lovely, slinky white number with a massive split up the side, showing off a toned leg. And you, Ta, you'll be my Maid of Honour and will be wearing a deep purple puff ball of a dress."

Taha boomed out a laugh. "Can you imagine the look on your parents' faces if we both actually did that?"

Hunter laughed at the image. "Never mind my parents. Can you imagine what Gavin would do?"

"Even though I have yet to meet him, I imagine he would laugh his head off."

Hunter sighed. "Yeah, he really would." He sobered. "What am I going to do about Gavin and keeping him safe?"

Taha put down his spatula and grabbed the two plates, bringing them over to the island and putting one in front of Hunter. "There is nothing you can do for the moment except be careful and mindful of your surroundings. I'll contact Troy after breakfast and see how quickly he can come."

Hunter nodded. "Thanks. I'm keeping my fingers crossed that this is just a mistaken house situation."

Taha nodded. "It probably is, but better to be safe than

sorry. Now, I slaved over breakfast for hours; eat up before it gets cold."

Hunter laughed just as Taha intended him to and dug into breakfast.

∽

Breakfast at the vampire coven was in full swing, with everyone laughing and joking.

Mathis and Raz kept looking at Gavin, for although he was laughing, it wasn't full-on like normal. Raz wondered what time Gavin got up, as when he went to check on his brother earlier, his room was empty.

Troy was laughing with the witches when his phone pinged. He grabbed it out of his pocket and looked to see who was contacting him, and if it was a job off and if it would be worth doing. Being one of the best mercenaries in the industry made him a popular person.

He looked at the message and frowned. It was from his friend Taha, saying that Hunter Marsden, his partner in Area 51, found a strange message in his house and there were no signs of a break in. He cursed out loud when he read the message. The sudden silence around the table made him realise how loud he had been.

"Really, Troy, and you kiss Cairo with that mouth," Annie said in mock disapproval.

"I do a lot more than kiss him with my mouth, Annie, and some of the things I do are really filthy," Troy said, grinning.

Cairo gave a happy sign. "They really are."

There were titters around the table.

"What's wrong kitty?" David asked him.

"A message from a friend who might be in trouble."

"I thought you were a loner," Dave said, remembering one of their first conversations.

"I am or was considering I'm now surrounded all the time. But this one I've known forever. He's never asked for my help before though."

"I'll come with you if you want," Cairo offered.

Troy smiled at him. "Sure. I'd like for the two of you to meet."

"Oh, and before I forget, Gavin," Sean suddenly said, "I sent you the photos to use as you see fit."

Gabriel, Kayden, and Gavin laughed, and Gavin grabbed his phone to have a look.

"What photos?" Dave asked, smiling. "Anything fun?"

Gavin silently laughed, and putting his phone down, he signed to Dave.

Dave's mouth fell open and he looked at Sean. "You took photos of the Twister game?"

"*What?* You sneaky witch," Seth said. "I demand you delete those photos at once."

Everyone laughed, Sean laughing the loudest.

"You need to send me those photos," Gio said with a massive smile.

"And me," Kevin said.

"And me," David added. "The thought of the three of them in a tangled heap still makes me laugh."

Dave groaned. "Show me the pictures, Gav," he said, holding out his hand for the phone.

Gavin shook his head and laughed just as Dave made a grab for his phone. They had a playful tussle for a moment, which Gavin won, and Dave flopped back in his chair in defeat.

Gavin patted his arm and silently laughed. He put his phone down and glanced at the screen when the colour suddenly bled from his face and a look of horror covered it.

"Gavin, what's wrong?" Mathis asked urgently from across the table.

THE VAMPIRE AND THE TATTOOIST

Gavin ignored him and picked his up phone, hoping that he was mistaken. But there it was, clearly showing that the message had been sent.

"Gavin, what is it?" Dave asked urgently.

He dropped his phone and signed.

"You accidently sent a message to Hunter?" Kayden said.

Gavin nodded.

"Was it a message telling him you were a vampire?" Seth asked him.

He shook his head and passed his phone to Dave to read it aloud.

I miss you too Hunter, so much. Something horrible happened and I really need you. Can you come?

Gavin started signing, quickly and with agitation.

"I didn't mean to send the message. I wrote it out and meant to delete it. I really wanted to see him, but I can't," Gabriel translated.

"I'm sorry, Gavin. You might want to message him and say you've changed your mind. Chances are he'll be here soon," Dave told him.

"Gavin, your mate is called Hunter?" Troy asked.

Gavin nodded and signed.

"Gav says yes, and he's a tattooist," Dave translated.

Troy wiped a hand over his face. "That's what I was afraid of."

"What's wrong, kitty?" David asked him.

"The friend who messaged me earlier is Taha Lewis. He opened a tattoo shop with his best friend Hunter Marsden called Area 51. The message Taha sent me this morning is that Hunter might be in trouble," Troy explained.

Gavin jumped up in a panic. He needed to do something but didn't know what.

Kayden stood and put his arm around him. "Sit back down and let's think of a plan to help your man. Chances are, if he got your message, he's on the way here now. Maybe Troy could message Taha and tell him to come with Hunter," he said, pulling Gavin back down to his seat.

"That's an idea," Troy said, picking his phone up and shooting off a message and the coven address. He looked at Gavin. "Try not to worry. If Hunter is in trouble, I'll protect him."

"What the Kitty means is *we* will protect him," David said. "As your mate, Hunter is part of this coven. We will do whatever we need to keep him safe."

"And we'll help, as well, you know we will Gavin. I have to pop back to my coven, but I'll be here in a flash if you need me," Gabriel said, torn between staying or going home. But he needed to get back. They still had children to find.

Gavin nodded and signed.

"Nonsense, you're important, as well. Hopefully I'll find the location of the children today," Gabriel told him.

"I'll send Ian with you, witch, then I can stay here and help Gavin," Kevin said.

"Thank you," Gabriel said before looking at Mathis. "Stay with your brother. I'll be back as soon as I can. But if any of you need me sooner, just shout," he said, looking at everyone.

"Be safe, little witch," Mathis said, pulling him in and kissing him senseless.

They finally pulled apart after lots of cat calls.

"Gabriel, would you be offended if I sent two vampires with you, as well?" David said.

Gabriel shook his head. "Not at all, thank you. If your vampires don't mind coming to a witches coven."

"They won't. I would ask Olly to help, but he's away on a new assignment. Neill, Ivan, your latest assignments have finished. Go with Gabriel and Ian. There may be things you can do to help."

Both vampires nodded.

"Can you give me two minutes to grab my tablet and then I'll be ready to come?" Ivan asked.

At Gabriel's nod, he jumped up and shot out of the kitchen.

"Sean, Kayden, are you both staying here?" Gabriel asked them.

Kayden shook his head. "No, there's lots to do at home, too much for just you. We'll come with you," he said before looking at Gavin. "But we'll be back in an instant if you need us."

Gavin nodded and smiled at him just as Ivan rushed back in.

"Ready," he told them.

The witches, Ian, and Neill stood up, and Gabriel opened a portal for them all to walk through.

"See you all later," he said, smiling at Mathis before walking through the portal and closing it.

A moment later, the doorbell rang.

CHAPTER 11

*H*unter was clearing up the kitchen when his phone pinged. He dropped the dish cloth and pulled his phone out of his pocket. He smiled when he saw it was from Gavin and opened it, the smile falling off his face as he read the message.

Forgetting to message back, Hunter hurried out of the kitchen and bumped into Taha. "Gavin needs me. I'm running over to his place to see him."

"I'll message Luke and ask him to rearrange your appointments. I heard from Troy and he's actually in the area. He's calling around later." Just as he said that, his phone pinged. He pulled it out to have a look. "Troy said we should go round instead. He said he's currently staying at Gavin's home."

Hunter looked confused. "Your friend is staying with my Gavin?"

"Looks like. Let me message Luke that he needs to change both of our appointments and then we can go and see what's going on."

Hunter nodded. "I'll drive."

Taha nodded, texting as he followed, remembering to grab his keys and lock his house up before getting into Hunter's car. With Taha giving directions, Hunter drove faster than he probably should have, but Gavin needed him and Troy was staying with Gavin.

His mouth fell open when he pulled into the drive and saw the size of the house…. Mansion? Castle? Whatever it was, it was *big*.

"Holy cow," Taha exclaimed. "Who knew writing computer games paid so well?"

"We are *so* in the wrong profession," Hunter said, pulling to a stop, turning the engine off, and quickly jumping out, not waiting for a reply. He hurried up the front steps and rang the bell just as Taha joined him.

~

DAVE JUMPED up as the bell dinged. "I'll go. You know a friendly face might help." And before anyone could say anything, he rushed out and opened the front door, smiling when he saw Hunter and another man who must be Taha. "Hey, Hunter."

Hunter shook his head and smiled at the man. "Hey, Dave. Thanks for helping me yesterday. Gavin messaged me."

"So, you came running?" Dave asked him.

Hunter nodded. "Yes. This is Taha, my business partner."

"And best friend," Taha put in.

"I'm Dave. Come on in. Gavin's at the breakfast table. Follow me."

Hunter didn't bother looking round, too intent on getting to Gavin.

Taha, though, looked around, and he stopped as he passed what could only be a ballroom. Was that seriously a banner saying, 'I killed my first person? And were those fangs and red teardrops? That had to be a joke, right? Taha pulled himself away and finally followed the other two.

Dave led Hunter into the kitchen, which was suddenly filled with silence. Hunter didn't care; all he cared about was Gavin.

Gavin saw him and jumped up, throwing himself into Hunter's arms.

"I have you," Hunter said, closing his arms around Gavin and hugging him back. He dropped a kiss on Gavin's head and rested his cheek against his head.

Finally, Gavin pulled back and signed, forgetting for a moment that Hunter didn't know much sign language. He was shocked when Hunter caught his hands.

"Enough, sweetheart. You needed me, so here I am," Hunter said gently, smiling down at him.

Gavin leaned against him for a moment.

"Taha, good to see you again," Troy said, standing up.

"I would say the same, but I'm not sure at the moment. Was that ballroom really decorated for a kill party?"

"Crap," Dave said. "No one closed the door."

"A kill party?" Hunter queried, looking up.

"It's a long story," David said. "Have a seat and we can talk."

Hunter moved and grabbed Gavin's hand before sitting down next to him, Taha sitting on the other side.

"My name is David D'Angelo, and I run one of the world's largest security companies. Troy said you were in trouble and needed help. We can help you."

Hunter sighed. "I'm not even sure if I'm in trouble, to be honest."

"Tell us everything. If it's nothing, we can tell you and relieve your mind. If it's something, then we can help you," Gio said.

"Okay. I noticed something strange in that every time Gavin and I met, someone was following us."

Gavin gave a start at this and frowned at David, then his brothers, before pulling his hand out of Hunter's and angrily signing.

"I didn't catch all that Gav. You've gotta slow down," Raz said.

"Gavin is telling you, your brother, and my son off for having someone follow him," Stefan said, who had been sat quietly at the table the whole time.

"Wait, you had professionals following us?" Hunter queried.

"I did, although they obviously need a refresher course in stealth. Gavin, did you really think I wouldn't send someone out to watch over you? You hardly ever go out. When you went to the library and met Hunter, that was the first time you'd been out of the house in months. I didn't want you alone if you had a panic attack or you got into a situation you couldn't deal with," David told him before grinning. "Plus, can you imagine what your brothers would have done to me if I let you go alone?"

"You know, if we had known, both Raz and I would have stalked you ourselves." He looked at Hunter. "I'm Mathis, by the way, and this is our brother Raz."

"We met at the library," Hunter said.

"We did," Raz replied for him.

"So now you know the stalker was harmless. What else happened?" Gio asked.

"Someone broke into my house last night, except I have no idea how they got in. I checked all the doors and windows and couldn't find anything amiss."

"What was taken?" Troy asked.

"Nothing. It was something that was left." Hunter shifted

and put his hand in his pocket, pulling out the piece of paper that had been left.

"Can I see it?" Mathis asked.

Hunter handed it over.

Mathis read it before swearing.

"What?" Seth asked. "What does it say?"

"You will die for what he did. He killed the Master. We will kill you," Mathis read, dropping the piece of paper and running his hands over his face.

"You know what this means," Taha asked; it wasn't a question but a statement. "Does it have anything to do with the kill party?"

"We're going to need Gabriel here for this," Mathis said.

CHAPTER 12

Gabriel closed the portal and looked around. They had come out in his office.

"Shall we start here?" Ian asked.

Gabriel shook his head. "No, we need to go to Leonard's rooms and look in his secret room. Hopefully everything we need will be there," he said, walking to the door and unlocking it with magic before opening it and waving them all out so he could lock the door afterwards. There were few people he trusted in the coven, so locking all important rooms no one else could enter was necessary.

Sean and Kayden led the way towards the stairs. The coven house was quiet, which worried Gabriel. "Sean, Kayden, can you guys have a wander round and find out if everyone is still hiding in their rooms or have even packed up and left?"

"We can do that," Sean said. He and Kayden changed directions and walked down the hall towards the kitchen while Gabriel led Ian, Ivan, and Neill up to Leonard's room.

"I take it it's not always this quiet?" Neill asked.

Ian snorted but didn't say anything.

"No, coven members took to their rooms when the bombings started," Gabriel told them before stopping and looking at them. "Sorry, I should have asked if you knew what happened here."

"We've heard chatter. That your brother and a man called Kay and some others tried to kill you, killed some coven members, and were into illegal stuff," Ivan said.

"Pretty much. We found out that one of the big things they were into was paranormal child trafficking. There was also money laundering and probably a host of other things we don't yet know about," Gabriel replied.

"But you've caught everyone involved?" Neill asked.

"Honestly, I have no idea. The ones we questioned said it was only them, Roberto, Kay, and Leonard, but David offered his expertise in looking into everyone."

"Yep, he asked me to do a deep background on everyone belonging to the coven. I have a programme running now doing deep searches on everyone," Ivan told him.

"Thank you," Gabriel said, carrying on walking before stopping at a door and looking it over. "Someone has tried to break down my spell."

"Do you know the magic?" Ian asked.

"I'm not sure. I'll get my magic to remember it so I can look later."

"You can do that?" Ian asked in surprise.

Gabriel grinned. "I guess we'll find out." He looked at the door and placed his hand on it, opening it. "Let me check the room first," he said, standing in the doorway. He sent his magic out looking for any bombs. He found three. "I need to defuse three bombs. Once I do that, you can come in."

"Do you know where they are?" Neill said, looking around confused.

"I do. You can come and look, but stand where I tell you, and if I say move, move."

Gabriel walked to the first one, which was on one of the bedside tables. "Okay, come and stand round me, but stay behind."

The three walked over.

"I don't see a bomb," Ivan said, looking confused.

"Witch bombs 101," Ian said. "They're different from anything you've ever seen. It could be a strand of hair, a chip on something, anything can be a witch bomb."

"Look at the lamp. At a quick glance, it looks perfect, right?" Gabriel asked.

"Yes," Neill said.

"No, there is a slight chip on the left side at the base. The chip is lying next to it," Ivan said.

"And that's the bomb," Gabriel said. He pushed his magic into the lamp and deactivated the bomb and fixed the chip. "There, one down, two to go."

"That's actually incredible," Neill said.

"It really is," Ian said. "The one we encountered was a random strand of hair."

"How did you undo it?" Ivan asked.

Ian shook his head. "We didn't. We tripped that sucker before we could figure out how to undo it."

"Where is the next one?" Neill asked.

"Over here." Gabriel led them to the wardrobe. "Now I'm going to help you slightly with this one. It's on this side," he said, pointing to the left side. "Have a look without moving forward and see if you can find it."

The three men looked, and after a minute, Ian spoke. "Third scroll down, the flower on the left, the petal is pointing the wrong way."

Gabriel nodded. "Yes."

"That's so tiny," Ivan said.

"It is. That's why witch bombs are so hard to find." Gabriel pushed his magic into the bomb and diffused it, and the petal went back into its proper position. "Now this one, I'm not sure I would have discovered it without my magic," He led them to the fireplace. "Don't move in front of me but see if you can find it."

The three men looked, and after a few minutes, Neill let out a frustrated breath. "I can't see it. Everything looks normal."

"I think I've found it," Ivan said. "One of the threads is broken on the spider's web."

Gabriel nodded. "Yes."

Ian whistled. "I never would have got that one."

Gabriel disabled the last bomb. "And now the room is safe. We just need to find his secret room."

Just then, Sean and Kayden walked in. "Can you not find the secret room?" Sean asked.

"We haven't started looking yet. We — and by we, I mean Gabe — had to sort out the bombs first," Ian told them.

"What did you find out?" Gabe asked his friends.

"So, there has been no new killings. Those that work outside the coven house are still going to work, but otherwise, people are sticking to their rooms for the moment," Kayden said.

"The bodies in the dining room have been taken away, but we couldn't find out where they were taken or who took them, and Rafe is with Sheldon, keeping him company," Sean added.

"Well that's something, at least," Ian said.

Just then, Gabriel's phone rang. He pulled it out. "It's Mathis," he said, clicking the answer button. "Hey, vampy."

"Hey, little witch. Can we borrow you for a few minutes?"

"Yep, give me two minutes and I'll be there."

"See you in a moment."

"You will," Gabe said, hanging up. "I'm needed at the

vamps. If I find the secret room, can you five start having a look and I'll join you as soon as I can?"

"We can do that," Kayden said.

Gabe sent his magic out, and the bookcase swung open. He also checked for bombs but there weren't any. "There you go. Have fun, and I'll be back soon." And with that, he opened a portal and reappeared in the vampires' kitchen.

CHAPTER 13

"What's going on?" Hunter asked. "You obviously know."

No one said anything for a moment.

"Oh, for heaven's sake," Annie said. "What everyone is trying to figure out is how to tell you that pretty much everyone here is a vampire, or in Troy's case, a jaguar. Kevin here is a wolf and Dave, Willard, and I are the only humans currently here. The party was for Gavin, who yesterday killed a very bad witch to save a friend. We threw him a party to try and cheer him up."

"You're a vampire?" Hunter asked Gavin in surprise.

Gavin nodded and signed.

Dave translated. "I wanted to tell you so badly, but I was scared you would think I was an evil monster and want nothing to do with me."

"I promise, you two are perfectly safe here," David assured them.

"That club in Cuba takes on a whole new meaning now," Taha said to Hunter.

Hunter nodded. "Yeah, it really does."

"What club?" Seth asked.

"When we went travelling, we stopped off in Cuba. We went to a club one evening. We thought we'd entered an EMO club, but I swore I saw someone with pointed teeth bite into someone's neck."

"So did I but put it down to a trick of the lights," Hunter put in. "But bringing things back to now. That letter was obviously meant for me because of what happened yesterday. But how did they get into my house?"

"Let me ring Gabe and get him here. Maybe he can help," Mathis said, picking up his phone and making the call.

A moment later, a portal opened, and Gabriel walked out.

Hunter and Taha both jumped up.

"What the hell is that?" Taha asked.

"A witch's portal. It's a quick way to travel," Gabe said, smiling at him and closing the portal.

"Witches, vampires, cats. Just what freaky rabbit hole have we just fallen down?" Hunter demanded.

Gavin hung his head. His mate didn't think he was evil, just a freak. He didn't know which was worse.

"Are you calling us, calling *Gavin* a freak?" Raz demanded, standing up, his eyes swirling red in anger.

Hunter glared at him. He was scared and wanted to run away and never look back, but then he would have to give up Gavin, and he couldn't do that to the man he loved. "No, I said we had fallen down a freaky rabbit hole. I did not say any of *you* were freaks. Am I concerned about this strange new world? Yes, I'd be lying if I said I wasn't. Am I scared? Sure, who wouldn't be when they discover vampires are real and other paranormals that I've only read about in books are real. I'm human. I'm allowed to be concerned, especially as I might have a paranormal killer after me."

"Raz, calm down and sit," David ordered.

Stefan looked at Hunter and Taha. "I know this is a lot to

take in and you need to process and probably have a freak out, but I promise as King of the Vampires, you are safe here. We only want to find out who is after you and protect you."

Hunter looked at him for a moment before nodding and sitting down. Taha sat, as well.

"So what did I miss?" Gabe asked, sitting down next to Mathis.

"This," Mathis said, passing him the piece of paper.

Gabe read it and sighed, looking at Hunter. "This was left in your house?"

Hunter nodded. "Yes, but I can't see how they got in. Now would someone tell me what this is all about?"

"It's connected to me, I'm afraid. I have recently, like very recently, like yesterday, become head of my family coven and head of the Southern witches. My brother Roberto was leader before, but he was straight jacket insane. He let a witch into our coven called Kay Cameron-Webb. We found out that Kay along with some coven members were involved in some very unsavoury things. The leader of this group was a witch called Leonard Banning.

Yesterday, there was a battle in which Kay was killed, but Leonard kidnapped Gavin and a wolf shifter friend, Ian.

"Leonard planned on killing them both and blaming it on me. He used magic on Ian, but before Leonard could kill him, Gavin killed Leonard instead. Gavin killed his first person to save his friend."

"Gavin isn't like the rest of us. He's gentle without a mean bone in his body, and killing someone, no matter how evil, upset him, hence the party," Seth said.

Hunter caught up Gavin's hand and gave it a squeeze.

"We thought we had captured all those involved, but it seems we missed one," Gabriel said. "This letter was delivered to your house by a witch using the same kind of portal I used. When I returned home earlier, I went to Leonard's room, and someone had tried to break in. The magical signature attached to this note is the same one that was used on the door."

"Do you know who?" Mathis asked him.

Gabe shook his head. "No, but you can be damn sure I'm going to find out. I need to have another chat with the lemmings."

"I'll come back with you and talk to them," David said.

"Why is there a sign in the ballroom for a kill party?" Max asked from the doorway.

Dave looked at him and grinned. "Do you really want to know?"

Max shook his head. "Probably not. If anyone needs me, I'll be in the library." Max turned and walked away, saying, "Of all the people in the world, Davy had to fall in love with a vampire. He couldn't have fallen for an accountant could he..."

His voice faded as he walked further away.

"Well, he's not wrong," Dave said, grinning at David.

"But just think how boring your life would have been," Seth said with a smile. "And just think it's all thanks to me saving you."

"Kidnapping," Dave pointed out.

"You were kidnapped?" Hunter exclaimed.

"There was a whole mistaken identity with a Russian mob brat and me," Dave said. "It's all sorted."

"Hunter, Taha, what foods do you like?" Annie asked them.

Before either could answer, Kevin's phone rang.

"That's Ian's ringtone," he said, grabbing his phone. "What's up Ian?"

"You remember that Russian hacker from the other day, Olay Ivanov?"

"What of him?"

"Looks like he was involved with all of this stuff at the coven," Ian said.

"Of course he was. Thanks. Keep looking." Kevin hung up and put his phone down. He looked at David. "You heard?"

David nodded. "Yes. Mathis, has anything been done with his computer yet?"

Mathis shook his head. "Not yet, but I can go and get started and see what I can find."

"Thank you."

"What did Ian say? Clue the pesky humans who don't have super hearing in, would you?" Dave said, looking at David and Kevin.

"It would seem Olay Ivanov was involved with Kay and Leonard," David told him.

"Well crap. Shall I call the Russians and see what they know?" Dave asked.

"Russians?" Taha asked.

"Russian mob," Dave supplied helpfully.

Hunter snorted out a laugh. "Of course you know the Russian mob, why wouldn't you?" He looked at Gavin. "Can we go somewhere and talk?"

Gavin nodded and stood up, Hunter standing with him.

"Excuse us for a bit," Hunter said.

"Hunter, I would prefer if you didn't leave the house or grounds. If you need to, I'll send a bodyguard with you until we've caught the witch that is after you," David said.

Hunter nodded. "I understand."

"Hunt, I'm going to head to the shop. Ring if you need me," Taha said.

Hunter pulled out his keys and tossed them at Taha. "Take my car."

"Thanks," he said, catching them.

Hunter nodded and walked out of the kitchen with Gavin. "Lead on," he said to Gavin.

Gavin nodded and led him up the stairs and to his bedroom.

As they walked, Hunter looked around. The decorations of the house were lovely. He had expected a house of this size to be over-decorated, but everything was understated. The pictures that graced the walls looked amazing. He didn't recognise any of the painting styles, but that didn't detract from their beauty. As an artist himself, Hunter loved all forms of art, not just the famous painters.

Gavin opened his bedroom door and stood out the way to let Hunter walk in first.

Hunter walked in and smiled; this room was so Gavin. The room itself was large. In the middle of the room was a large double bed flanked by two bedside tables. There was a sofa, coffee table, and a couple of chairs towards the back of the room by large windows. The other corner of the bedroom was set up with two desks, covered with computers and three screens. There were papers and notebooks scattered around the desk, indeed, over the whole room.

Gavin walked in behind him and closed the door. It felt strange having Hunter here, in his room. He still wasn't sure what Hunter thought about him being a vampire, and that had him worried.

Hunter turned round and grinned at him. "If I had to design a bedroom for you, this is what I would have designed. It looks perfect."

Gavin nodded and grinned, then signed, "Thank you, I love it."

Hunter walked over to him and stood looking down at him. He was about a head taller than Gavin and had more muscles, a fact that Hunter loved. He could think of nothing worse than having a partner who was the same height and build as him.

He saw a look of apprehension in Gavin's eyes. Hunter

raised his hand and touched his cheek. "We have so much to talk about, sweetheart," he said gently.

Gavin raised his eyes and looked at Hunter and saw the tender look in his eyes. There was so much he wanted to say, but he didn't want to move.

Hunter smiled. "I know, sweetheart," he said before bending his head and kissing him. He moved his hand from Gavin's cheek and placed it behind his neck, his other arm wrapped around Gavin's waist, pulling him closer.

Gavin was in heaven. He had only kissed Hunter once, and that was a quick barely-there kiss. He wrapped his arms around him and sighed into the kiss. He loved the fact that Hunter was taller than him and had more muscles. Sure, Gavin was much stronger, but that didn't matter to him. He felt surrounded, safe.

Hunter was in heaven. The one time he had kissed Gavin had been far too brief, a barely-there kiss at the end of their last date. This was so much better. He felt Gavin sigh against his lips and used that to map out Gavin's mouth with his tongue.

When they both needed air, Hunter pulled back, but not far. "Just perfect," he said, not releasing Gavin. "Jump up."

Gavin did and wrapped his legs around Hunter's waist, who walked them over to the sofa and sat down with Gavin sitting astride him. He moved his hands, so they rested on Gavin's waist.

Gavin smiled at him before signing, "You are not scared of me?"

Hunter shook his head. "No, I'm not scared of you. I don't think you're a freak, evil, a monster, or anything else that probably went through and is going through your head right now. If I did, there would be no way I would have kissed you like I needed to more than anything else in the world. Do I wish you hadn't had to kill someone, even to save a friend?

Yes, but then I would wish that for anyone I knew that had to kill." He paused. "I understand why you didn't tell me. I probably wouldn't have said anything until I knew you better if that was me. But sweetheart, no more secrets. If we're going to work, we need to be open and honest with each other."

Gavin nodded and smiled at him. He loved looking at Hunter. His eyes were a lovely green, his dark brown hair hung in waves to his shoulders. To Gavin, Hunter was perfect, and if he had made Hunter the hero in his next game, well, that was up to him. Gavin signed. "I'm sorry I didn't tell you. I didn't know how. Thank you for learning sign language for me."

Hunter smiled. "Well, I wanted to understand you without you having to write everything down. It's something I should have thought about before even meeting you. Have you noticed that you say a lot with only a few hand movements?"

Gavin gave a silent laugh. He wasn't the one that was a chatty Cathy. But Hunter seemed to know what he was thinking and answered questions accordingly.

"Now enough chat," Hunter said, pulling Gavin closer. "I need to kiss you again."

Gavin was all for that.

CHAPTER 14

*I*an couldn't believe that Olay Ivanov had been involved in everything that was going on. In his and Kevin's research on him, they found no connection between the Russian or the witches.

Once Gabe left to go see the Vamps, the rest of them had walked into Leonard's secret room. Ian was expecting something small, but this room was massive. There were bookcases filled with folders, cabinets filled with files, and a laptop.

Kayden and Sean had started looking through the folders on the shelf, Neill was going through the paperwork found on the desk, Ian was going through filing cabinets, and Ivan was trying to hack into Leonard's computer.

It was in one of these cabinets that he found paperwork involving the Russian. There was a whole file on children Ivanov had sent to Leonard, but nothing yet about where any safe houses were.

"Am I the only one surprised at how much stuff is in here?" Sean asked generally.

"I'm still wondering how all of this was going on under

our noses and not only did we not know, but you vamps didn't know, either," Ian said, frowning.

"It makes you wonder what else has been happening that we don't know about," Neill said.

"I wouldn't beat yourself up about this. Don't forget witches were involved. They could have used magic to cover so much up," Kayden said, flicking through a folder. "Here's something. It's a list of houses and I'm guessing warehouses. They all have lines through them, so I guess they're no longer in use. But I'm wondering if it would be worth going to look at them."

"It would give us a good idea on what type of house or dwelling they use and an idea of the locations they like to use," Ivan said before he scowled at the screen. "Just unlock, dammit."

"Try hitting it," Ian said to him. "That's what I usually do."

"No, I've never been beaten by a computer, and I'm not about to let a mad witch break my streak."

Sean leant over the desk and touched the computer, grinning. "Bibbidi-Bobbidi-Boo."

Everyone laughed until Ivan said, "Holy crap, that worked!"

"Really?" Sean asked, as surprised as everyone else.

"No, idiot," Ivan said, laughing.

"Well, it was worth a try," Sean said, shrugging.

"I have other tricks I can use," Ivan said and went back to getting lost in computers.

"Oh," Sean suddenly said. "Leonard was called The Master, if that helps."

Ivan smiled. "Probably. Let me try something," he typed in something then smiled. "I'm in."

"What was his password?" Ian asked.

"Masters of the Universe 1."

"Gah, what a twatwaffle," Kayden muttered, not looking up from his folder.

"Here's something. I clicked into his calendar, and it looks like he's shorthanded his entries. There's nothing in for today, but tomorrow evening it says, 'MC 2 Dks.'"

They all looked at him. "MC to Dks?" Kayden asked.

"The M and C are capitalized, the two is the number 2, and the D is capitalized but the k and s are small," Ivan told them.

"So, move children to… somewhere," Ian said, thinking.

"But what could Dk mean?" Sean asked.

"Docks?" Ian asked. "I mean, it's only about thirty miles to the nearest port. What if the children are being loaded into a container and shipped out from there? Ivan, can you run a search on his system and look for any mention of crates and ships."

"I can do that. Give me a sec."

"Kayden, are any of the files you're looking through named?" Ian asked him.

Kayden looked. "With shorthand. Let me look and see if I can find anything that mentions Dks."

"This would be much easier and quicker if Gabe was here. He could just send his magic out and look for what we needed," Sean said.

"Can you not just use your wand and pull the information out?" Ian asked him.

Sean looked at Kayden, who shrugged. "No idea, to be honest. It won't hurt to try."

"Go on, babe, give it a go," Sean said to Kayden.

Kayden grinned and grabbed his wand, putting his intentions into his magic and then flicking his wand around the room.

Suddenly, a secret draw flew open.

"It worked," Kayden said, sounding and looking shocked.

"Well done," Ian said, walking to the draw. "That's impressive. We would never have found that drawer," he said, looking at it before picking up the paperwork and starting to flick through it.

Sean got up and hugged Kayden. "Well done."

"This is it. It lists the location the children are at and gives their names and species. Looks like they're being moved tomorrow from one location to the docks. The container is due to be packed onto a cargo ship bound for Columbia," Ian said, reading through it. "They're scheduled to be moved from their current location early tomorrow evening. The boat leaves at midnight."

"How are they going to get the kids out of their present location, to the docks, and onto a container without being seen? Neill asked.

"Either drugging them or using magic," Sean said.

"A portal maybe?" Ian suggested. "We need to move out and rescue those children." He grabbed his phone and dialled Kevin again.

CHAPTER 15

Kevin was still sitting at the table talking to everyone. Hunter and Gavin had left as had Taha.

"I'm going to the library to work with Max," Dave said. He had just stood up when Kevin's phone rang, and he sat back down.

"What's up, Ian?" Kevin asked on answering.

"We found a location for the missing children. They are due to be shipped out tomorrow," Ian said.

"Come back with the address and we can go and rescue them," Kevin told him.

"Will do. Can you get Gabe to open a portal?" Ian asked.

"Yep, see you in a bit," he said, hanging up. "Gabe, can you open a portal for Ian?"

"I can," he said and waved his hand, opening a portal.

"What's going on?" Dave asked as Ian came through the portal carrying a folder.

"Thanks, Gabe," Ian said. "As for what's going on, we have an address for some of the missing children. They're due to be shipped out to Columbia tomorrow evening."

"Then we have time to rescue them," Kevin said, standing up. "I'll call for backup, and we can go and get them."

"Before you go, let me take a copy of the names and we can start searching for their families," David said.

"Here," Ian said, handing the list over to him as David grabbed his phone and took photos.

"Do you want some vampires to go with you?" Dave asked.

"It probably wouldn't hurt," Kevin said.

"I'll come, as well, in case you need a witch," Gabe said.

Mathis looked at him.

"I have to help, vampy," Gabe said softly, putting his hand on Mathis' arm. "My brother and coven were involved with all this. I have to help make things right."

Mathis grabbed his hand and kissed it. "Okay, little witch."

"I can go with Kevin," Creed said.

"I can go, as well," Seth offered.

"Not without me," Gio said.

"You know this is what we do, right? I'll be fine, babe," Seth said. looking at him.

"I'm not doubting you my Seth, but I'm coming, anyway," Gio told him.

"We can go, as well," Rickon said, pointing to the others.

David looked at them for a moment before nodding. "Mathis and Raz will go with you, as well. But if Kevin, Ian, Seth, Mathis or Raz tell you to do something, you do it. This will be your first rescue mission, they are all trained professionals."

"Do you want me to call Sean and Kayden to come, also?" Gabe asked.

"I'd rather they stayed looking through those files, if you don't mind, Gabe," Kevin said.

"Nope, I don't mind. I think I would rather keep them

safely looking through the files," Gabe paused. "Well, as safe as they can be in the coven house."

"Don't forget Ivan and Neill are with them, as well," Mathis pointed out.

"That's true," Gabe agreed before looking at David. "I wonder if you can look at the lemmings and see if you can find out who the missing witch is."

David nodded. "We can bring the lemmings here and I can do that. I will extract everything they know for you."

"You might need to use the potion on Giles if he clams up again. If you do, have Sean or Kayden come and say the spell for you, but thanks," Gabe says with a deep sigh.

"Gabriel, remember we're all here to help. You don't have to do any of this alone," Kevin said. "I feel partly responsible. This happened under my nose, and I didn't even get a hint of something this bad was going on."

"The same with me. I prided myself on knowing everything that's going on in and around this area. Knowing we missed something this big, that children have been kidnapped practically under our noses, is unsettling," David said.

"I wouldn't beat yourselves up too much. Don't forget witches were involved. They could have hidden everything with magic," Gabe said.

"That's practically word for word on what Kayden said," Ian commented.

Gabe grinned. "We can't both be wrong, then."

"Thank you, Gabe. Everyone who is coming, it's time to go. We'll head to my place and make plans before we rescue the children," Kevin said, standing up.

"Does this mean I get to meet your brother?" Creed asked him, smiling.

Kevin sat back down sighing. "Most probably."

Ian snorted out a laugh and looked at his phone. "Nope,

your brother was called away this morning. It's safe to go home."

"Then let's go before he comes back," Kevin said, standing up again.

"I can't wait to meet your brother," Dave said, laughing.

"I'll record the meeting," Ian said, laughing as he stood up.

"Stay in touch, and if you need more help, shout," David said.

"Will do," Kevin replied as those that were going left the kitchen.

"I'm off to the library while you do your woo-woo stuff on those witches," Dave said, giving David a quick kiss and standing up. "If you need me, text me." And with that, Dave left the kitchen.

CHAPTER 16

Hunter and Gavin were still sitting on the sofa. Gavin had laid his head on Hunter's shoulder and fallen asleep, and Hunter was happy to sit there and let him sleep, his arms around Gavin. Knowing how sweet Gavin was, Hunter was sure that Gavin hadn't got much sleep last night and if being in Hunter's arms helped him sleep, then Hunter would stay here all day if necessary.

Hunter laughed to himself, never in his wildest dreams did he think that the man he would fall in love with would be a vampire. He sobered up when he remembered that he now had a killer witch after him. Well, he didn't know anything about witchcraft, but he knew how to punch someone. He was pretty sure punching a witch in the face would stop them. The one thing he wouldn't do was get Gavin to kill another witch.

His arms tightened around Gavin. No, he would do whatever was needed to ensure Gavin never had to kill again.

THE VAMPIRE AND THE TATTOOIST

Dave reached the library and found Max sorting a shelf out.

"How's it going, Max?"

"I thought I would sort this shelf out since my hands were getting twitchy."

Dave laughed. "I know what you mean. Mine have been itching to start tidying the shelves."

"We need to get a scanner and computer down here. I'm sure a lot of these books need digital recording." Max said, stroking the cover of the book he was holding.

Dave nods. "Yeah, David said these were one of a kind books, and they need preserving. I'll look into getting everything we need to scan them. I know Stefan wants to create a central paranormal library. Apparently, before Kevin offered to help me, different paranormal groups didn't mix or work together."

"Why not?" Max asked.

"No idea, but now look, there are witches, wolves, jaguars, and a witch doctor."

"So, what's the story with the kill party?" Max asked, leaning on one of the shelves.

"Gavin killed a bad witch yesterday to save Ian's life," Dave told him.

"Gavin's the computer game wiz, right?"

Dave nodded. "Yeah, he and Ian were kidnapped, and to save Ian, Gavin shifted into his vampire form and killed the witch."

"That must have been hard for him. You told me he was a gentle soul."

"He is. He was so distraught that Mum decided to throw him a party, her reason being that you can't cry at your own party. Dad went out and got decorations, and he and Stefan decorated the ballroom."

"Is there anything we can do to help him?" Max asked.

Dave smiled and pulled Max into a hug. "Thanks," he said before pulling back. "He has Hunter looking after him."

"What, tattoo artist Hunter?" Max asked in surprise.

"Yep, they're mates. But Hunter has a killer witch after him."

"Because Gavin killed that bad witch?"

Dave nodded. "Yep. Let's sort more of these shelves and I can fill you in on everything you missed."

∼

Kevin pulled up in front of the pack house. The house was a large wooden three-floor structure with lots of windows. It looked like a wooden lodge, but on steroids.

"Wow, this is just as big as the D'Angelo coven house," Creed exclaimed.

"It is. Those who don't live in the pack house have houses all around this area, we even have our own shop, pub, school and cinema."

"So you have a pack town," Creed said.

"Please tell me it's called Wolf Creek or something close to," Rickon said with a laugh.

Kevin laughed. "Sorry to disappoint, but no. The town is called Sleepy Magna."

"Well, that's disappointing," Jessamy said, opening the car door.

Everyone met by the pack house door. Kevin walked in, holding Creed's hand, the others following.

He smiled at Creed. "Welcome to my place. I'll show you around later, but for now, let's go to the conference room." Kevin says, leading the way. "Ian, see who's around and can supply us with food and drinks while we research everything."

"I can do that," a woman says, walking out of one of the rooms they passed.

Kevin stopped walking and smiled. "Mother, what are you doing here?" He dropped Creed's hand and pulled his mother into a hug.

She hugged him back. "Where else would I be when your brother tells me you've stopped returning his calls, that your consciousness went missing, and that you found your mate?"

Kevin pulled away. "I can't believe that loser snitched."

"He was concerned about you. Where have you been and when can I meet your mate?" His mother asked.

Kevin smiled. "Right now." He turned back and grabbed Creed's hand, pulling him forward. "Mother, my mate, Creed Brooks, Creed, my mother Lissa Mellor."

Creed held his hand out. "It's lovely to meet you, Mrs. Mellor."

Lissa laughed and took his hand and patted it with her other one. "Call me Lissa, dear, and it's lovely to meet you as well." Lissa grinned at Kevin. "You scored yourself a vampire. Very nice."

Kevin laughed. "I did. The fates sure smiled kindly on me."

Lissa looked around the group. "And a human?"

"I'm a witch. Gabriel Augusta," Gabe said, smiling at her.

Kevin introduced everyone.

"It's lovely to meet you all. But what's going on?"

"We're planning to rescue some kidnapped paranormal children. They're being shipped out tomorrow and we need to save them," Kevin replied.

"In that case, go and start planning, and I'll supply you all with refreshments. Your brother will be upset he missed you. He was called away this morning. But Kevin, and you, Ian," she said, looking his way. "Start answering his calls, don't make me use my annoyed voice."

Everyone laughed.

"I'll make sure he does," Creed told her.

Lissa patted his cheek. "I knew I liked you, dear."

"Annie's going to love meeting you," Ian says.

"Who's Annie?" Lissa asks.

"Our coven leader's mate's mother. She's currently staying at our coven," Creed says.

"I've invited her and Queen Louise, the vampire queen, over here to play with our pups anytime they want to," Kevin said.

"She's the lady that keeps feeding you all," Lissa said, remembering some of the pack talking about her.

"That's the one," Ian replied.

"Then I can't wait to meet her or the vampire queen. Now run along and start your strategizing' and I'll start making food."

"Thank mum," Kevin said, leading everyone into the conference room.

CHAPTER 17

Gavin had been asleep for a few hours now. Hunter had moved him around so he'd be more comfortable, and Gavin hadn't stirred. But Hunter was getting hungry and could really do with a drink. He was just debating whether or not he should text Dave when there was a knock on the door. Hunter hoped it was one of the vampires and that they had super hearing, so he called out a gentle, "Come in."

The door opened and a man stood there holding a tray. "I thought you might both be hungry and in need of coffee. I'm Thomaz, by the way."

"Hunter, and you are literally a lifesaver. I was about to message Dave to see if he could grab me a coffee. Gavin's been asleep for a while, and I didn't want to wake him," Hunter told him.

Thomaz walked over to them and put the tray on the table. "Under the platter are sandwiches, sausage rolls, and the like, and Gavin's favourite biscuits. If you tell me what you like, I can make sure I have your favourites on hand."

"Thanks. I'm not picky. I like anything but cakes with vegetables in them," Hunter told him.

Thomaz gave a small laugh. "I can promise I'll never make anything like that." He looked at Gavin. "He didn't sleep well last night. I found him sleeping in the kitchen next to Bruno this morning. I told him if he got scared, he could come into my room, but now you're here, so you can make sure he sleeps and hold him if he gets upset."

"I can. Why didn't he go to one of his brothers?" Hunter asked, frowning.

"They're both newly mated. I don't think Gavin wanted to disturb them."

"I can understand that. But yes, I'll help Gavin with whatever he needs," Hunter assured him.

"If at any time you want to have a freak-out, the freezer is stocked with ice cream, and I'm around. So is Dave if you need help. Mind you, everyone here will help."

Hunter smiled at him. "Thank you. I admit I was a bit freaked out earlier, but I'm okay now."

"I'll leave you now, but if you're not down for dinner, I'll bring something up for you both. Dinner is at seven."

"Thanks, Thomaz."

And with that, Thomaz left the room, closing the door behind him.

Gavin was slowly coming awake. He was pretty sure he heard Thomaz's voice and his door closing but couldn't be sure as his brain was still sleep-addled.

He felt Hunter's arms around him. He couldn't believe he had fallen asleep on him. He wondered what Hunter thought of him now. Gavin also realised something while he slept with Hunter's arms around him — he didn't dream. He gave a deep, happy sigh.

Hunter was about to lean forward and grab his coffee when

Gavin sighed and started to wake up. "Hello sweetheart," he said, dropping a kiss on Gavin's head. "I'm glad you managed to sleep. Thomaz has just been in with lunch. Are you hungry?"

Gavin nodded and sat up, only to realise that he was in a different position. He looked at Hunter.

"I wanted you to be comfortable while you slept."

Gavin smiled and kissed his cheek before signing, "Thank you."

"Thomaz told me he found you asleep with Bruno last night," Hunter said gently.

Gavin nodded and looked down, his cheeks having a faint blush on them.

Hunter used his finger and lifted Gavin's head, so they were looking at each other. "Never be ashamed or embarrassed that you need comfort, sweetheart. You seem to sleep well in my arms. How about I stay, and you can sleep wrapped in my arms."

Gavin smiled and nodded before signing.

"I'm sure, sweetheart. Now, how about we eat something and then we can take a walk outside in the gardens because I'm sure they are stunning."

Gavin smiled and climbed off Hunter's lap. He leant down and took the covers off the food: sandwiches, sausage rolls, chicken nuggets, mini pork pies, chopped raw veg. In fact, everything needed for a picnic. Everything Gavin loved to eat as he could pick while he worked.

"We should sit on the floor and have a picnic," Hunter suggested, looking at the food.

He loved Hunter's idea and giving a silent laugh, he picked up the plates and platters and put them on the floor.

Hunter laughed and grabbed the drinks as he sank down on the floor next to Gavin and handed one to Gavin.

"Cheers," Hunter said, holding his mug up.

Gavin clicked his mug against Hunter's and silently laughed.

～

Sean sighed. "We've been at this for hours. I think we should have a coffee break."

"That sounds really good," Neill said, putting down the papers he was reading through.

"Shall I bring everything up here or do you want to come down to the kitchen?" Sean asked.

"What will your coven think having vampires walking around?" Ivan asked.

Sean shrugged. "I don't really care."

"Someone should stay here to make sure no one comes in and tampers with anything," Kayden said.

"How about Neill and I go and grab refreshments, and you and Ivan stay here?" Sean suggested.

"That sounds like a plan," Ivan said.

"Be back in a bit," Sean said, as he and Neill walked out of the secret room.

Kayden looked around and shook his head. "You would think Leonard would have a better filing system. I mean, the files themselves seem to be related to the same thing, but instead of being together on the shelf, they're all dotted around different shelves."

"Maybe it's a date thing: the newer projects are closer to hand; the older ones further away," Ivan said.

Kayden shook his head. "No, I've been checking the dates as I go along. They're all mixed up."

"You would think due to running such a large operation, he would want things in order."

"Maybe this was his system in case it was ever discovered."

Ivan thought for a moment. "Maybe the person who tried to get in here messed everything up. Maybe Leonard wasn't the real leader of all this," he said, waving his hand around the room.

"I need to message Gabe. Someone will need to talk to the lemmings again," Kayden said, grabbing his phone and shooting off a text.

A few moments later, Sean and Neill walked back in, both carrying trays with drinks and food.

"We bring refreshments," Sean said, smiling.

"Did you run into anybody?" Kayden asked, taking two drinks off Sean's tray and putting them on the bookshelf.

"Rafe and Sheldon were eating in the kitchen. Sheldon said he had the bodies removed from the dining room. A few others are out and about, but many are still staying in their rooms," Sean replied, passing a drink to Ivan and putting one on the table for Neill as Neill handed out cakes.

"At least we know who arranged for them to be removed," Kayden said. "I've just texted Gabe, as Ivan wonders if Leonard was actually the leader of all this…" And he went on to explain their thoughts.

"Gah, can't we catch a break?" Sean asked, sounding frustrated.

"We will soon," Neill said optimistically.

"Well, I've found something," Ivan said. "I think Leonard thought just deleting files from his trash would erase them off his system."

"You mean that doesn't?" Sean asked in surprise.

Ivan snorted. "No, which is good for us as I can see everything Leonard tried to delete."

"What did you find?" Sean asks, coming to stand behind Ivan and looking at the screen. "I'm not liking the look of that list. That's a long list."

"So, as you know, I took his hard drive out and connected

it to my computer. I was looking at his deleted files and this came up. I think this is a list of all the kidnapped children. But going by the dates on here, this list goes back nearly ten years."

"But Kay was only here for five years," Sean said.

"I think this group has been doing this for longer than we realise. We know from what Mathis said, reading the file that Kay was doing things like this before he came here." Kayden said. "I wonder if this is a big network that spans different witch coven houses?"

"I think this goes beyond just witches. The children listed are from all paranormal groups. I think there is a massive underground paranormal network involved in all of this," Ivan said.

"We need to let the others know our thoughts," Kayden said, grabbing his phone again.

CHAPTER 18

*P*lans were being made in the pack conference room when Gabe's phone beeped. He pulled out his phone and frowned at the message.

"What's wrong, little witch?" Mathis asked him.

"Kayden and Ivan don't think Leonard was the actual leader of all this," Gabe said.

"If not him, then who?" Ian asked.

Gabe ran a hand through his hair. "That is the question. I need to ring David. Hopefully he can find out from the lemmings," he said, pulling up David's number and hitting the call button and then the speaker button.

"Hi, Gabriel. The lemmings have been brought over and I'm just on my way to talk to them," David said on answering.

"David, Ivan and Kayden think Leonard wasn't the actual leader of all this. Can you ask Giles what he knows?"

They heard David growl. "I'll find out the truth. How is the planning going?"

"We have plans and back up plans," Kevin replied for Gabriel.

"Good. Remember, if you need help, call," David reminded them.

"And if you need a witch, call Sean or Kayden," Gabe said.

"Will do. Chat later." And with that, David hung up.

Gabe put his phone down.

"Do you think Ivan and Kayden could be right?" Seth asked.

"I honestly don't know. At this moment in time, there are very few people I trust in the coven, which is a sad thing to say as I've known a lot of these people my whole life. I don't know what it's like with wolves or vampires, but unless someone mates outside of the coven, we don't usually get many new members."

"The same with packs. New members come through matings, occasionally because people move with their jobs and petition to join the pack. But we do thorough background checks first and then they're on probation for eighteen months before we fully accept them," Kevin said.

"Apart from new mates and Gio's guards, plus you guys," Seth said, waving to Gio's friends, "we've not had any new members since the coven started."

"But Kay wasn't born in your coven," Gio said. "Who else was new?"

Gabriel thought for a moment. "Giles Goodsir. I'm sure he joined a few months after Kay. The only other one I can think of is Jake Conway." Gabe smiled at Mathis. "He's the witch you knocked out in Kay's bedroom."

"I'm glad I did that now."

Before he could say anything else, Gabe's phone rang again.

"Hey, Kayden," Gabe said, again putting his phone on speaker.

"Gabe, we think we have a bigger problem," Kayden said.

"Really?"

"Yeah. From the information we're finding, we think this is bigger than just our coven. We think it's a massive underground paranormal network, including all paranormal groups."

"There is no way something like this could have been hidden from the paranormal council," Gio said, frowning.

"It could have been suppressed by Quintus Cameron-Webb. We need access to his computer and files," Gabe replied. "I could partition the paranormal council, but then they would swoop in and try and take over everything."

"Hopefully we can find Kay's computer in his room. It should have emails from Kay to Quintus. I should then be able to find Quintus IP address and hack his system, which could potentially give us some answers," Ivan said.

Gabe looked at Kevin. "I can pop back to the coven house and get Kay's computer for Ivan and be back before it's time to go."

Kevin nodded. "That would be helpful."

"Guys, I'm on my way back to you. See you in a moment," Gabe told them.

"You will," Kayden said, hanging up.

Gabe pocketed his phone. "Be back in a bit." He looked at Mathis. "Want to come?"

"Of course I'm coming, little witch. That other witch is still on the loose in your coven," Mathis told him.

Gabe swirled his hand and opened a portal into Leonard's bedroom, holding his hand out to Mathis, who took it.

"Back soon," Mathis said as he and Gabe walked through. Gabe closed it behind him.

CHAPTER 19

Hunter and Gavin enjoyed their floor picnic. Hunter was amazed how much he could understand from Gavin's signing, Gavin only needing to write things down occasionally. Gavin had been constantly smiling since he woke up, and Hunter loved that look on him, the way his eyes sparkled with happiness, a far cry from the look in them when Hunter had first arrived.

Seeing Gavin's happiness, Hunter leant forward and kissed him. He moved closer and put his hand around Gavin's neck, and as they kissed, Hunter laid Gavin down. He laid over Gavin, making sure to keep most of his weight off his stunning vampire.

He managed to pull his lips away and started kissing around Gavin's neck. He lifted his eyes to look at Gavin's face and saw pleasure covering his features and his eyes alight with passion. Hunter kissed Gavin on the lips again before pulling back. "Shall we move to the bed?"

Gavin smiled and nodded, the smile slipping slightly, and he started signing.

Hunter looked confused for a moment before he asked, "When we make love, you want to mate with me?"

Gavin nodded and signed again.

"You want to chomp on my shoulder and drink some of my blood?"

Gavin nodded, looking concerned.

Hunter smiled. "Will I become a vampire? Have increased strength? Super speed? I won't have to sleep in a coffin, will I?" he asked, suddenly horrified.

Gavin burst into silent laughter at the look of horror on Hunter's face.

A moment later, Hunter joined in, falling next to Gavin as they both tried to pull themselves together.

Hunter turned on his side and raised his hand, laying it on Gavin's cheek.

Gavin moved so he was now lying on his side, looking at Hunter. He loved the look in Hunter's green eyes, especially as they were now filled with happiness.

"I know I won't be sleeping in a coffin as you have a lovely looking bed in here. But what about turning into a vampire and all the other perks?"

Gavin shook his head.

"What, nothing?"

Gavin shook his head again, silently laughing.

"I would formally like to lodge a protest," Hunter said, smiling at him.

Gavin signed.

"I'll talk to Dave. I bet he's feeling left out on the superpowers front as well."

Gavin nodded and leant forward, kissing Hunter. He sighed. He could kiss Hunter forever and not have enough.

Hunter pulled back and gave him a gentle smile. "Yes, you can mate with me, but Gavin, should we not wait until this witch killer who is after me has been caught?"

The smile fell off Gavin's face, and he signed quickly.

"Sweetheart, you need to slow down. I'm missing most of what you're saying," Hunter said, grabbing Gavin's hands. "But I'm guessing you're saying that you'll mate with me now, that you're a fierce vampire and will protect me, plus, so will everyone here."

Gavin nodded and pulled his hands free and signed.

"Thank you for your promise, and I love you, as well."

Gavin smiled wide and pounced on Hunter, raining kisses over his face.

Hunter laughed, and with superhuman effort, rolled them before pulling away and standing up, pulling Gavin up with him and moving them to the bed. "Gonna make love to you now, Gavin," Hunter told him gently. "If you don't want this now, we can wait."

Gavin rolled his eyes and Hunter laughed before kissing Gavin and starting to strip him out of his clothes.

CHAPTER 20

Gabriel and Mathis smiled at their friends. "Did you miss us?"

"I'm sorry, who are you?" Sean said.

"Who are any of us?" Mathis replied quickly.

"Gah, don't start him down that path," Ivan complained.

Mathis laughed and looked around at the secret office and the piles of paperwork. "That's a lot to go through."

"It is," Ivan agreed. "That's why we need Kay's computer. It wouldn't hurt to have Giles' computer, as well."

"I can get them. Hopefully they'll be in their rooms and not in the Goodsir's house," Gabe said.

"We can hope. I mean, we must be due *some* luck about now," Neill replied.

"Mathis and I will go and search Kay and the lemmings rooms and see what electronics we can find," Gabe said.

"We have their mobiles. Seth and Cairo collected them before they were locked up," Mathis said.

"Good. I can go through them, as well," Ivan commented distractedly as he read the information off the screen.

"Did you find something?" Neill asked him.

"I'm not sure... more initials. It talks about a meeting they all had. Well, this is helpful; they even had an agenda for the meeting sent to all of them. The meeting was conducted by teleconference so certain people could remain anonymous."

"What initials?" Kayden asks.

"KW, QCW, GG, JC, DD, JT, SS, LB, RA, AT," Ivan read.

"So, we have Kay and his father, Giles, Alun, Robert, Leonard, The lemmings, and Jake Conway," Gabe said.

"So, one of them has to be the leader. I'm going with Daddy Cameron-Web," Sean commented.

"We'll get the other computers and gadgets and find out," Mathis said, turning to look at Gabe. "Ready, little witch?"

Gabe nodded. "Come on, then. Let's get this over with."

"That's the spirit," Kayden said with a laugh. "Want me or Sean to come with you?"

"You go, I went and got refreshments," Sean said to him.

Gabe laughed. "Yep, come on Kayden. You can carry everything we find."

"I think I'll stay here, thanks," Kayden said with a grimace.

"Too late," everyone said.

Kayden shook his head and stood up, laughing. "Remind me why we're friends again?"

"Because I'm just so awesome," Gabe deadpanned before looking at Kayden and burst out laughing along with the others.

"That you are, mate of mine," Mathis said, still laughing and taking his hand. "I'm glad you finally realised it."

"This is the last room. It's Jake Conway's room," Gabe said and knocked loudly on the door. "Jake, it's Gabriel. Open up."

"I can't hear any heartbeats from inside the room," Mathis told them.

"Then I'm going in," Gabe said. He put his hand on the

door to see if the room had been protected. "Now I know who put the message in Hunter's house and tried to get into Leonard's room."

"We can check his room and then look for him," Kayden said.

"We can," Gabe agreed and, muttering a spell, pulled down Jake's protection wards, then using his magic, opened the door. "Let me check for bombs first." And with that, Gabe sent his magic into the room.

Gabe sighed. "So, most of the room has bombs spread around it. Let me disable them first, then we can go in." He paused. "There, all done now." He looked at Mathis and Kayden. "You both might want to stay here while I go in."

Mathis snorted. "Sure, I'll get right on that." And with that, Mathis walked into the bedroom, Kayden following close behind.

Gabe shook his head and walked in after them.

"Well, this is a bust. It looks like Jake packed up and left," Kayden said while looking around.

He was right. The room was empty of personal effects; the doors to his wardrobe stood open showing nothing inside.

Mathis walked to a large chest of draws and pulled open each draw, but they were all empty, as well.

"His details should be in the office filing system," Gabe said. "We can find him but not today."

"Let's seal this room anyway and get back to the others. Ivan can go through all these," Kayden said, holding up all the devices he was carrying. They had found laptops and tablets in all the other rooms. Why they were left behind was anyone's guess.

"Yep, let's do that," Gabe agreed and followed them out of the room, with Gabe closing and sealing it behind them.

They then walked back to Leonard's room to join the others.

"I come bearing gifts," Kayden announced as he walked into the secret room, handing everything to Ivan.

"Nice, thanks. I should be able to hack these and get more information."

"Also, Jake Conway has packed up and left," Gabe told them.

"We should be able to find his details in the office," Sean said.

"Yeah, we thought of that. Mathis and I have to get back to the pack, but we can return and look later, or..." He paused and walked over to the bedroom door, placing his hand in it and muttering a spell.

The others walked out and watched him.

"There," Gabe said with a smile.

"What did you do, little witch?"

"I made it so Kayden and Sean can get into all the rooms I've sealed, so if I'm not around, you two can go into rooms and look for whatever is needed. When you're working in a room, keep the main door closed so no one else can walk in."

"Thanks, Gabe," Sean said.

"Gabe, can you send me back to the coven house so I can start looking through all these?" Ivan asked.

"I can do that," Gabe replied, swirling his hand and opening a portal.

Ivan gathered everything he needed. "Thanks. I'll let you know what I find. Good luck with the rescue, and if you need my help, just yell."

"Will do," Mathis said. "Can you also start looking through the Russian's computer? If you need help, ask Gavin."

Gabe snorted. "Pretty sure Gavin's busy with Hunter at the moment."

"I do not need to know that. Come on, little witch, we need to go, as well."

"Laters," Ivan said as he walked through the portal.

Once he was through, Gabe closed it and opened another to the pack house. "We'll catch up with you guys later," Gabe said.

Sean and Kayden hugged both Gabe and Mathis.

"Be safe, both of you, and good luck," Sean said.

"Thanks," Mathis said, and with that, he and Gabe returned to the pack house.

CHAPTER 21

"So what's new?" Ian asked Mathis and Gabe as they arrived back.

"Well, Jake Conway has packed up and left. Ivan found stuff but he's looking for more," Mathis told them.

"If this Conway is involved, he could be panicking and might move the children quicker," Seth said, sounding concerned.

Kevin nodded. "We'll have to bring the rescue forward. There's no telling what he could be doing." He looked at everyone. "The plan stays the same. Stick with your group, do everything you're told, and don't get dead. Let's go."

Just as he said this, his phone rang. He groaned and answered, "What's up, loser?"

"Where the hell have you been?" a voice growled down the phone.

"I've been busy. Listen, can I call you back later? We are literally just about to leave on a mission?"

"Fine, but you better ring me back, you turd, and tell Ian to stop ignoring my calls. If you don't phone me back tomorrow, I'm telling Mum."

"You're such a pain in the arse. I'll talk to you tomorrow." And with that, Kevin hung up. He looked at Ian.

"I heard. Come on. Let's head out."

"I can't wait to meet your brother," Creed said with a smile.

"Neither can we, Wolfie, and if he's a stick in the mud, you know Dave as well as Troy and all of us will razz the hell out of him," Seth told Kevin with a laugh.

Kevin laughed. "I can't wait to see that. But now, we really have to go."

~

Dave and Max walked into the kitchen. They'd tidied some shelves and started to get some of the books in order, but it was slow going.

Thomaz had brought lunch down to them, but they were both now in need of coffee and cake.

They walked into the kitchen and found it empty.

"It seems strange that no one is in here," Max commented.

"I know," Dave said, hunting around for the cakes. "What I find strange is how at home I feel here. I thought I would miss my house, but no."

"I've never seen you this happy, Davy."

He pulled out the cake box and smiled at Max. "I've never been this happy. Sure, I'm in a strange new world, but I have David, so it all balances out."

"That's good to hear, sweetheart," David said, walking into the kitchen with Stefan by his side.

"Hey, babe," Dave said, putting the cake box down, walking to David, and wrapping his arms around him.

David pulled Dave as close as he could and dropped a kiss on his head.

"We're making coffee and having cake," Max tells them. "Want some?"

"Yes, so very yes," Stefan replied.

Dave pulled back and looked at David and Stefan. "What's wrong?"

"Let's get coffee and cake first and then we'll tell you," Stefan replied.

"Okay," Dave said, moving to the coffee pot. Thankfully, it was full. He got four mugs and filled them whilst David got the milk and Stefan found the plates and a knife for the cake.

Once everyone was seated with cake and coffee in front of them, Dave asked, "So, what's wrong? Wait, you went and saw the lemmings. How did you get on?"

"We found out more than we knew before. The things those men were involved in is disturbing. We managed to pull out information from most of the lemmings, but we'll need Sean or Kayden to perform the unbreaking spell so we can access Giles Goodsir's mind. I know they are busy at the moment, though, and I don't want to pull them away from that."

"I'm sure they won't mind you ringing and asking for help," Dave said.

"They wouldn't," Ivan said as he walked into the kitchen.

"Ivan, when did you get back?" David asked him.

"A few moments ago. I have all the lemmings' gadgets and need to go through them. From what we found out, it appears Quintus Cameron-Webb might be the mastermind behind all of this. But a witch named Jake Conway has upped and left the witches coven. His name has been linked to everything as well. I left Neill, Sean, and Kayden looking through all the paperwork, and there is a *lot*. Gabe sent me back here while he and Mathis went back to the pack house."

Dave screwed his nose up. "I'm guessing that is the Cliff Notes version."

Ivan nodded. "Pretty much. I need to go through everything and pull-out relevant info, then try and hack into Quintus Cameron-Webb's computer. Is Gavin busy, do you know?"

"He was asleep in Hunter's arms when I took lunch up to them. I told them dinner was at seven if they wanted to come down, and if not, I would take food to them," Thomaz said, walking into the kitchen with Bruno at his side.

"Hey, Bruno, are you being a good boy?" Max asked the dog.

Bruno barked and ran over to Max, who slid to the floor and offered hugs and tummy rubs. "I'm glad you're all better now."

"Me, too," Dave said softly.

"Bruno needs a friend," Thomaz said.

"He has us. Or do you mean a doggy friend?" Dave asked.

"A doggy friend," Thomaz said. "I umm, might have found a German Shepherd puppy for sale. I was going to look at him later."

David laughed. "A dog convert?"

Thomaz nodded and grinned. "Maybe, plus I don't want Bruno to be lonely."

"Where did you find the puppy?" Dave asked.

"On that kennel club site you sent me. They are eight weeks old. Look," he said, pulling his phone out of his pocket and opening it up before handing it over to Dave.

"Oh, he's so cute," Dave said, looking at the picture before turning the phone and showing it to David. "Bruno and I can come with you if you want. It would be good for Bruno to meet the puppy and see if they like each other," Dave said.

Thomaz smiled. "That would make sense. Then if they do, we can stop off at the pet shop and buy everything the puppy will need."

"I think Mathis and Raz are still planning on getting a

puppy for Gavin. Maybe they should talk to Hunter, as well," Ivan added.

"That would make sense. If Gavin and Hunter come down for dinner, ask Gavin for help," David said to Ivan.

The vampire nods. "Will do. Now off to hack computers. See you all later."

"What time are you seeing the puppy, Thomaz?" Dave asked.

Thomaz looked at the time. "About an hour. I'll have to leave soon as it will take about forty-five minutes to get there."

Dave looked at David and grinned.

"No, you have Bruno and Troy," David told him.

Stefan and Thomaz laughed at that.

Dave grinned. "I'm going to tell Troy you said he was my pet."

"And before that, I'm off to work," Max said.

"When can you start here full time?" Stefan asked him.

"Four weeks. I don't think they'll let me go earlier on account of Davy being on holiday and then leaving."

"I've not handed my notice in yet," Dave pointed out.

"But when you do, it will be with immediate effect, won't it?" Max asked him.

Dave nodded. "Sorry."

Max shook his head. "Don't worry about it. I mean, when I finally do leave, I get to work in the most amazing secret library in the world. So worth it."

"You do know if you want to move in, there are enough rooms for you to pick one, don't you?" David told him.

"I might have to build up to that if you don't mind," Max said.

"We understand. Just know you will be more than welcome."

"Thanks," Max said. "Now I really do have to go."

"So do we," Thomaz said. "We can walk out with you."

Dave jumped up. "Bruno, harness."

Bruno walked over to Dave and stood while Dave put him in the harness and attached the lead before kissing David. "See you all later."

CHAPTER 22

The rescue party arrived at the warehouse trading estate and parked well away from the one they wanted.

"Gabe, can you detect any witch traps from here?" Kevin asked him.

Gabe closed his eyes and sent his magic out to have a look. "Yes, there are several bombs on some doors and windows and something else. My magic is saying there is demon magic in the warehouse."

"Can you undo all the magic?" Seth asked.

"The witch, yes; the demon magic… I guess we'll find out," Gabe said, sending out his magic to disable the witch bombs. "Huh. It didn't work."

"Why not?" Seth asked, sounding confused.

"They are tied to the demon magic. We can't get in via any doors or windows, I think the only way in or out is via portal."

"Any witch portal or a specific one?" Mathis asked.

"From the feel of things, any witch portal. I've also found out that there are twenty children in there, plus three shifters

— two bears and a lion — and two vampires," Gabe said, opening his eyes.

"Can you create separate witch portals at the same time at different ends of the warehouse?" Gio asked.

"There might be a few seconds delay between them, but I can do that, yes."

Kevin looked at those gathered. "Same rules apply. Stick to your groups, don't get dead, and see you on the inside."

"Everyone ready?" Gabe asked. "Seth, you and your team go in first. As soon as the last of you are through, the portal will close. We'll use the second portal." With that, Gabriel swirled his hands and the first portal opened, followed seconds later by the second one. The two teams entered with the portals closing behind them.

Seth and his team walked out at the back of the warehouse where numerous crates were stacked up two and three high in front of them.

Seth pointed to Cairo and, using hand signals, told Cairo to take some of the group and look on the right while he and the others would look on the left.

Cairo nodded, tapped Troy and Jessamy on the arm, and motioned others to follow him.

Seth motioned for the wolf shifters with them to spread out and keep watch. He then signalled for the others to follow him.

They quietly moved around the boxes. He looked into one of the crates and saw it had bars on the front and a child curled up, watching.

The child looked at Seth, who motioned for the child to keep quiet. The boy, and Seth was pretty sure it was a young boy, nodded and moved closer to the crate bars. He then pointed to the upstairs of the warehouse and pretended to hiss.

Seth smiled at him and gave him two thumbs up and

carried on moving forward, checking the other crates. A few were empty, but the majority held children of all different ages.

Suddenly they heard fighting coming from the front of the warehouse.

"Protect the merchandise," he heard someone call out.

He heard a roar and realised the lion was headed their way. Before he could say anything, he saw Troy shift, and he and some wolves went to stop the lion.

"Get the children out of the crates," Seth said, ignoring the fighting.

He, Gio, Bailey, and Raz started opening the crates and releasing the children. Each child they released they carried to some of the wolf shifters who were now in their wolf form and formed a protective ring around them.

From above, they heard a screech.

"Bailey and I will deal with him. You stay with the children," Gio said, drawing his sword as Bailey drew his and ran off.

"There are only fifteen children here. I thought Gabe said there were twenty," Raz said, doing a quick head count.

Seth looked at the children and saw the first child stood in front of the others, watching. Seth walked over to him. "Do you know where the missing children are?"

He nodded. "They took them to a room over there," he said, pointing to a door off to the side.

"Do you know what's in there?" Raz asked.

The boy shook his head. "I've never been in there. But they need saving, as well."

Seth nodded. "We'll save them."

Kevin and his team were fighting with some of the guards. The lion had shifted and ran off towards the back of the warehouse.

The two guards they found were easily dealt with, killing them before they could shift. Kevin's team had started to search the rooms around their part of the warehouse when more guards appeared. They'd just killed those guards when even more arrived.

"Where the chuff are they coming from?" Ian asked.

"That room," Creed said, pointing to an open door where more guards were running through.

"They must have a portal in there and sent a message for help. I'll go and close it," Gabe said, quickly running that way.

Mathis and Ian joined him and fought their way into the room where they saw the open portal.

Gabriel grabbed his wand and threw his magic at the portal. They heard a scream from the inside, and though the portal didn't close, no more guards came through. "I've managed to stop anyone else from coming through, but demon magic was used to create this portal. It will take me a while to close it."

"Ian, do you want to go back and help the others and I'll stay with Gabe?" Mathis said.

"Will do. Stay safe," Ian replied, running out of the room.

Gabe raised his other hand and pushed more magic into the portal, but whomever was on the other side of the portal pushed back. The battle to close the portal was on.

CHAPTER 23

*H*unter sighed as his arms tightened around Gavin. Gavin was lying on top of him and moved his head to kiss Hunter's chest.

"So, is my chomp mark going to scar? You know, like in those vampire films where they have two bite marks on their neck that they have to cover with fancy scarves?" Hunter asked with a smile in his voice.

Gavin looked up, nodded, and smiled. He moved and signed.

"No, sweetheart, I don't mind. I also don't care who sees it. You're mine, I'm yours, the whole world can know for all I care."

Gavin smiled, leant down, and kissed Hunter. He would try and heat things up, but after making love three times, he was tired and hungry. As proven by the loud rumble of his stomach.

Hunter pulled back and laughed. "Let's shower and dress and then go and feed you."

Gavin nodded but then flopped down on Hunter.

THE VAMPIRE AND THE TATTOOIST

Hunter laughed. "That's the opposite of getting up, sweetheart."

Gavin lifted his head and poked his tongue out at Hunter before moving off him.

Hunter laughed and got off the bed, holding his hand out to Gavin, who took it. Hunter then pulled Gavin out of bed and into the bathroom.

Forty-five minutes later, hand in hand, Hunter and Gavin walked into the kitchen just as the final dish was being put down.

Dave saw them first and jumped up, hugging both Gavin and Hunter. "Well, you both look happy."

"That could be because we are," Hunter replied.

"Good. Dinners ready. Come sit," Dave said walking back to his chair.

Gavin pulled Hunter to the table and they both sat down. He looked around but didn't see his brothers, so he looked at David.

"Mathis, Gabe, and Raz are still with the pack rescuing the children," David told him. He looked at Hunter. "Gabriel might also have a lead on the witch who threatened you, but he's with the rescue mission at the moment."

Hunter nodded. "The children need saving first."

"Hey, Gavin, with your brother busy, can you help me go through some of the lemmings' gadgets?" Ivan asked.

Gavin nodded and then looked at Hunter.

"I don't mind, sweetheart. Help your friend."

"Ivan," Ivan said.

"Hunter."

"Thanks, Hunter." He looked back at Gavin. "Can you do it straight after dinner?"

Gavin nodded.

"While you do that, I can pop home and get some more clothes."

Gavin frowned.

"Hunter, until the witch is caught, I'd rather you didn't leave the coven house or grounds. Can your friend drop off some clothes for you?" David asked.

Hunter sighed. "Yeah, he won't mind," he said, taking his phone out and sending Taha a message.

"It's not forever," Dave said. "How about after dinner, you and I go somewhere and chat about how we don't get any superpowers after mating a vampire."

Hunter laughed. "Yes, let's do that."

"Thomaz, how did you and Dave get on seeing the puppy?" Stefan asked.

Gavin sat up straighter and signed, "Puppy?"

"Yes, a puppy, a German Shepherd puppy. I thought Bruno needed a friend. The puppy was so cute and snuggly, and Bruno liked him. We pick him up at the weekend," Thomaz replied, smiling.

"He didn't snuggle with me, but he latched onto Thomaz," Dave said.

"And we have time to buy everything we need for the little guy," Thomaz said.

Gavin signed.

"If you want a puppy, I'm sure we can find you one," Hunter said. "You know puppies are hard work, right? They need training and walking, and they pee everywhere."

"Not if they are trained properly," Dave put in. "Plus, Bruno will help."

As they were talking, dishes were passed around, and suddenly Thiago appeared, smiling.

"Just in time for dinner, Thiago," Annie said, smiling at him.

Gavin jumped up and gave him a hug.

"Hello, everyone." He looked around. "Where's Raz?"

"He and some others went with Kevin and his pack to rescue some kidnapped children," David told him.

"Then I will go and help." And just as suddenly as he arrived, Thiago vanished.

GABRIEL WAS STILL STRUGGLING with closing the portal. He had managed to stop anyone else from coming out but still couldn't shut it down. Each time he thought he had it and could close it, more magic poured in from the other side, and Gabe was getting tired. He wasn't sure how much longer he could keep a hold on the portal, but he needed to close it.

"What can I do, little witch?" Mathis asked gently.

"Nothing. Whoever is on the other side of this portal is strong. I'm still trying to close it. I can't leave it open, vampy."

"Can you find the end, so we know where it originated?"

Gabe shook his head. "No, I'm stuck in the middle. I'll keep trying."

While Gabe was dealing with the portal, it didn't take long for Kevin and his team to incapacitate the new guards. Once done, they thoroughly searched their end of the warehouse. All the rooms were empty.

Kevin sent his team to go and help Seth's. He walked over to the room where Gabe and Mathis were and saw Gabe struggling to close the portal. "Don't forget, Gabe, you can do this," he said from the doorway.

"I can. It's just taking time," Gabe replied, not looking away from the portal.

Kevin left him to it and went to join the others at the back and looked around.

"Where is Seth and Raz?" he asked.

Bailey nodded towards a room off to the side. "Some children were taken in here. Seth and Raz went to help them."

Kevin rushed to the room, Creed at his side. They found Raz standing guard in front of five children and Seth fighting with a guard. The speed at which they are fighting meant Seth was fighting a vampire.

"Creed, help Raz to get the children out and put them with the others."

Creed ran over, and once they gathered the children, Raz and Creed rushed out of the room.

Just then, Gio came running into the room, took one look at the fight, and jumped into the fray. The next moment, Seth was falling into Kevin after being shoved out of the way by Gio.

Kevin caught him before they could both fall to the floor.

Seth was fuming. "Oh, he did *not* just shove me out of a fight."

Kevin patted his head. "There, there."

Seth swatted his hand away. "Giovanni, you are so sleeping on the sofa tonight," he shouted angrily.

A loud growl was heard from Gio, and the next moment, the other vampire was thrown into the wall. He went through the wall and lay unconscious. half in and out of it. Gio turned to look at Seth.

"Don't even talk to me right now," Seth said to him.

"But my Seth—" Gio started, but Seth turned and stomped out of the room.

Kevin looked at Gio and shook his head. "Oh, Gio."

Gio looked a bit sheepish. "I guess I shouldn't have done that."

"No. This is what Seth does and he's good at his job," Kevin said.

"I know, but I've not been there for over thirty years. I just want to keep him safe," Gio explained.

"Talk to him and grovel nicely," Kevin said, offering those

words of encouragement as he walked out of the room with Gio following.

"We need to get the children somewhere safe," Creed said.

"Gabe can help. He can create a portal for us," Ian said.

"Gabe was trying to close that other portal," Kevin said.

"Maybe I can help," Thiago said, appearing next to him and looking around.

Raz smiled and walked to his side just as a loud explosion sounded from the direction of the portal.

They took off at a run. The vampires reached them first, followed closely by the shifters.

The room was filled with smoke, and with a wave of his hand, Thiago got rid of the smoke and saw both Gabe and Mathis on the floor near the far wall, eyes closed.

Raz ran to his brother and Kevin to Gabe with the others crowding around.

"Gabe?" Kevin said, kneeling next to him.

"I closed the portal," he said, opening his eyes and rubbing the back of his head. "Mathis?"

"I'm here, little witch. I would just like to go on record as saying that hurt." He moved and let Raz and Thiago help him up just as Kevin and Ian were helping Gabe.

"But I closed the portal," Gabe said, waving his hand around to show the portal was gone.

"Can whoever opened it re-establish the portal into the warehouse?" Kevin asked.

"No, I took care of that," Thiago said.

"Hey, Thiago," Gabe said, walking to his side and hugging him.

Mathis pulled him into a hug, as well. "When did you turn up?"

"A few moments ago. I went to the coven house to join Raz for dinner when David told me you were all here. I came to see if you needed help."

"Now that the portal is closed, we should be good to get the children out of here," Gabe said.

"Where can we take them?" Creed asked.

"We'll take them back to the pack house. Our healer can check them out and we can keep them safe while we look for their families," Kevin replied.

"We can help you protect them, as well, if needed," Seth offered.

"Thanks, I'll let you know," Kevin said, resting his hand on Seth's shoulder for a moment. He turned and walked towards the children where some of his pack were still in wolf form surrounding and protecting them.

"Okay, children. My name is Kevin, and my pack is protecting you. We've gotten rid of all the guards and will get you all out of here in a moment. For now, you'll come with me to my pack while we look for your families."

The children gave an excited mutter. The one who spoke to Seth stepped forward, looking at Kevin as if sizing him up. "How do we know we can trust you? Those guards said the same thing, that we were being taken to our homes, but we knew they were lying."

"I swear to you on my honour as an Alpha, I will help you all to find your families and get you home."

"So will I," Seth said. "Along with my coven."

"As will I," Gabe said.

The boy stared at them all for a moment before turning to the other children. "This guy says he can find our families and get us home. Let's go with him. If we don't like it, we can run away."

Ian snorted out a laugh. "That you can, my young friend. Now, how about we get out of here. I'm sure if we ask someone nicely, they can provide bacon sandwiches and cakes."

"Plus, you know, maybe a bath and clean clothes," Gio

added, looking over the children who were wearing dirty clothes and, going by the smell, none had washed in a while.

Gabe turned and opened a portal to the pack house. "This will take you home. I need to go back to my coven, but call if you need me, and I'll update you on everything the others found out."

"Thanks, witch. We'll talk tomorrow. All those coming to the pack house, through the portal. Ian, you first," Kevin said.

Ian grinned at the children and walked through the portal, motioning them to follow. It took a while, but finally Kevin kissed Creed and walked through, Gabe closing the portal behind them.

Gio looked at Creed. "You didn't want to go with him?"

"I did, but I have his car keys. I'll drive his car over to the pack house, but if you need me for anything, just call."

"We will," Seth said. "I've got my car, so I'll drive back to the coven house. Anyone want a lift?"

"I'll come with you, my Seth," Gio said, smiling at his mate.

Seth scowled at him. "Anyone except Giovanni, who will be sleeping on the sofa tonight."

"But—" Gio started to say, but Seth stomped off.

"I'll come with you, Seth," Gabe said, walking to catch up with him.

"I'm joining them," Mathis said, pointing to Gabe and Seth.

"I have my car, so I'll drive back," Cairo said.

"And I'm going with him," Troy said.

Gabe paused and turned round, opening a portal to the vampire coven. "It will close when the last person walks through," he called back.

"I guess I'm using the portal," Gio grumped out, walking through it first, the others following.

CHAPTER 24

The portal brought them out into the kitchen where dinner was still being eaten.

"Welcome back," David said, looking them all over.

Dave jumped up and hugged everyone. He looked around. "We're missing people. Where are they? And are the children safe?"

"Everyone is safe. We took no serious injuries. The children are with the pack," Raz said, smiling at Gavin. "The others are driving back."

"Gio, where's Seth?" Louise asked.

"Driving back with Gabe and Mathis. I wasn't allowed to go with him," Gio grumbled as he sat down at the table.

"What did you do?" Dave asked him, grinning. "I bet you did something. Did you stop him fighting or demand he stayed hidden?"

"I pushed him out of a fight and took over," Gio admitted.

Everyone at the table groaned.

"Oh, Gio," Stefan said. "Are you sleeping on the sofa, as well?"

Gio nodded. "I was only trying to protect him. I've not been able to do that in forever."

"He knows that darling. But remember, this is what Seth does," Louise told him.

"I know," Gio said with a big, heartfelt sigh.

"There's plenty of food for you all. Dig in," Annie told them.

"Then, once you've eaten, you can tell us everything," Dave says.

Raz looked up and saw Gavin staring at him. "I promise, Mathis and Gabe are fine. They were knocked out for a few moments when a portal blew up, but they are both fine."

Gavin's fingers started flying.

"Gavin asked how the portal blew up," Dave translated.

Raz shook his head. "No idea. Gabe can tell us when he gets back here. You look happy, little brother."

Gavin signed.

Hunter grabbed his hand and kissed the back of it. "You make me happy, too, sweetheart."

"I look forward to getting to know you, Hunter," Raz said, sending him a smile.

"Thanks. I look forward to getting to know you, as well."

∼

Seth was driving home silently fuming.

"What did Gio do?" Gabe asked.

"He threw me into Kevin so he could take over fighting the vampire," Seth spat out. "You know, because I've never fought a vampire in my life. If he doesn't trust my skills, we're going to have problems."

Mathis leant forward from the back seat and touched Seth's shoulder. "Did you ever think that he just wanted to protect you? He's not been able to do that for a long time."

"He knows you can fight and know what to do. But think of how he feels. He's just gotten you back, Seth, so of course he wants to protect you," Gabe added.

"Stop talking sense. Now I can't stay mad at him," Seth huffed out.

Mathis and Gabe laughed. "Make up sex," they both said at the same time.

Seth grinned and drove faster.

~

Kevin looked at the children sitting around the large pack table, eating sandwiches as if they were starving, which they probably were.

"Once they've eaten, we'll find them beds for the night, and I have some pack members getting clothes. When they've had a bath we can get them to bed," Lissa said. "Your healer isn't here at the moment but should be back tomorrow."

"Thanks, Mum. Is king loser back yet?"

Lissa shook her head. "No, your brother is still away. He won't be back until tomorrow, but he phoned to get me to remind you to phone him."

"I'll call him now," Kevin said, pulling his phone out of his pocket and dialling his brother.

"About time you phone, dweeb," his brother said.

"What's up Dirty Gerty?" Kevin replied.

Ian snorted out a laugh and Lissa rolled her eyes.

"What have I said about you calling me that?"

"To call you that all the time," Kevin said, laughing down the phone.

"You're such a dick," his brother grumbled.

"So, I'm calling you back as you demanded. What's up?"

"What's up? How about my brother ignoring all my calls and messages. How about Ian ignoring them as well. You can't leave me

a message saying you're celebrating finding your mate and having your consciousness back and not tell me the details."

"There is too much to tell you over the phone. So, the Cliff Notes version is we're friends and working with the D'Angelo coven. It was there I met my mate, Creed. We're also friends with the Augusta witch's coven."

"You're friends with Roberto Augusta?" Bert queried in astonishment.

Kevin snorted out a laugh. "Hell no. He's dead, never to return after having his heart ripped out. No, with Gabriel, his brother, who is now head of the coven and head of the Southern Witches. It was while we were helping Gabe that we discovered kidnapped children and a lot of other dodgy stuff that we're all working together to sort out. I've also invited Annie and Louise to come and play with our pups."

"I've heard of Annie. She's the human who keeps feeding the pack."

"She is."

"Who is Louise?"

"The vampire queen,"

"So since I've been gone, you've made friends with witches and vampires?" Bert queried.

"And a jaguar," Kevin added.

"Please tell me it's not Troy Nettles."

Kevin laughed. "If it helps, David D'Angelo wants to either maim or kill him."

"So why doesn't he?"

"Dave, his mate, won't let him. Listen PITA, I have to run. I'll give you full details when you get back."

"And you can introduce me to your mate and new friends. It's about time we all worked together, and I would like to meet the vampiric Royal family."

"You will soon enough. Be safe and chat soon." And before his brother could say anything else, Kevin hung up.

Ian looked over at him and laughed. "He'll get you back for that."

Kevin shrugged. "He can try. I'll just set Dave on him."

Lissa shook her head. "One day I hope the three of you have sons who are just like you."

"Mum, that's just mean," Kevin complained.

"Welcome to my world, darling."

CHAPTER 25

Seth, Gabe, and Mathis arrived back at the coven house at the same time as Cairo and Troy.

"Forgiven Gio yet?" Cairo asked Seth as they walked up the front steps.

"Yeah," Seth replied. "I couldn't stay mad at him."

Mathis opened the door and they all walked in, heading for the kitchen.

"Welcome back," David said, as they entered the kitchen.

Gavin jumped up and hugged Gabe and Mathis and signed.

"We're both fine. The explosion just blew us off our feet and gave us a little bump on the head," Gabe assured him.

Gavin nodded and smiled, pointing to the table.

"Yes to food. I'm starving," Gabe said.

Gio saw Seth enter and jumped up, moving to stand in front of him. "I'm sorry, my Seth—"

He didn't get any further as Seth pulled Gio into his arms and kissed the stuffing out of him. He pulled back. "Thank you for wanting to protect me. But no more shoving me out of a fight."

"I promise, my Seth."

"Aww, you two are so cute," Troy said, laughing their way.

Cairo grabbed Troy and dragged him to the other end of the table.

"You love living dangerously, kitty," David said.

"What can I say? It keeps me on my toes."

"We kept food back for you," Thomaz said, bringing fresh, hot dishes to the table.

Gavin sighed happily. His brothers and their mates are home and safe. He had been worried for a while there. He leaned into Hunter's side, and Hunter put his arm around him.

"Hunter, I meant to ask what your favourite food is so we can cook it for you," Annie enquired.

"Roast pork with all the trimmings is my absolute favourite, but I'll happily eat anything unless it's cake with vegetables in it," Hunter replied.

"Oh, a nice big roast dinner. Thomaz, we'll have to do that one Sunday," Annie said happily. "Louise, I was thinking of going over to Kevin's pack tomorrow. I thought we could maybe reassure the children they're now safe and play with puppies."

"That sounds like a good idea. I'll come with you," Louise said, smiling Annie's way.

"I'll message Kevin to let him know to expect you," David said.

"And ask him if he wants us to bring anything," Louise said.

"Will do."

Everyone chatted while the latecomers ate their dinner, but once they were finished and everything cleared away, David asked what happened.

"You mean apart from the love of my life throwing me out of a fight and into Kevin?" Seth asked with a laugh.

Gio picked his hand up and kissed the back.

"Yep, apart from that," David replied.

Seth told them what they found out and everything else that happened. He shook his head. "They kept the children in small crates. Who even does that?"

"Sick people whom we will stop," David said.

"Some of the wolves and I took on a lion. I'm pleased to say we won," Troy told them.

"I thought a lion would always win against a jaguar," Hunter remarked.

"In the jungle maybe, but we're shifters and I had the wolves helping. It was still hard, but we all survived. Well, not the lion, but the rest of us did."

"Someone opened a portal and kept sending guards and other nefarious people through, which Kevin and the others stopped. It took work to close the portal," Gabe told them. "Whoever was on the other end was a strong magic user. But I closed it in the end."

"And caused it to explode," Gio added.

Gabe shook his head. "I don't think that was me. I think it happened when I negated the other magic."

"It felt like demon magic," Thiago said.

"That would explain the power in that magic. Any idea who it belonged to?" Gabe asked him.

Thiago shook his head. "No, but I can go and find out."

Raz took his hand. "Can you do it safely?

Thiago nodded. "I can. How about you come with me when I go back and you can see the underworld, where I live, and what I do?"

Raz gave a huge smile. "Yes, please and thank you."

Gavin looked at Thiago and started signing.

"You will, Gavin." He looked at Raz. "Your brother was concerned he wouldn't be able to contact you in the underworld. All electrical devices will work down there."

E. BROOM

"You have Wi-Fi in hell?" Dave asked shocked

"No, we have Wi-Fi in the underworld. Hell is a completely different place that none of you will *ever* be seeing," Thiago said.

"So hell and the underworld are two different places?" Willard asked as if trying to figure it out.

Thiago nodded. "They are. The underworld is just like this world but down there and is where demons live. Hell is basically a large torture chamber with a lot of different levels, depending on the crimes committed."

"Wow, that's amazing," Dave said. "I hope one day I can see where you live. I imagine it would be, well, I'm going to say amazing again, but how about fascinating?"

"I will see what I can do. We can bring mates down, but it's frowned on to bring anyone else down without permission."

"Who do you need to get permission from?" Raz asked.

"I can put a request in to Lucifer."

"Wait," Hunter said. "*The* Lucifer, the fallen angel, the devil?"

Thiago snorted. "Lucifer and the Devil are two different entities. The Devil is the evil one. Lucifer is ruler of the underworld. He's still an angel, just a down below angel and not an above angel."

"I think my mind is literally blown right now," Dave said. "I want to come down even more now."

"Me, too," Hunter said. "Being with all of you and a part of this world is certainly eye opening."

Thiago smiled. "I'll put a request in as soon as I get back."

"I'm afraid I need to get back to my coven. I need to catch up with the others and look into Jake Conway," Gabe said.

"I can grab my laptop and come back with you," Mathis offered.

Gabe nodded. "I'd like that, unless you're needed here."

"Go with Gabe, Mathis. Gavin said he would help Ivan with some research," David told him.

"I'll just run upstairs and grab some clean clothes. Be back in a bit," Mathis said, standing up and walking out of the kitchen.

He had just passed the front door when the bell rang. "I'll get it," he called out and pulled the door open and looked at the man standing there, holding a bag.

"You're Hunter's friend," Mathis said.

"Taha. He asked me to drop off some clothes and I've brought his car back."

Mathis nodded. "Come on in. Hunter's in the kitchen. Just down there on the left."

"Thanks," Taha said, walking in and heading towards the kitchen while Mathis closed the door and went upstairs.

Taha walked into the kitchen and saw Hunter sitting at the table, Gavin was leaning into his side, both of them looking happy.

Annie saw him first. "Hello. Taha, isn't it?"

Hunter looked up and saw his friend.

"It is." He held up a bag. "I've got your stuff, Hunter. I've also brought your car back."

Hunter stood up and walked over, giving him a bro hug. "Thanks, Ta. How are you getting home?"

"Luke's waiting outside in his car. I also thought I should remind you that you have Mrs. Sargent coming in tomorrow."

Hunter nodded. "I've not forgotten. I'll be at the studio tomorrow."

"Hunter, you still have the witch after you," David said.

Hunter nodded. "I know, but I need to work tomorrow. I know how to punch, and Taha is an expert in martial arts."

"Taha really is good," Troy agreed.

Gavin clicked his fingers, and when Hunter looked at him, he started signing.

"I'll be safe, I promise. And I won't go anywhere alone," Hunter assured him.

Gavin silently huffed.

"I like him," Taha said, grinning at Gavin. "We call that the Hunter huff."

Gavin gave a silent laugh.

"Ignore Taha. He talks nonsense," Hunter said with a laugh.

Taha handed over the bag and Hunter's keys. "Right, I'm off. I'll see you tomorrow. Do you want me to come and pick you up?"

Hunter was about to say no when he looked at Gavin. "Yeah, that might be best."

"Pick you up at nine. Bye, everyone," Taha said.

"I'll see you out," Hunter said, following Taha out into the hall. He dumped his bag by the stairs and walked to the front door.

"You look really happy, Hunt," Taha said, grinning at him. "I can't wait to get to know Gavin."

"Me, either. Thanks for helping out."

"That's what friends are for. I'll see you tomorrow morning."

"You will," Hunter replied, opening the front door. He saw Luke sitting in his car and waved.

"See you tomorrow," Taha said, giving him another bro hug before descending the front steps.

With a final wave, Hunter shut the door and walked back to the kitchen. There was silence as he entered. Hunter sighed. "I'll be careful; I promise. If it was any other client, I'd change the appointment, but I can't change Danni's," he said, sitting down.

"Why not?" Gio asked him.

"Danni is a cancer survivor. Her tattoo tomorrow is to cover up her surgery and treatment scars. She has been through so much and needs this to help her mental health."

"I can send someone with you tomorrow," David said, not trying to talk Hunter out of going to work.

Hunter looked at Gavin. "Would you feel better if I had a vampire with me?"

Gavin nodded and signed.

"I know, sweetheart. If it will put your mind at rest. You realise, though, that if when we mated you had passed on some of your abilities to me, I wouldn't need anyone watching over me."

Gavin silently laughed.

"Hunter, I feel your pain," Dave commiserated.

"You poor humans, you," Seth said with a laugh.

Mathis chose that moment to come back into the kitchen, carrying a bag and backpack.

"Right, we're off. Call if you need us," Gabe said, standing up and walking to Mathis' side. "Portal or car?"

"Portal; it's quicker," Mathis replied. He smiled at his brothers. "See you later."

Gavin jumped up and hugged them both before signing.

"We'll be safe," Gabe assured him, and with that, he opened a portal, and with a final bye, they both walked through, the portal closing behind them.

CHAPTER 26

Gavin was sitting at his brother's desk. He had been upstairs and got his tablet, bringing it down so he and Ivan could run searches for the children's families and to see what else they could uncover.

Ivan had hard drives and other electronics from the witches' coven house he was also going through.

Gavin knew searching for the families was important, but for the first time in his life, his mind wasn't on computer things. It was on his mate, Hunter. The most perfect man he had ever met. Hunter who seemed to get him and understand him without words.

He knew Hunter had to go to work, but that didn't mean he wasn't going to worry about him while he was out of the house.

"You have it bad, my friend," Ivan said with a laugh.

Gavin looked up and grinned before nodding.

Ivan sobered. "We'll all do that we can to keep your man safe. You know that, right?"

Gavin nodded and signed.

"I know you're worried. You're allowed to be."

THE VAMPIRE AND THE TATTOOIST

Gavin signed.

"Love makes everyone crazy," Ivan told him.

Gavin signed again.

Ivan shook his head. "I've not had time to go back to the library and see Jamie. I'm not even sure if I should."

Gavin gave a silent huff and signed again.

"I didn't get all that, but did you say everyone deserves love?"

Gavin nodded.

"Maybe," Ivan replied.

Gavin picked up a pen and threw it at Ivan, who caught it, laughing.

"Let's get back to research and see what we can find."

Gavin grinned and nodded.

∽

HUNTER WAS SAT in the library with Dave.

Dave thought of this library as his and Max's, but as Max wasn't around, it was a good place for them both to talk.

"We need some sofas down here," Dave said. He and Hunter were currently sitting at Dave's desk.

"Sofas would be good. I can't believe there is a massive library here, under the house."

"I know. This is literally my dream job, curating this library and bringing order to the total chaos that's here, and I don't even need to leave the house," Dave said happily while looking around.

"Did you really get kidnapped?" Hunter asked him, looking curious.

Dave nodded. "I really did." He went on to explain everything that had happened since Seth brought him here. He left nothing out. Hunter deserved to know the truth.

"Wow, that's a lot going on," Hunter said, shaking his head at the understatement.

"It is, and now just think, you are part of this crazy family, as well," Dave paused. "Are you okay with that?"

Hunter nodded. "I think so. I mean, I love Gavin with my whole heart, and if I have to become part of this world to have him in my life, then so be it. I might ask one of the vampire guards to teach me self-defence. I mean, I can throw a punch, but fighting has always been Taha's thing."

"You can join our lessons when they start. David insists my parents and I learn self-defence, it would be no problem including you as well," Dave assured him.

"If only we got cool abilities when we mated, that would solve everything. I feel jipped."

Dave laughed. "Me, too. I was hoping for super speed or super hearing, but we get nothing but a permanent vampire hickey."

Hunter snorted out a laugh. "Plus, we get the man of our dreams."

Dave sighed. "We do. You know everyone will keep you safe, don't you?"

Hunter nodded. "I know, and I know Gavin would prefer I stayed here until the witch was caught, but I really can't put Danni off."

"Gavin understands, he really does. It's a mate thing, wanting to keep your loved one safe," Dave told him.

"I feel the same way about Gavin. I know he's a vampire with super abilities, but I don't see that when I look at him. What I see is the amazing man he is, who makes me smile and laugh, and who I want to wrap up in cotton wool."

"I think we all feel the same about him. He has this air of gentleness about him, which even though he killed that witch, he hasn't lost. Thomaz told me Gavin slept in the kitchen last night with Bruno."

Hunter nodded. "He told me the same. Hopefully Gavin will sleep better tonight, wrapped in my arms, knowing how much I love him."

"I'm sure he will," Dave agreed.

∽

Gabe sighed as the portal closed behind them. He brought them to his bedroom so Mathis could drop his bag off.

Mathis put his bags on the bed and pulled Gabe into his arms. "You okay, little witch?"

Gabe wrapped his arms around Mathis, leant on him, and nodded. "I'm fine, vampy. I just need a moment with just the two of us."

Mathis dropped a kiss on his head. "You can have all the moments you want."

Gabe pulled back. "I just need you and me somewhere away from all of this where we can just focus on us, and not any of this other crap we're dealing with."

"And we will," Mathis assured him. "But for now, we need to focus on all this crap. Before we do, though, I'm going to kiss you."

Gabe smiled. "Good plan," he said as Mathis dipped his head and kissed him.

Finally, they both pulled back.

"Perfect," Gabe said, smiling.

"Yes, it was, and it will keep being perfect. But for now, let's go and see Sean, Kayden, and Neill and make sure they're not buried under paperwork."

"Hopefully they remembered to stop and eat," Gabe replied, pulling out of Mathis' arms and taking his hand.

Mathis snatched up his laptop bag and went with Gabe.

They found Sean, Kayden, and Neill still hard at work. There were piles of papers everywhere and empty shelves.

"You've been busy," Mathis said as he walked in.

They all quickly looked up, with Sean and Kayden jumping up and hugging both Mathis and Gabe.

Mathis looked at Neill. "What, no hug from you?"

Neill laughed. "Maybe next time."

"Did the children get rescued?" Kayden asked them.

"They did. They're currently at the wolf pack being looked after until their parents can be found," Gabe told them.

"Thank goodness for that," Sean said, breathing a sigh of relief.

"Have you eaten?" Mathis asked them.

"No, not yet," Neill said. "We ordered Chinese. We're just waiting for it to arrive. I asked the takeaway place if they would text me when they arrive, and I'll go down and get it."

"We can all go down. You guys look like you could use a break from all this," Gabe said.

"Yeah, we really do," Kayden said with a sigh.

Neill stood up, stretched, and gave a tired sigh. "I think I'm getting old."

Mathis snorted. "You *are* old."

"How old are you, or is it rude to ask?" Kayden asked.

"I stopped counting when I hit five hundred," Neill replied.

"You're over five hundred years old? You look good for your age," Sean said, grinning at him.

Gabe looked at Mathis. "How old are you?"

"Mathis is still a baby vampire," Neill said, chuckling.

"I'm three hundred and ninety-nine," Mathis replied.

"We'll have to throw you a four hundred year birthday party," Gabe said. "We can hold it at your home."

Mathis shook his head. "You don't need to do that."

"I can just see Dave, Gabe, and Gavin now, decorating the hell out of the place," Neill said, laughing as they left the secret room and then the bedroom. Gabe sealed it again as the door closed.

Mathis groaned. "They would, too, and Seth would help."

"Ian, as well, I should imagine," Gabe replied, laughing. "This will be so much fun. We can make it fancy dress."

"Yay, fancy dress parties are the best," Sean agreed.

Mathis looked at Neill. "I blame you."

Neill nodded. "I would, too."

By this time, they reached the kitchen just as Neill's phone pinged. He smiled looking at the message. "Foods here," and with that he strolled off to the front door to get the food.

The others walked into the kitchen. A few people were sat in there eating. Gabe shook his head. He wondered what it would be like for the whole coven to eat together. It was something to think on anyway.

"Hey. Gabriel," one of the witches said. Incidentally, it was the witch who told Gabe to make Kay's trousers fall down.

"Hey, Brian, Stan, Danny. How are you three doing?"

"We're good. We made extra food if you want some," Stan said, waving to the dishes on the table.

"You all can join us," Brian offered, smiling at everyone.

"We have Chinese coming. You can share that with us if you want," Kayden said, walking to the cupboard and getting some plates while Sean got drinks.

Neill walked in, and the smell coming from the bag he was carrying was amazing.

"That smells amazing. I almost wish I'd not eaten now," Gabe says, flopping into a chair.

Neill brought the bag to the table and set everything out before taking a seat. He looked at everyone, "Help yourselves."

"Neill, this is Brian, Stan, and Danny. Guys, this is Neill, and you know Mathis." Gabe said.

"Homemade Chinese food and takeaway Chinese food, nice," Sean said, putting food on his plate and passing containers around.

Everyone except Mathis and Gabe were happily munching on the food.

"How is your search into the dodgy stuff going?" Brian asked.

"There is so much to go through, but thankfully, we rescued the last lot of kidnapped children," Gabe told them.

Stan shook his head. "How could all this stuff be going on in our coven and none of us knew?"

"It's a sophisticated operation. Thankfully, the vampires and wolves are helping, as this is way outside of things I know," Gabe said.

"You know if we can help in any way, we will," Danny said, pointing at the three of them.

"What do you know of Jake Conway?" Mathis asked them.

"I know he was one of the names on the dualling list," Stan said. "But apart from that, I didn't have much to do with him. He always struck me as a bit of a loner."

"Same here," Brian said. "He always stood apart from everyone in meetings, but now that I think about it, I'm not sure I saw him watching any of the duels."

"I don't remember seeing him, but I didn't really focus on anyone. I was more focused on watching Kay or taking part in duels," Gabe said.

"I don't remember seeing him, either," Kayden added. "But like Gabe, I didn't look to see who was there and who wasn't."

"I've not seen Jake for a couple of days, though," Brian said. "He might still be hiding in his room. I know some of the other witches are."

Gabe shook his head. "We checked his room. Jake had packed up and left."

"What an idiot. I mean, that's a sure sign he's involved with all this stuff," Danny said.

"But you said you would still investigate anyone that left," Brian added.

"We are. If he's involved, he'll not escape justice," Mathis replied.

"Good. He deserves everything that is headed his way," Stan replied.

CHAPTER 27

Hunter and Dave had been talking for hours when they finally emerged from the library.

After saying goodnight, Dave went to hunt down his mate, while Hunter went to look for Gavin.

Dave had given him directions to the office. and hoping he had the right one, he knocked on the door. He entered when he heard a, "Come in."

Gavin smiled when he saw Hunter and jumped up, walking around the desk and into his open arms.

Hunter dropped a kiss on Gavin's head, wrapping his arms around him before looking up and smiling at Ivan. "Sorry. Hi, Ivan."

Ivan laughed. "Hey, Hunter. How was your chat with Dave?"

"Interesting," Hunter said.

Gavin pulled back and looked up at Hunter, a question in his eyes.

"We're starting a support group for humans who mate vampires and don't get superhuman abilities."

Ivan laughed and Gavin gave a silent laugh.

THE VAMPIRE AND THE TATTOOIST

"How is research going?" Hunter asked.

"It's going. We have searches running for the families, financials, and I'm hacking into these devices," he said, waving his hand at the electronics on his desk, "to pull out all the information I can."

"I would offer to help, but I'm not that good with computers."

"That's okay. We have programmes running. Why don't you take Gavin off to bed? He didn't sleep well last night."

Gavin turned and scowled at Ivan before signing.

Ivan huffed. "Like Thomaz or your brothers haven't told Hunter already. There is nothing more you can do for tonight, so go with Hunter, little brother, and you can get back to this tomorrow."

Gavin signed again.

"I promise I'll get some sleep, as well, and yes in my bed and not at this desk."

Gavin nodded, signing.

"Night, Gav. Night, Hunter."

"Night, Ivan," Hunter said, taking Gavin's hand and leading him out of the office.

Hunter closed the bedroom door behind them and smiled at Gavin, dipping his head and kissing him.

Gavin stepped as close as he could to Hunter and wrapped his arms around him, loving the feel of Hunter in his arms, but he needed more. He moved his hands and pulled Hunter's top up.

Hunter groaned at the feel of Gavin's hands on his skin, but now he wanted Gavin naked and under him. He tapered the kiss and smiled down at Gavin. "How about I'll strip me, you strip you, and we go from there?"

Gavin smiled but shook his head. Before Hunter could do anything, Gavin was suddenly a blur, and in a moment, they were both naked.

Hunter's mouth dropped open before he smiled. "Handy trick." He picked Gavin up and laid him on the bed before climbing over him and leaning on his arms, keeping most of his weight off Gavin. "Love you, Gavin."

Gavin smiled at Hunter, linking his hands behind Hunter's neck and mouthed the words back, pulling Hunter down into a toe-curling kiss before they made love.

～

Kevin was tired. After the children had been fed, bathed, and given clean clothes, beds were found for them with different pack members. A couple of the children were housed in the main pack house, hopefully fast asleep.

He was sat in his study, catching up on work and researching anything he could think of. He couldn't believe so much black-market stuff was happening under their noses. Kevin prided himself on knowledge and knowing everything he could. To find out there were things he didn't know was disturbing.

He felt Creed walk up behind him and wrap his arms around him.

"How about you leave this for now and come to bed. I can guarantee tomorrow will be busy."

Kevin laid his hands over Creed's and leaned back. "That sounds like a good idea." He locked his computer and moved to stand up, Creed moving back dropping his arms.

Kevin moved away from his desk and smiled at Creed, stepping close and tangling his hand in Creed's hair. "You have the best ideas," he said, leaning forward and kissing him.

～

THE VAMPIRE AND THE TATTOOIST

Morning seemed to arrive way too quickly in Hunter's opinion. He groaned quietly as his alarm sounded loudly. He managed to snag his phone and silence the annoying beeps. He pulled his arm back and wrapped it again around Gavin, who was sleeping soundly in his arms. They were both lying on their sides with Hunter spooning Gavin.

Hunter had slept lightly, wanting to stay aware of Gavin in case he had any nightmares, but from what Hunter could tell, Gavin had slept well.

He gently kissed Gavin's shoulder. Never in his wildest dreams had he imagined he could be this happy, or be so deeply in love, but that was before he had met Gavin. Sure, their meeting had been unexpected, but Hunter was so glad he sat on the floor in the library.

Hunter was under no illusions that being mated to a vampire didn't come with a few dangers. He quietly scoffed. *That* was an understatement. He already had a killer witch after him, but he meant what he'd said: he would take a bodyguard with him to the studio if it put everyone's mind at rest.

He felt Gavin waking up and tightened his arms around him.

Gavin lifted his hand and kissed the back of it before turning over and smiling at Hunter, moving his head to kiss him.

Not being stupid, Hunter kissed him back and pulled Gavin on top of him, not breaking the kiss, and running his hands up and down his back.

Gavin broke off the kiss and started kissing Hunter around his neck, Hunter moving his head to give him better access. He licked over the mating mark.

"If you need to drink love, drink," Hunter told him.

A moment later, Hunter felt Gavin's fangs bite into his mark and sighed as pleasure shot through him.

A little while later, Gavin retracted his fangs and licked over the mark, sealing the wound before moving to kiss Hunter, who rolled Gavin onto his back before making love to him.

It was a happy couple who walked into the kitchen for breakfast that morning.

Gavin could never remember being so happy. That was a lie; he'd been this happy when Mathis had attacked their father. Their father had never liked him, but it had gotten worse when he found out Gavin was mute. He could remember coming home from seeing a healer and running to hide behind Mathis and Raz to get away from his father's anger.

What he didn't expect was for the man to come into his bedroom that evening and try and kill him. He never knew what drew Mathis into his room, but Mathis literally saved his life and attacked their father. Gavin could remember smiling and being this happy when they left. He was safest with his brothers, well Hunter and everyone in the coven.

He was pulled from his thoughts when they got a round of good mornings. He smiled at everyone while Hunter said, "Hello."

Dishes were passed around, and they dug into breakfast.

"Hunter, I've asked Owen to guard you today. He's back from his latest assignment and can protect you," David told him.

Hunter sighed. "Thanks, I hope he won't be too bored. He does know he won't be able to come into my room while I'm working, right?"

Gavin glared at him.

"No," Hunter said. "Not with the tattoo I'm doing today."

Gavin started fast signing.

Hunter closed his hands around Gavin's. "I promise I will

do whatever Owen thinks is best, but he can't come into my appointment with Danni," Hunter said gently.

Gavin huffed out a silent breath.

Hunter bopped him on the nose and grinned. "Love you, too, sweetheart."

Gavin screwed his nose up at him.

"I'll make sure Owen knows," David assured him. "As vampires, we have enhanced hearing as well as speed. If anything happens, just shout and he'll come running."

"Thank you. Normally I could possibly pass your man off as an apprentice, but for today, I can't do that," Hunter said, not wanting anyone to think he was being difficult. "Taha said he will pick me up at nine, but I can message him and drive Owen and myself in."

"Would he mind?" Dave asked him.

"Nope, it would save him a trip. Let me message him now," Hunter said, pulling his phone out of his pocket and sending the message. "Done."

"Mum, Annie, I messaged Kevin earlier about you both going over to the pack to see to the children and play with the puppies. He said you are more than welcome. I'll come with you; Gio and Seth, I'd like you to come, as well."

"We can do that," Seth said.

"I think I'll come, as well," Willard said, looking at Stefan. "We can't let our wives have all the fun."

"Quite right. We shall go, as well," Stefan agreed.

"Bailey, Jessamy, and Rickon can come with us, too, then," Gio said.

"We need to stop at the shops and buy treats for the children, both the kidnapped ones and the pack children. I'm not sure I have enough time to make lots of biscuits," Annie said, frowning.

"Shop brought biscuits will be fine, Mum. You could look at those large cookies they have," Dave said.

Annie smiled at her son. "Perfect, thank you, Davy."

"Morning," a voice said from the doorway.

"Hey, Max," Dave said, jumping up and hugging his friend. "I'm off to play with puppies today."

"Puppies?" Max asks, smiling.

Dave nods. "Wolf shifter puppies."

"That will be nice," Max said, his smile only slipping a little.

"You're getting better, Max. You didn't freak out," Dave said with a laugh.

"Give me a year and this will all seem normal," Max said. He looked at those gathered at the table. "Have fun. I'm off to the library." And with that, Max headed off, muttering as he left.

Dave turned and grinned at those sitting at the table. "At least he's no longer freaking out."

"Indeed," David replied.

"And on that note, I need to go," Hunter said. "Where will I find Owen?"

"I'll message him for you," David said, pulling his phone out of his pocket. "He'll meet you by the front door in a few moments."

"Thanks." Hunter looked at Gavin and raised his hand to Gavin's cheek. "Have a good day and I promise to stay safe."

Gavin nodded and leant in to kiss him goodbye.

"Break it up, you two. I don't want to see my little brother making out with his mate over breakfast," Raz said as he walked in.

Gavin smiled into the kiss and pulled back, turning his head to look at Raz and poking his tongue out at him.

"Morning, Raz. Bye, Raz," Hunter said with a quick grin before standing up and collecting his dirty crockery.

Gavin put his hand on Hunter's arm to stop him and signed, "I'll tidy up for you."

"Thanks, sweetheart," he said, putting it back down. "See you all later."

And with a round of goodbyes, Hunter left the kitchen, walking to the front door. He saw a man waiting for him. He couldn't remember meeting Owen before, but he had met so many people since he turned up yesterday, he might have done.

"Hi, I'm Hunter," he said, smiling at the man.

"I'm Owen and I'll be your bodyguard for the day," the vampire replied with a grin.

Hunter nodded and opened the front door, pulling his keys out of his pocket and letting Owen close the door behind them. "You don't mind if I drive, do you?"

Owen shook his head. "Nope, go ahead, I'll keep an eye out."

"Thanks," Hunter said, clicking the key fob and unlocking his car.

Once they were under way, Hunter asked. "Were you told about not being able to come into my room today?"

Owen nodded. "I was. That's fine. I'm fast. If you need me just call for help."

"I will do, thanks. I hope you won't be too bored today."

Owen grinned. "I doubt I will. I've never been to a tattoo studio before."

Hunter laughed. "Then prepare to be amazed."

It didn't take them long to get to Area 51. Owen laughed at the name.

"Taha and I are SyFy nerds. We both came up with that name at the same time."

"Nice. Is it just the two of you?" he asked as Hunter parked.

"No, there is Luke who also does tattoos, and Shelby who does piercings. Come on, I'll introduce you."

CHAPTER 28

Kevin and Creed were up early, intent on going downstairs and getting breakfast started, but his mum was already there and cooking up a storm.

"Hey, Mum," Kevin said, walking over and kissing her cheek. "What are you doing up so early?"

"I thought I'd cook breakfast for everyone. Plus, the children are all coming here for breakfast," she replied. "Morning, Creed, dear," Lissa said, smiling his way.

"Morning, Lissa," he replied, kissing her cheek. "Thanks for this."

"You're welcome, dear."

"Mum, the king and queen of the vampires, as well as their two sons, will be visiting today. Plus, Annie and Willard."

"Oh, how lovely," Lissa said. "I can't wait to meet them."

There was movement by the kitchen door and a young boy stood there. The boy who had helped Seth and took charge of the children.

"Morning, Jack," Kevin said, smiling at him.

"Hey. Are the vampires that helped us escape coming today?" Jack asked.

Kevin nodded. "Most of them, yes."

"Good," Jack said. "I'm going to check on the others. Spencer should be down in a minute."

"Jack, everyone is safe here on pack grounds. The children will be here for breakfast soon," Kevin told him.

Jack looked uncertain.

"Why don't you stay here and check on them when they come in for breakfast?" Lissa suggested softly.

Jack nodded and crossed his arms over his chest, leaning against the door frame and waiting for the children to arrive.

Hunter walked into the studio, Owen by his side.

"It's so light and airy in here," Owen said, looking round.

Hunter laughed. "You were expecting something dark and depressing?"

Owen laughed. "I honestly didn't know what I was expecting."

"Let me show you round," Hunter said, leading the vampire further in. "Here is the kitchen — help yourself to anything in here." Hunter led him down a corridor, pointing out rooms. "This is Taha's room, that's Shelby's, Luke's is there, and this is mine," he said, opening the door and walking in, Owen following.

Owen looked around. There were two windows on one side of the room, letting in lots of light but with frosted glass so no one could see in. Under one of the windows was a sink and a countertop with different things on its surface. There was a seating area and a table with chairs surrounding it. He also noted the tattoo chair and small roller table and a stool.

"This should be easy enough to protect you. You only

have one door, and the windows look secure. Thankfully, your room is quite near the front of the shop. Will your door be open or closed?"

"Closed. There will be some I can keep the door open for, but not this one," Hunter told him.

"What is different about this one?" Owen asked, curiously.

"The lady I'm tattooing is a cancer survivor, but she had to have both of her breasts removed. Today I'm tattooing her chest to cover up the surgery and treatment scars," Hunter told him.

"Poor thing," Owen said. Vampires didn't get cancer, but he had seen enough people in his long life who had the horrible disease and saw the knock it could do to their self-confidence.

Hunter led them back to the main reception area. There was a reception desk by the far wall with a chair behind it. A sofa was positioned in front of a large window and chairs with a coffee table were at the front of the area. The walls were decorated with pictures of different tattoos, and there were a couple of binders on the table with more pictures inside. There was a price list on the wall behind the reception desk, and large potted plants dotted around. The whole area looked warm and inviting.

The front door opened, making the bell jingle, and two laughing men walked in. They saw Hunter and hurried over, offering hugs.

"Are you alright? And your Gavin?" one of the men asked.

Hunter nodded. "We're both good, Shell. Did Ta tell you everything?"

Shelby shook his head. "No, just that there were family issues."

"There are a few issues. Can I introduce Owen to you both? Owen, this is Shelby and Luke. Guys, this is Owen."

Luke looked from Hunter to Owen and back again. "You have a *bodyguard*? Just how bad are the family issues?"

"Bad. But you're both safe, I promise," Hunter assured them.

"We can see that," Shelby said, looking back at Hunter. "We have a cute bodyguard here."

"I'll keep out of your way," Owen assured them.

"Well that's a shame," Luke said, grinning at him.

Hunter shook his head as he looked at his friends. He was about to say something when the door opened again and Taha walked in. He saw Hunter and grinned. "You made it in, then."

Hunter nodded. "Yep, this is Owen," he said, nodding to Owen.

Taha turned to look at Owen, who suddenly hissed and his eyes swirled red. A moment later, Owen was stood in front of Taha, raising his hand to Taha's cheek.

"Mine," Owen said, leaning forward and kissing Taha.

Taha was so momentarily stunned by the declaration and by Owen kissing him that for a few seconds, he froze before kissing the vampire back. His hand went round Owen's neck and tried to pull him closer.

"What the hell!" Luke exclaimed. "What was that?"

Hunter sighed and rubbed the back of his neck. "That was Owen and Taha realising they are made for each other."

"But Owen hissed, and his eyes went weird," Shelby pointed out.

"Wait," Luke said, sounding excited. "Is Owen a paranormal? Is that really a thing? Please tell me the books I read are real."

"How amazing would that be if there was a whole paranormal world out there," Shelby said, just as excited.

"You wouldn't be freaked out if you found there was?" Hunter asked.

"No, I mean can you imagine people that can change into animals? How amazing would that be?" Luke said. "Or finding out wizards and witches are real."

Hunter turned to look at Taha and Owen, who were just coming up for air, both looking stunned.

Owen smiled and rubbed his thumb over Taha's lips. "Amazing."

Taha nodded. "It was indeed. I'm Taha."

Owen leant in and gave him a quick kiss. "It is so nice to meet you. I would love to continue this, but I'm here to protect Hunter."

Taha nodded and took a step back. "I'm glad he has someone other than me watching his back."

"Hey, we have his back as well," Shelby reminded him.

Taha shot them a smile. "Sorry, I know you do. I think that kiss just addled my brain."

Owen laughed.

"I should imagine it did. It looked smoking hot," Shelby said, fanning his face.

"Do you want me to contact David and ask him to send someone else so the two of you can go off and get to know each other?" Hunter asked them.

Both Taha and Owen said no.

"I'll stay and protect you like I was asked to," Owen said.

"And I'll stay as you're my best friend," Taha added.

Hunter nodded. "If you're sure, but the offer is there, and now I have to get ready for my client." And with that, he left the others and walked back into his room.

He always kept his room sterile and clean, disinfecting it after every client and again before he went home. He also cleaned it when he first got it. After disinfecting all surfaces in his room, he collected his drawing pad and the design he had ready to go on the tattoo transfer paper. He then went to his cupboard and pulled out everything he would need. He kept all his supplies in the cupboard in his room. They did think of having a central storeroom where they could keep everything, but he, Taha, and Luke all liked different equipment.

He wrapped up everything he needed, put foil over his tray, and set everything up. He would pour the ink out while the stencil was setting.

It took a while to set everything up. He had surprised more than one person by how much he had to do before the client came in. Once he was set up, he grabbed his phone and sent a message to Gavin.

H: Hey, sweetheart. Guess what? It would seem that Owen and Taha are mates. Who'd have guessed? xx

He hit send and laughed to himself. Who indeed would have guessed that his best friend would also be the mate of a vampire?

He didn't have to wait long for Gavin to message him back. He smiled as he opened the message.

G: For real? Sweet. Owen is awesome, and from what I've seen of Taha, he seems nice. Just warn Taha that Owen has his shoes handmade and they usually cost upwards of £10k.

Hunter's mouth dropped open. People really pay that for shoes? He hit reply.

H: £10k for shoes???? That's just mad. I think the most expensive pair I have ever brought were £150.

A moment later Gavin replied.

G: Same. But Owen does love his footwear collection. Those that are going to the wolf pack have left for the day. I'm going over everything the computer picked up last night, along with Ivan. BE SAFE and go nowhere alone. xx

Hunter smiled to himself. He would stay safe if only to put Gavin's mind at rest.

H: Promise. Love you, sweetheart.

G: Love you more x

He still wasn't used to anyone apart from his family saying that to him and hearing it from Gavin gave him a happy glow inside of him. But now he needed to get his head in the game. Danni Sargent was due in a few minutes, and he would need to concentrate. He pulled a hair tie out of his pocket, tied his hair back and left the room.

CHAPTER 29

Gabe was in the office with Mathis, Neill, Sean, and Kayden having a catch-up on what they found yesterday. They touched on things briefly after dinner, but Gabe told them all to head up to bed and fill him in properly this morning.

"So, tell me what you found in all the paperwork," Gabe said.

"We have records of money laundering, drug supplies, weapons smuggling, exotic animal smuggling, and child trafficking," Sean told him.

"We're hoping Ivan finds evidence of those involved as at the moment we only have initials, which wouldn't hold up in a court," Neill said.

"We need to close all these lines down, so they don't get moved somewhere else," Kayden added.

"I'm sure at the moment we have closed some streams, but until we've caught everyone involved, it could all start again," Mathis said.

"That reminds me…" Gabe started, standing up and going to the filing cabinet. "Let's look at Jake Conway." He rifled through the drawer until he found the folder with the man's name on it. Pulling it out he shut the drawer and walked back to the desk, dropping the file on top and sitting down. He opened the file and looked over the paperwork inside. "Huh, according to this paperwork, Jake Conway is a cousin of Kay."

"I never knew they were related," Kayden said.

"Me, either," Sean said.

"Apparently, they're related on Quintus's side. Now we know how he's linked to this and why he ran," Gabe said as he kept reading. "I have his parents' address, but the chances of him going there are slim to none."

"Maybe he's hiding out at Giles' place. I mean, everyone has been caught. Who would think about one of the group members hiding out there?" Sean suggested.

"It's what I would do. I'll message David and see if he can send someone over to have a look," Mathis said, pulling out his phone and sending the text. "Done."

"It would be good to know what David got out of the lemmings," Gabe said.

"We can set up a meeting for later," Mathis said, looking at his phone. "Everyone is now at the wolf pack."

"To look after the missing children?" Sean asked.

"That and to play with puppies," Mathis replied.

※

It was a procession of cars that arrived at the wolf pack.

"This looks amazing," Dave said, looking around. "It's like they have their own little town or village."

"And look! Kevin, Creed, and Ian are waiting for us," Annie said happily from the back seat.

David parked the car, smiling as he got out and looked around. As Dave said, the pack lands did look amazing.

"Welcome to my pack lands, vamp," Kevin said, walking over to meet them and shaking David's hand.

"Thank you for letting us come. Mum and Annie wanted to check on the children and play with the puppies," he replied.

"I am so excited to be here, and I know Louise is, too," Annie said happily, walking over to them.

"I am indeed," Louise agreed, coming to stand with them.

"Welcome to my home," Kevin said to her and Stefan. "Can I introduce you to my mother?"

"Oh, that would be lovely," Louise said, smiling.

Kevin led them over to the pack house steps where Lissa stood waiting, a smile on her face. "Mum, can I introduce you to the vampire royal family: King Stefan, Queen Louise, Prince David, and Prince Giovanni. Guys, this is my mother, Lissa Mellor."

"It's so lovely to meet you all," Lissa said happily, shaking hands as pleasantries were exchanged before David introduced everyone else.

"It's so lovely to meet you," Annie said happily. "Why don't you show us to the children? We brought goodies for them. Willard, Davy, grab the boxes."

"I'm sure they'll love that. They're playing in the back garden," Lissa said, leading the way.

As they were walking to the back of the pack house, they heard children's laughter.

"We brought the pack children over to play with them, hoping that would put them at ease ," Lissa explained.

"Judging by the laughter, that was a good idea," Louise said.

Lissa opened the garden gate and led them into the garden.

"Oh, how pretty," Annie exclaimed.

The garden was stunning. It had flower borders filled

with colourful blooms in front of laurel trees that surrounded three sides. It was also a good size — roughly two acres — with a selection of different seating areas, an outdoor kitchen, and a massive waterfall towards the back of the garden.

The children were playing, both in human and shifted forms.

"I thought shifts didn't happen until they reached a certain age," Dave said, sounding and looking confused.

Ian snorted. "That's just in stories. In real life, shifters can shift from birth. It's not uncommon to see a wolf puppy wearing a nappy."

"If I see that, I'm taking a photo to send to Gabe and Sean," Seth said, looking around. He saw one child standing off to one side as if watching over everyone and recognised him as the young boy who had helped them. Seth left the others and walked over to him. "You don't want to join in?" Seth asked him softly.

Jack shook his head. "I'm fine watching over the others and making sure nothing bad happens to them. I couldn't help much in the warehouse. I did what I could, which wasn't much when we were all caged, but here I can make sure nothing bad happens to them."

"You're all safe here," Seth assured him, internally shaking his head. He was too young to be watching over the other children. Seth guessed he couldn't have been older than ten or eleven.

Jack nodded, but Seth could see in his eyes he wasn't sure.

"We brought yummy treats with us. Look, they're being put on that table there," Seth said, pointing to where the others were gathered, and the boxes had been placed.

Jack still looked uncertain.

"How about we both walk over there, and you can have a

THE VAMPIRE AND THE TATTOOIST

look and see what we brought and decide if it's safe," Seth suggested.

Jack looked like he was thinking about it before he nodded.

"Good lad."

"Jack," the young boy said.

"And I am Seth," Seth replied, smiling at him.

"It's hard to stop looking after them," Jack confessed softly.

Seth touched his shoulder. "You don't have to. You can still have fun while watching out for them."

Jack nodded and moved closer to Seth's side as they walked to the table.

"Jack," Lissa said, smiling at the young boy. "Our friends brought yummy treats for everyone."

Jack nodded. "Thank you, I'm sure everyone will enjoy them."

"Here," Gio said while picking up a box and offering it to him. "Choose the one you want before we call the others over."

"I can wait and make sure everyone has one first," Jack said.

"Nope, if you take one, the others will come and have one. They're watching you to see what you do," Seth told him.

Jack looked up and saw some of the children watching him. He grinned at them before looking back at the cake box and picking up a chocolate muffin. "Thank you," he said, turning back to the children. "We have cakes."

He moved away as the children came running over and all took one.

Jack groaned when he took his first bite and unconsciously leaned into Seth's side.

"Good?" Seth asked, slipping an arm around his waist.

Jack nodded and held it out to Seth. "Want some?"

"Thanks," Seth said, breaking off a small piece and eating it. "Can I tell you a secret?"

Jack nodded.

"That was nice, but Thomaz and Annie make better ones."

Jack looked at him in surprise.

"Seth's right," Ian said, walking over to them. "They have the best cakes there."

"Maybe one day I can try some," Jack replied almost shyly.

"I'll make it happen," Seth assured him.

CHAPTER 30

Kevin was standing with David off to one side.

"We should gather the others and have a catch-up," David said. "We can update everyone on what's been found."

"That sounds good. Shall we call them here now?"

David nodded. "Yes, it would be easier. I'll message Ivan if you want to message Gabe."

They both got their phones out of their pockets and sent messages.

Within a few moments, a portal opened, and Gabe, Mathis, Sean, Kaden and Neill arrived.

"Did you miss us?" Sean asked, smiling at everyone.

"If they didn't, I did," Dave said, hurrying over and hugging them all.

"Gabe, can you open a portal from the coven for Ivan and Gavin?" David asked.

"I can," he said, swirling his hand. The next moment, a portal opened, and Ivan and Gavin walked through.

Gavin saw his brother and rushed over to hug first him and then the others.

"Where is Raz?" Mathis asked.

"Thiago took your brother off to visit the underworld and to get permission for us all to visit," David replied.

"See if I can come, vamp. That would be an amazing trip," Kevin said with a grin.

"I'll ask Thiago when he comes back," David assured him.

"Where's the kitty?" Ian asked, walking over to join them.

"He and Cairo are looking for the witch Jake Conway. They've gone to look at the Goodsir house," David replied.

Ian nodded. "Makes sense to hide out there."

"Let's move this over to that seating area there," Kevin suggested, pointing to a large round outdoor dining table that was already set up with cold drinks and covered cakes.

As they sat down, Stefan came over and joined them, as did Gio and Seth. Everyone else was playing with the children, and Annie, Louise, and Lissa were sat on the floor with wolf puppies jumping all over them, talking and laughing.

"Looks like the mums are bonding," Seth said, smiling their way.

"Good, it might keep my mum round for a while," Kevin said, looking over at them.

"She doesn't live here?" David asked, surprised.

Kevin shook his head. "No, she still lives in our old pack. I keep asking her to move here, so hopefully she will now."

"I'm sure Mum and Annie can work their magic on her," Gio said, sounding full of confidence.

"I take it your brother isn't back," Seth asked him.

"No, thank goodness. Hopefully, he'll not be back today, either."

Creed laughed. "I hope he is. I can't wait to meet him."

Kevin just shook his head and looked at the others. "We thought we would have a catch-up and fill everyone in on what we currently know."

"As you can see, we rescued all the children that were in

the warehouse. They were kept in crates before being taken off to a separate room," Seth told them.

"What happened in that room?" Mathis asked.

"I don't know. But whatever it was, it wasn't good," Seth said, just as Jack wandered over and leant against his chair.

"I don't know what happened in there, either. None of us do. But there was a lot of screaming and crying and then silence. Those that were taken in there were never seen again," Jack told them.

Seth slipped an arm around him. "When Raz and I went in to look for the children, they were huddled in the corner of the room and a guard was walking towards them. Needless to say, he didn't get to them."

"I closed the portal that was being used to bring guards into the warehouse. It was a struggle to close, as it had demon magic attached to it," Gabe added.

"So we have a demon to deal with, as well?" Stefan asked.

"Possibly. Thiago said he would see if he could find the demon involved," Gabe said.

"We've not found any more records of children being taken after these ones, but it still might be worth checking the addresses we found just to be on the safe side," Kayden suggested.

"We were moved from a house to the warehouse if that helps," Jack said.

"It does, thank you, young man," Mathis said.

"Jack," Jack said.

Mathis nodded.

"Did you find everyone's families?" Jack asked.

"Most of them. If you're Jack Martins, we couldn't find yours or a boy called Spencer Stevenson's," Ivan replied.

"Spencer told me last night his family is all dead and he kept running away from his foster parent's place. He said that's how he was taken because he was walking the streets one evening trying to get away," Jack told them.

"What about your family?" Seth asked him gently.

"It was only me and my grandma. She died and it was just me in the cottage for a bit before I was taken." He looked at Seth. "Can I come and live with you?"

Before Seth could answer, Gio said, "Sure you can. Seth and I will look after you."

Seth and Jack, well, everyone turned to stare at Gio with different looks on their faces from humour to shock.

Gio grinned at David. "I'm now the favourite son. I just gave Mum and Dad a grandson."

David laughed and Stefan looked at Jack. "Welcome to the family, Jack. I'm Stefan, Gio and David's father."

"Not to mention king of the vampires," Dave happily added.

Jack's mouth dropped open. "For real? A real king?"

"For real," Stefan replied, smiling.

"If you ask nicely, he might even show you his crown," Seth added.

Jack smiled. "Would you?"

"I think that can be arranged. We will also sort out the paperwork so Seth and Gio can formally adopt you," Stefan said.

Jack looked from Seth to Gio; Seth still had his arm around Jack. "Would you do that? You don't know me."

"You don't really know me either," Seth pointed out. "But you feel safe with me and hopefully Gio, as well."

"I do," Jack replied, nodding. "Thanks, but what about Spencer? He needs a family, as well. Can he come with me?"

"If he wants to, yes, but the decision needs to be his," David said.

"Thanks, I'll go and talk to him." And with that, Jack rushed off to find Spencer.

"Congratulations, it's a boy," Ian said, laughing at Seth and Gio.

Gio grabbed Seth's hand. "Is that okay, my Seth?"

Seth nodded. "I was going to ask you if he could come and live with us."

Gio blew out a sigh of relief and everyone laughed and offered congratulations.

CHAPTER 31

Once everyone had calmed down, they carried on catching up.

"So, all the records we've been through so far in Leonard's secret office — and let me tell you, there are thousands of them — detail everything he was into but give no names, just initials," Kayden said. "Quintus' initials feature in a lot of them, but there are some I don't recognise. It might be worth cross-referencing them against the covens Kay and Jake came from."

"We can do that," Ivan said. "Shoot them over to me and I'll do a dig."

"Will do," Kayden replied. "Last night I typed up a lot of notes, giving as much information about all the activities we've uncovered and breaking it down as much as I could. There's still more to add, but I can send you all copies if you want."

Gabe looked at his friend. "Did you sleep at all?"

Kayden nodded. "I did."

Sean huffed out a sigh and grabbed Kayden's hand. "Not much, though."

"Wait... I've just remembered. It's your wedding anniversary today," Gabe suddenly said, looking at his two friends. "You should be off enjoying your day. Leave this for now and go and have fun."

Sean shook his head. "No, we spoke about taking some time off from all this, but we didn't want to. There's still so much to sort out."

"In that case, we shall have a celebration BBQ for you both here today," Kevin said. "I'm sure Gabe can arrange the decorations, and we always have enough food for a BBQ."

"Oh, wow, thank you. But you don't need to," Kayden replied, looking surprised.

"Babe, Wolfie wants to throw us a party. Just smile and say thank you," Sean said, grinning.

"Wolfie?" Dave questioned, sitting forward with a beaming smile.

"This is now a no-party zone," Kevin grumbled out as the others laughed.

Annie walked over with Spencer and Jack. "You're having a party?" she asked.

"Well, we were going to have a celebration for Sean and Kayden's wedding anniversary today, but not anymore," Kevin told her.

"Oh, how exciting. Let me grab Louise and Lissa and we can start making cakes. Jack, you and Spencer can come and help." And just that quickly, Annie rushed them off in the direction of Louise and Lissa.

Kevin shook his head. "No one listens to me anymore," he lamented.

"That's probably because you're a dweeb," a voice said from behind him.

"Gah," Kevin mumbled, looking over his shoulder at his older brother. "What's up, Gerty Berty?"

"For once in your life, behave," Bertrum said, scowling at him.

"Hey, Mum, Gerty Berty's being annoying," Kevin shouted to his mother.

"You're such a PITA," Bert muttered.

"Behave, boys. Don't make me come over there," Lissa warned.

Kevin laughed and stood up to hug his brother. "I suppose it's good that you're back. Let me introduce you around," he said, pulling back.

Everyone at the table stood. "King Stefan D'Angelo of the vampires, meet Alpha King Bertrum Mellor."

The two men shook hands.

"It's good to finally meet you, Alpha King," Stefan said.

"The same, but please call me—."

"Gerty Berty," Kevin supplied quickly.

Bert's hand shot out and hit the back of Kevin's head. "No," he said, scowling at his brother before looking back at Stefan. "Bert will be fine."

Stefan laughed. "And you must call me Stefan. Let me introduce you to everyone."

The others came forward and hands were shaken.

Dave held his hand out and shook Bert's when Bert suddenly jerked him closer and took a sniff, and he growled.

Quick as a flash, David rushed forward and pulled Dave away, shoving Dave behind him.

Seth and Gio moved to flank Dave as Gabriel moved in front of them, wand at the ready.

"What the hell, wolf? Dave is *my* mate," David growled out angrily, his eyes turning red as he shifted into his vampire form, now practically nose to nose with the Alpha King.

"Bertrum?" Kevin queried as Bert's Beta and guards came to stand behind them, the vampire guards standing by Dave.

"The human smells like my mate," Bert replied.

"Shit," Kevin said, running a hand down his face.

"*You* don't smell like my mate," David spits out.

"It doesn't matter. He still smells like my mate," Bert shot out.

"What do you mean it doesn't matter?" David demanded angrily.

"Everyone, Gavin is trying to say something," Gio announced.

They all turned to look at him and he quickly started signing.

"Gav, slow down. I'm missing half of what you're saying," Mathis complained.

"Gavin is saying that earlier this morning, Dave hugged Max. It could be that *Max* is the Alpha King's mate," Kayden translated.

Silence met this announcement before Dave sniggered, then he moved forward and touched David's arm. "Relax, babe. We know we're mates and it's just the two of us, but what Gavin says makes sense." He turned to look at Bertrum. "Could that be it?"

Bertrum nodded, taking a step back from David. "It could be, yes, as the scent is getting fainter. Who is Max and why were you hugging him?" he demanded.

Dave narrowed his eyes, and without looking away, he said, "Kevin, I see what you mean about your brother. Now look here, wolf; you don't get to use that tone with me. Max is my best friend, my human best friend. We hug, get used to it. Max is also freaked out about the paranormal world, and you having this crappy attitude won't help. Now, we are in the middle of a serious meeting, so leave us be so we can carry on." And with that, Dave turned his back on Bertrum and walked back to his seat at the table.

"I so want to be you when I grow up," Sean said, walking over and joining him at the table.

Bertrum stood there for a moment, not sure what he should do.

"You should apologise for being a dick," Jack said from behind them.

Bertrum turned and looked at Jack. "I wasn't being a dick," he protested.

Jack wasn't the only one who snorted.

Bertrum rolled his eyes and turned back to the group. "I apologise for my behaviour. I was stunned when I smelt my mate, and my brain took a dump."

David settled down. "Apology accepted. I would probably have done the same thing," he grudgingly admitted.

"Thank you," Bert said.

"Don't you have something urgent you need to do at, like, in the other end of the country?" Kevin asked him.

"No, Bacon, I don't, but maybe I can help with whatever you're discussing," Bert offered, hoping that would show he really was sorry.

There were sniggers around the table.

"Bacon?" Gabe queried, smirking.

"Don't ask," Kevin said.

Gavin silently laughed and started signing.

Kayden snorted out a laugh. "That would make sense."

"What did Gavin say?" Sean asked.

"Gavin says Bacon refers to Kevin Bacon," Stefan told them.

"O.M.G., I think that's even better than wolfie," Dave said, grinning like mad.

"I hate you so much right now," Kevin said to his brother.

"Pull up a chair and join us," Stefan said to Bert.

"Thank you," Bert replied, pulling a spare chair over and sitting at the table. His second, Drake, came to stand behind him as all the guards moved back out of the way.

"Before you start the meeting again, Annie asked how

long you've been married for?" Jack asked, looking at Sean and Kayden.

"Ten years," Kayden said at the same time Sean said, "Nine years."

"Good to see you both know how long you've been married," Ian said, laughing at them.

"Ten years?" Sean asked, looking at Kayden.

Kayden laughed. "Yeah, sweetheart, it's ten years."

"My only excuse is that time has no meaning when I'm with you," Sean tells him.

"Nice save," Gabe said, laughing at him.

Kayden and Sean laughed. "Ten years," Kayden said to Jack.

"Thanks, I'll tell Annie," Jack said, then walked away.

CHAPTER 32

"Right, back to the meeting," Kevin said, retaking his seat as the others settled down. "For the sake of his nibs, here, I'll do a quick recap on what we know," he said, running through everything.

Bert shook his head. "How could all this be happening and none of us picked up even a hint of anything?"

"I'm pretty sure the witches covered a lot up, especially Quintus. Plus, if there's a demon helping, they could have hidden a lot," Gabe said.

"That would make sense," Bert said. "What has the council said?"

"Nothing. I'm not telling them until we have sorted everything or if we have to," Gabe told him. "Quintus Cameron-Webb was our council representative and is up to his neck in all of this. We think he's been removed from his post for not stopping his son, but I don't know for sure yet."

"I suggested that Gabriel document's everything in case the council does get involved. At the very least, everything will be recorded for when this underground network has

THE VAMPIRE AND THE TATTOOIST

been stopped and charges are brought against those involved," Stefan said.

"If you have any problems with the council, let me know. I'm happy to go and bash heads together," Bert offered.

Gabe laughed. "Thanks. I'll let you know if it comes to that."

"Ivan, Gavin, what did the two of you discover?" David asks them.

Gavin nods to Ivan. "I've hacked all the electronics we found. It would seem that they recorded a lot of their meetings."

"Seriously?" Mathis asked in surprise, leaning forward.

"Oh, yeah. They dimmed the colour to hide their faces but didn't disguise their voices. Like Kayden, I've put an initial document together. I can email it over to you all. The only issue I'm having is hacking Quintus Cameron-Webb's computer. I was hoping that Gabe might be able to magic it to me."

"I can give it a go," Gabe replied and muttered a quick spell. The next moment, a laptop appeared in front of him.

"Nice one," Seth said, high-fiving him.

"You're so much stronger than your brother was," Bert said, smiling at Gabe.

"Thanks. I'm still learning what I can do. He suppressed my magic for years."

"I'm not surprised," Bert said.

"Like we said earlier, Gavin found addresses for everyone except Spencer and Jack, so we can start getting the children back home," Ivan added.

"If you send me the addresses, my pack can start getting them home today," Kevin told them.

Gavin nodded, picked up his phone and sent the list to Kevin. While he had his phone out, he also sent a quick message to Hunter. He knew Hunter couldn't reply, but at least he would know Gavin was thinking about him.

"Where's our party invite?" Troy asked, walking over to them with Cairo.

"Kitty cat," Bert said by way of a greeting.

"Puppy. This is my mate Cairo. Cairo, this is the Alpha King, Bertrum Mellor."

Bert looked at Cairo. "You have my sympathies."

Cairo snorted out a laugh.

"The puppy thinks he's funny," Troy said.

"He's the only one," Ian mutters as the others smile.

"Did you find Jake Conway?" David asked him.

Cairo shook his head. "No, the place was deserted."

"Figures," Gabe said, sagging a little. "Nothing to do with this is easy, so why would finding him be different?"

CHAPTER 33

Hunter was hard at work with Danni's tattoo. They had to occasionally stop because of the pain Danni was feeling and so he could sit up and stretch. He was just finishing up the left side of Danni's chest and wiped away a bit of ink.

"So, this is the main outline done for this side. Do you want me to do the smaller, fallen leaves while I'm on this side or would you rather I start on the other side?"

Danni blew out a breath. "Can you start on the other side, please?"

"Yep," Hunter says, rolling around to the other side. "Truthfully, Danni, how are you doing? We can stop for today and carry on in a day or so."

"No, I can do this, but I might leave the fallen leaves and shading for another day."

"That's no problem. Same as before, if you want me to stop so you can take a moment, just let me know."

"I will. Thanks, Hunter."

Hunter patted her arm. "You're doing great, honey."

Danni smiled. "Thanks. I've impressed myself that I'm not a blubbering mess, to be honest."

Hunter laughed and dipped his needles in the ink. "You'd be surprised how many tough guys I get in here who cry their eyes out."

"Really?"

"Oh yeah," Hunter said as he started working again. "I tell them there will be pain, but they somehow never believe me."

"Did you cry the first time you got one?" Danni asked with a laugh.

"No, but I did swear like a sailor," he confessed. "Apart from the woman that tattooed me, no one else knows that."

Danni laughed. "Your secret is safe with me."

Just then, Hunter's phone dinged with a new message.

"Do you need to get that?"

"No, that would be my boyfriend just checking in. He knows I can't answer him just yet."

"Nice, what does he do?"

"Writes computer games. I couldn't believe it when he told me the games he wrote, I have most of them. He has some serious skills."

"I'm afraid the only games I play are things like online Monopoly and online Yahtzee."

"Both good games. Mind you, I find Monopoly frustrating."

"The online version is different. You don't interact with anyone in person. But I still get annoyed when someone steals my money or tries to destroy one of my buildings."

"I can imagine," Hunter says.

"Tell me more about your boyfriend — unless you'd rather not."

"I could happily talk about Gavin until the cows come home, and now as you've asked and can't go anywhere, I can wax lyrical about him."

THE VAMPIRE AND THE TATTOOIST

Danni laughed and let Hunter talk.

A couple of hours later, Hunter was finished. "There, all done," he said, putting his machine down and wiping the last of the ink off. "Let me grab the mirror and you can have your first look." He picked up the mirror and showed Danni her new chest design.

"Oh, Hunter, it's even more perfect than it looked on paper."

"The redness will calm down..." Hunter went on to explain about aftercare as he wrapped the tattoo. "How about we wait a week or so and then we can do the fallen leaves and start the shading?"

"I like that idea. Let's do that," she readily agreed.

"Come with me to reception and I can book you in," Hunter said, leading the way out.

He smiled to himself as he passed the kitchen and saw Taha and Owen wrapped in each other's arms.

"They look happy," Danni commented as they passed them.

"They are," Hunter agreed.

Mark Sargent was sitting in the reception area waiting for Danni to come out.

"I hope I haven't kept you waiting long," Hunter said to him.

Mark stood up and smiled at him and Danni. "No, I've only been here a few minutes."

Hunter left Danni and Mark to talk as he grabbed the diary and looked at his appointments. "Danni, how does a week Tuesday sound?"

Danni pulled her phone out and looked. "Yep, that works, about 10.30 again?"

"Yep," Hunter said, picking up a pencil and writing her in. "I've booked you in. Remember the aftercare we talked about, and you have the leaflet, but if you have any issues, just call."

"Will do. Thanks, Hunter," Danni said.

"Yes, thanks," Mark said, taking her hand and leaving the shop.

Hunter put the diary down and headed back to his room to clear up and sanitise everything. He paused in the doorway of the kitchen and looked at Taha and Owen, who were still wrapped in each other's arms. "It's a good job that killer witch isn't around," he said with a laugh.

They both looked at him.

"You're safe. It's fine," Taha said, grinning.

Hunter snorted a laugh.

"I would still have heard you call for help," Owen assured him.

"I'm just messing with you," Hunter told them.

"Shell went out and got some lunch. Yours is in the fridge," Luke said, walking into the kitchen and rolling his eyes at Taha and Owen.

"I'll clean up my room and then have some," Hunter said, turning and walking back to his room.

He tidied everything up, threw away what he needed to, and put everything that needed sterilising into the machine. Finally, he got the disinfectant and sanitised every surface. Once finished, he went to the sink and washed his hands. He was just drying them when he heard a noise behind him. He turned round, expecting to see one of his friends, but saw a strange man standing behind him instead.

The man was roughly his height at six-foot-six but was lanky with close-cropped hair and a sneer on his face.

Hunter couldn't remember seeing him before. "Can I help you? Do you have an appointment?" he asked.

The man shook his head. "I don't, but *you* do. You have an

THE VAMPIRE AND THE TATTOOIST

appointment with *death*." And quick as anything, the man raised his hand.

It was only then that Hunter saw his wand. Before he could call out for help, the man flung a spell at him. Hunter jumped out of the way as the spell hit the sink and it exploded. "Owen, help!" he yelled as he hit the floor.

Hunter saw a blur, and the next moment, the witch was in a crumpled heap on the floor.

Taha raced in and rushed to Hunter's side. "Are you alright?"

Hunter nodded and sat up, rubbing his arm. "I got out of the way in time." He looked at Owen. "Thanks."

"Stay there while I put the fire out," Taha said, running into the hall to grab a fire extinguisher and rush back in with Luke and Shelly at his side.

"What the hell!" Shell exclaimed as Taha put the fire out, smoke filling the sink area.

Luke and Shelly ran to Hunter's side.

"Are you alright?" Luke asked, holding his hand out to help Hunter up.

"A sore arm, but I'll live," Hunter replied, taking the offered hand and standing up.

"Do you know how he got in?" Taha asked with a final squirt of the extinguisher before opening the windows.

Hunter shook his head. "I didn't hear the bell ring. I think he might have portalled in. I turned round and he was just there."

"What do we do with that soon-to-be-dead man?" Luke asked.

Hunter looked at him. "Soon to be dead?"

"Yeah, Owen is a paranormal. They kill the bad guys," Luke said, rolling his eyes as if the answer was oh-so-obvious.

"Unfortunately, this witch's demise will have to wait. I need to take him to Gabriel. Pretty sure this is the witch they are after," Owen said, pulling out some zip ties from his pocket. He rolled the man onto his stomach and tied his hands behind him. "I can message David and see where I need to take him."

"I need to message Gavin," Hunter said, grabbing his phone. He opened his messages and smiled.

G: At the wolf pack. Met the Alpha King... he's strange. We're having a celebration later for Sean and Kayden's 10th anniversary. You have to come. X

Hunter sent a message back.

H: Would love to come. Just to let you know, we caught that murdering witch. Owen has him tied up.

Hunter waited for a message, but the next moment, a portal opened.

CHAPTER 34

*P*lans had been put in place, and Kevin's pack were starting to take the children home. There was still lots to do, but with every child that left and returned home, it helped settle something in everyone.

There was still more to talk about, but no one wanted to do that over food.

Sandwiches and nibbles had been brought out and eaten when Gavin's phone pinged. Hunter's name popped up and he smiled, opening the message just as David's phone rang. He gave a silent gasp at what Hunter wasn't saying.

"What's wrong, Gav?" Mathis asked his brother.

Gavin thrusted his phone at Mathis, who read the message.

"Little witch, can you open a portal to Hunter? They caught your witch," Mathis said.

"They did indeed. Owen has just phoned me," David said.

"Finally," Gabe said, standing up and opening a portal.

Gavin jumped up and ran through first, running straight to Hunter. He stopped just in front of Hunter and signed.

"I hurt my arm, but that's it. I jumped out of the way in

time. The sink was killed, though," he said, pointing to the smoky, blackened area, "and luckily the fire alarm didn't go off."

Gavin sighed and wrapped his arms around Hunter.

Hunter pulled him closer and rested his head on top of Gavin's.

"Yes, this is Jake Conway," Gabe said, squatting down by him. "We should be able to get most of the information we need from him." Gabe grinned at the vampires. "And by we, I, of course, mean you guys."

David nodded. "I can get the information from him, that won't be a problem. I also need to update everyone on what else I found from the lemmings."

"Umm, Hunter, you have a magical portal in your room?" Luke said, staring at it.

"It's a quick way to travel," Hunter replied.

"You must be Gavin. Hunter told us all about you and sighed happily, spoke more about you and sighed again. Really, there has been a lot of sighing. I'm Luke, by the way."

"I didn't sigh," Hunter protested.

Gavin pulled out of Hunter's arms and turned, smiling at Luke.

"Oh my God, you're gorgeous. I'm Shelby, and seriously, you're stunning. But if you don't mind me saying, your clothes are a bit plain, and you were born to stand out."

Gavin silently laughed and blushed, then signed.

"It's nice to meet you, too," Luke said. "I've only just started learning sign language, so I apologise now if I misinterpret something."

Gavin smiled and signed again.

"So that was you're welcome and it's nice to meet us?" Shell asked.

Gavin nodded.

Hunter put his arm around Gavin's waist.

Shelby sighed. "So unfair. Look, Luke, Hunter and Gavin look perfect together, and Taha and Owen look perfect together. We need to find ourselves some cool paranormal's."

"It's not all it's cracked up to be. You don't get any upgrades, no super speed, no super hearing, nothing," Hunter told them.

"Oh, you poor human, you," Mathis said, grinning at him.

They stopped talking when they heard a groan coming from Jake.

"Your witch is waking up," Mathis said, squatting down so he was the first face Jake saw when he woke up. Mathis gave him an evil grin. "Hello, buttercup. Remember me?" he said, patting Jake on the head.

"You can't keep me here. We will destroy you; *all* of you. Our plans have already been set in motion."

"What plans?" Gabe asked him.

Jake scowled at him. "You'll see."

"We need to find out what he knows," Gabe said.

"Let's take him back to the wolves. I'm sure Kevin would like to chat with him, as well," David said.

"Not to mention the Alpha King," Mathis said, again patting the man's head."

"Alpha King?" Jake asked paling.

"Look at that reaction. Definitely the Alpha King," David said. "Owen, you can carry him."

Owen grumbled and picked Jake up, throwing the witch over his shoulder.

"I demand you put me down," Jake said, struggling.

"I'll get right on that," Owen said, rolling his eyes.

"It might be worth bringing the lemmings, as well," Mathis said.

Gabe nodded. "Yeah, we still need to know what was found out."

"Let me collect the lemmings and I can fill you in. Can you open a portal to the coven house?" David asked.

"I can do that," Gabe said, opening a portal.

"Thanks. Mathis, you can come with me. Seth," David called out.

Seth walked through the portal. "What's up, bossman?"

"We're going to collect the lemmings and bring them to the wolf pack," David told him.

"Off we go, then," Seth said, walking through the second portal.

"See you in a bit, little witch," Mathis said following.

"When you're ready, text me and I'll open another portal for you," Gabe told him.

"Will do," David replied.

They watched David walk through the portal and then Gabe closed it.

"So cool! Can you teach me how to create portals?" Shell asked, smiling at Gabe.

"Only if you're a witch," Gabe replied.

"I'm not a witch, but I am fabulous. Does that count?"

Gabe laughed. "Alas, it does not."

"Bummer."

CHAPTER 35

Everyone was back at the wolf pack and Jake and the lemmings were currently being held in the wolf cells. Gabe added protection around them so no one could use magic.

Spencer had seen Jake carried through the portal, shouting his head off and struggling to get down. He let out a cry of terror and ran to hide behind Stefan, grabbing the back of his shirt and pushing himself against Stefan's back, hiding.

Stefan put his arm around the frightened boy and made sure he was hidden from Jake until Owen followed Ian to the cells. As soon as Jake was gone, Stefan turned round and hugged Spencer. "On my word as King of the Vampires, I will keep you safe," Stefan assured him.

Bert was standing beside Stefan and touched Spencer's shoulder. "I promise my protection, as well."

Spencer pulled back and looked at them, his eyes full of tears. He sniffed. "You both promise? He was the one who took me. I tried to fight him off, but he used magic on me and beat me up." He pulled his top up and showed them his bruises.

Bert growled. "I will revisit every bruise he gave you on him. I shall make him sorry he ever got involved with any of this."

"And when the Alpha King has finished, I will drain every drop of blood from his miserable body," Stefan added.

Spencer screwed his nose up. "Bet his blood is nasty. I can save you a cake so you can eat it afterwards."

Stefan laughed. "Thank you, but you eat your cake. Annie will always make more."

Bert looked at Spencer. "You okay now? If you want, we can go and annoy my brother."

Spencer moved out of Stefan's arms and wiped his face. "I'm okay now. What did you have in mind for your brother?"

~

Hunter was standing off to one side with Gavin in his arms, watching what was going on. Taha was standing next to him, replying to a message from Luke.

"Luke and Shell all right?" Hunter asked him.

Taha nodded and smiled. "Wishing they were here. They've also cleaned as much of your room as they could and contacted your customers for the next few days and rearranged your appointments."

"That should give me time to sort everything out. It should be easy enough to fix, just rip out the damaged units, replace them and get a new sink," Hunter replied.

"And paint and pretty sure you'll need to buy new inks, needles, etc. as your store cupboard was killed, as well," Taha told him.

Hunter groaned.

THE VAMPIRE AND THE TATTOOIST

Gavin pulled away and turned, signing at Hunter.

Hunter nodded. "You're right, it could have been much worse. Plus, I have insurance."

"You could always ask your dad for help," Taha told him.

"No, he's busy. This's why we have insurance."

"How will you explain what happened on an insurance form? Pretty sure witch spells aren't covered," Dave said, having been filled in earlier.

"Yeah, that could be tough. I'll figure something out," Hunter assured him.

"We always have money put away for emergencies. If needed, we can just use some of that," Taha said.

Gavin started signing.

"I didn't get all that, but did you offer to help with all the heavy lifting?" Hunter asked.

Gavin nodded.

"I will definitely take you up on that," Hunter said, grinning at him.

"I'm sure I can get Owen to help, as well," Taha said.

"Sorry, Taha, I should have congratulated you and Owen," Dave said to him, Gavin having told them all earlier that Owen and Taha were mates.

"That's okay, everyone is distracted, as they should be," Taha replied.

Gavin started signing at Taha.

Taha shook his head. "Sorry, Gavin, I've only just started learning."

"He said, 'Has Owen told you about his impressive shoe collection?'" Dave translated.

"No, he's not said anything about it," Taha replied.

"Just to let you know, he has his shoes handmade, and they're usually around ten thousand pounds," Dave told him.

"Seriously?" Taha said in surprise. "People actually spend *that* much money on shoes?"

"Yep, I only found that out when Bruno chewed and then tried to bury one of his shoes. I don't think Owen knows about that yet," Dave admitted.

"I'm not telling him," Taha said.

"Me, either," Hunter added.

Gavin signed, "No."

"Have you two met Sean and Kayden yet? They're witches from Gabe's coven. It's their tenth wedding anniversary today, so we're having a party later," Dave told them.

"Did we hear our names?" Kayden said, walking over with Sean.

"You did. I was telling Hunter and Taha it's your wedding anniversary today," Dave told them.

"It is. But we honestly don't mind not celebrating it today," Kayden said.

Dave snorted. "I'll let you tell my mother, Louise, and Lissa that."

"Yeah, maybe not," Sean said. "Has Gavin told you we're designing a computer game together? Vampires vs. Witches."

Hunter shook his head. "No, but I can't wait to play it."

Gavin smiled at him and leant back against Hunter, wrapping Hunter's arms around him.

Hunter dropped a kiss on Gavin's head.

"Do you know what's going to happen in the game?" Taha asked.

Gavin mimicked zipping and locking his mouth closed.

"You'll never get Gav to tell. I can guarantee until the game is written, the only people who will know what happens in it will be Sean, Kayden, and Hunter," Mathis said, walking over to them.

"Should you not be interrogating the lemmings?" Dave asked.

"David is going to fill us in on everything he learnt from the lemmings, then we'll question Jake Conway." He looked

THE VAMPIRE AND THE TATTOOIST

at Sean and Kayden. "Do you mind if we talk to them before your party?"

They both shook their heads. "Nope, we need answers and it's best not to wait," Sean said.

"We'll go and bring them up then," Mathis replied.

"Maybe ask Mum to keep Spencer and Jack with her," Dave suggested.

Mathis nodded. "Will do." And with that, he walked off back into the pack house.

Dave looked at Taha and Hunter. "You might not like what you're about to see and hear. Do you want me to get Gabe to send you both back to the coven house?"

Hunter shook his head. "No, I might not like what I see, but these are members of Gavin's family. I'll stay and watch."

"So will I. I know Owen is a vampire, so I should see what they can do," Taha said.

Gavin smiled at Hunter, leaned up and kissed his cheek.

As they were talking, Bertrum walked over to them.

"How are you doing? Especially with scenting your mate earlier," Kayden asked him.

Bert gave a small smile. "Impatient to meet him, but it can wait until we question the witches. Apparently, this Jake Conway paled at the mention of my name."

"I can't imagine why, puppy," Troy said, sauntering over to them.

Bert sighed. "How no one has killed you yet is a mystery."

Troy laughed. "Not really. Dave won't let David kill or maim me."

Dave looked at Troy and grinned. "Did you know I'm not allowed to get a puppy because I have Bruno and you?"

"I am not your pet," Troy ground out.

"Aren't you, though?" David said, walking over to join them with Kevin at his side.

"Pets don't usually fell people, and I felled you," Troy pointed out, grinning.

"I felled you, as well. Remember? With a not-so-little scratch," David shot back with a scowl.

"You're so cute when you scowl like that, old bean," Troy taunted.

David went to step forward when Cairo pulled Troy out of the way, shaking his head at his mate.

"You love living dangerously, don't you?"

Troy laughed. "I love you more."

"Aww, now who's being all cute?" Bert said with a laugh.

"Hey, bossman," Seth called out. "The gangs all here."

CHAPTER 36

All the kidnapped children were on their way home, thanks to Kevin's pack mates, except for Jack and Spencer who were staying in the kitchen with the mums.

The pack children had all gone home and would be coming back later for the BBQ. No one wanted the children to be around when the witches were interrogated.

And now the lemmings and Jake Conway were bound to garden chairs.

Standing in front of them were David, Kevin, Gabe, and Bertrum. Everyone else was standing further back, watching. The Alpha King's guards were standing with the vampire guards, ready in case anything kicked off.

David turned to look at everyone. "Before we start interrogating them again, as per Gabe's request, I went down and got more information out of them."

Stefan coughed.

David grinned. "And by I, of course, I mean Father and I."

Snorts were heard from those watching.

"We haven't got our friend Giles here to talk yet, but the other witches told us everything they knew," David said.

"I'm sure they hoped that by telling us what they knew, their punishment wouldn't be so severe," Stefan added.

"Idiots," Dave muttered.

"Right?" Sean said. "After being involved with all of this crap, what did they think, that Gabriel would pat them on the head and say, 'Okay then, I'll let you all go scot-free?'"

"Well, they don't seem to be the brightest of bright people," Hunter said.

"Indeed," David agreed. "So, these delightful lemmings told us more about everything they were involved in, which has already been discussed. It would seem that it's not just child trafficking, but child *sex* trafficking."

Gasps were heard from those around them.

"With Giles and Jake here being the main two involved with that part of the network."

"Sick freaks," Kayden muttered.

"They are indeed. The lemmings, however, don't know where the sex clubs are," Stefan said, sounding disgusted.

"Are there these kinds of clubs here in the UK?" Taha asked, shocked.

"From what we can tell, some are... those ones we can find. It's the international ones we'll have problems locating," David added.

"And that's if those children are still alive now," Kevin said. "I have some international contacts I can message, they will help."

"I also know people that can help," Bertrum said. "As Alpha King, I can get international wolf packs involved."

"As can I," Stefan added.

"Thank you," David said, looking at them. "I'm sure there will be details of where they were sent somewhere on the devices we have."

"That's a safe bet, considering they recorded all their meetings and didn't disguise their voices," Ivan said.

"Like Hunter said, not the brightest of bright people," Gio remarked.

"I didn't tell you earlier, but we also ran a search on all their financial records, and when I say we, I mean Gavin," Ivan said, smiling over at him while pulling his phone out of his pocket. "Over the last five years, they had all received large payments from a dummy corporation called The Masters. We still have searches running for more information on this corporation."

"All that money, along with all your assets, now belong to the coven, to be redistributed as I see fit," Gabriel told the bound witches.

"I'm thinking a lot of children's charities might be seeing some of that," Mathis said.

Gabe nodded. "They will indeed, and all the rescued kidnapped children."

"I don't need money," Jack said, coming to stand next to Seth and Gio. "But I need that one there punched in the face."

"Giles?" Gabriel asked, looking at him.

Jack nodded. "He kidnapped me. Told me I was to be his new plaything. That I was to be kept in a cage in his bedroom and that when he took me out of the cage, he was going to tie me to his bed. I don't know what he was planning after that... well I can guess, but before he could say anything else, I kneeded him in the nuts and bit his hand, so he used magic to tie me up and threw me into the boot of his car."

Gio walked forward. "That boy is my son," he snarled out before punching Giles. Blood spurted from his broken nose, not that he complained as the punch knocked Giles out.

"And now we can't question Giles," Owen commented.

"He deserved it," Seth said, his arm around Jack's shoulder. "If Gio hadn't punched him, I was going to do it."

Jack leaned into Seth and smiled at Gio. "Thanks. Someone needs to punch that one for taking Spencer."

"I'm sure that will happen soon, but we need answers first," Bert said. "I'm sure more than one of us wants the pleasure of punching him. But for the moment, Jakey boy here needs to start talking." Saying this, he walked over to Jake and stood in front of him, crossing his arms over his chest. "So, rumour has it you have set some kind of plan in motion and paled when my name was mentioned."

Jake gave an evil smile. "Your time as Alpha King is coming to an end."

"How?" Kevin demanded, walking to his brother's side.

Gabriel ignored them and started to look around. Something was in the air, but he didn't know what. He pulled his wand out.

Noticing, Kayden asked softly, "What's wrong?"

"Something strange is in the air. Can't you feel it?"

"Now you mention it, I can," Sean said, pulling his wand out, as well.

"We need a shield around all of us and the pack house right now," Gabe said urgently, and he threw his magic out, creating a shield.

Kayden pulled his wand out, and he and Sean added their magic to the shield just as an explosion sounded from around them, before flames engulfed the shield.

CHAPTER 37

The shield took the full impact but didn't break as the three witches kept sending out their magic.

Everyone exclaimed or gave a startled yelp, and Hunter hugged Gavin tighter.

Hunter looked up and saw Taha was in Owens's arms, Mathis was stood by Gabe, Dave was wrapped up in David's arms, and Kevin was standing by Creed, holding hands.

Seth and Gio surrounded Jack.

"Sean, Kayden, keep the shield up for a moment as I deal with the flames," Gabe commanded.

A moment later, they could all see the flames dying down until they'd all gone.

"Guys, release the shield," Gabe told them.

Sean and Kayden pulled their magic back and the shield dropped.

Everyone looked around at the devastated garden where the explosion had destroyed it. The ground looked like several bombs had gone off, and the only part of the garden left in its former glory was where the shield had been.

"What the hell!" Ian exclaimed.

"Anyone hurt?" Kevin asked, looking around.

"Only the garden," Dave said, pulling out of David's arms and looking around.

Gabriel pushed his magic out, and soon the garden was once again pristine and perfect.

Kevin looked at the three witches. "Thank you for protecting our home and us and Gabe for fixing the garden."

"You're welcome."

Bertrum looked at Jake. "I'm going to go out on a limb and say your plan just failed."

Jake paled.

"I know you protected the pack house, as well, but I'm going to check on those inside," Ian said.

"No need," Willard said, walking out. "We're all fine. What was the explosion?"

"A pathetic attempt to kill us," Bertrum said.

Willard looked at the still unconscious Giles. "Who punched him?"

"I did," Gio said proudly.

"Probably should have punched that one, as well," he said pointing to Jake.

"We will. We need answers first," David told him.

"Jack, why don't you come with me back to the kitchen? Lissa is about to pull sausage rolls out of the oven and we need another taste tester."

Gio looked at Jack. "Hot sausage rolls are the best."

Jack nodded. "They are. Thanks, Willard."

Willard nodded and they both walked back into the pack house.

"I love your dad, Dave," Seth said.

Dave smiled. "Me, too."

"So, Jake, tell us everything you know," Bertrum said.

"You'll get nothing from me."

Bertrum wasn't the only one who laughed at that. "Oh,

Jakey boy, I can either beat the information out of you or the vampires can literally rip the information from your head. The choice is yours, and to help you decide, I'm going to destroy your family and those who tried to blow my brother's pack up. If I wanted my brother dead, I'd kill him myself."

"Love you, too, Gerty," Kevin replied from just behind him.

"Can you imagine the lecture Mum would give me if someone else killed you?" Bert said to him.

"You'd probably get a bigger one if you killed Kevin yourself," Seth helpfully pointed out.

"Justifiable killing. She'd understand," Bert replied.

Kevin wasn't the only one to laugh at that.

Bertrum partially shifted and stepped forward, picking Jake up by his neck, his wolf claws piercing his flesh. "Now, start from the beginning and tell me everything."

Jake went ghost white and a wet patch formed on the front of his trousers, then shaking, he told them everything.

Sometime later, the lemmings, Giles and Jake were back down in the wolf cells.

"We need to confirm everything he said and all the names he gave us. Have everything documented," Stefan said.

"I wish we had recorded everything he said," Bertrum lamented. "We could have used that as evidence."

"Gavin did," Hunter said as everyone turned to look at him. "He pulled his phone out as soon as you grabbed Jake by the neck."

"Nice, bro," Mathis said to him.

"Yeah, thanks, Gav. Can you send us all copies of the recordings?" Kevin asked.

Gavin nodded and started attaching the recording to an email and sent it to everyone present he had numbers for.

Phones started beeping.

"Thanks, Gavin," Kevin said, looking at the email.

"Can you send it to me?" Bert asked his brother.

"Already have," Kevin replied.

"Thanks." He looked around the group. "Can you copy me in on all the information and reports that have already been compiled?"

"We can," David assured him.

"If you need more help going through physical copies of paperwork, I have people that can help."

"Thanks, Bert, I'll let you know," Gabriel said.

"In the meantime, I'll send some guards out to see what they can find," Bert said, walking over to them.

"Ian, go inside and check on the food status, it must be time to light the BBQ. I don't think I'm the only one who needs a good party now."

∽

The BBQ was in full swing, and the scent of cooking meat was in the air. The garden was decorated, courtesy of Gabe, with balloons and a congratulatory sign for Sean and Kayden.

Laughter could be heard from all around them.

"Thanks for having your anniversary today. I think we all needed this BBQ," Seth said to Sean and Kayden.

He was standing with them, Hunter, and Gavin.

"We can celebrate again if you want. Or we could have a party when the adoption goes through," Kayden commented.

Seth shook his head. "My life is weird. A few days ago, I was dying and Gio was cursed, and now we're both healthy, happy and have a son."

"Is it rude to ask what kind of paranormal he is?" Hunter asked. "There are probably a lot of rules I need to learn."

"Not really. We try and keep the paranormal world a

THE VAMPIRE AND THE TATTOOIST

secret, but it's like an open secret nowadays," Seth replied. "As for what paranormal Jack is, he's a red fox."

"So awesome," Sean said.

They heard a burst of laughter and saw Gio, Dave, Spencer, and Jack playing together.

"I had given up on ever hearing Gio laugh like that again," Seth said softly.

"But he's laughing and having fun," Creed said, joining them. "He's back to the old Gio he once was."

"We should thank Roberto. Because of him, we are all now friends," Sean said.

"I think I'll pass on thanking him, but I'm glad we all met," Seth replied.

Just then, Bertrum walked over. "Mind if I join you?"

"Nope," Creed said. "You can tell me all your brother's secrets."

Bert laughed. "I can, and I have embarrassing photos."

"You have to share them," Sean said, grinning at him.

"I will."

Gavin passed his plate to Hunter and started signing.

"I'm doing all right actually," Bert said.

Gavin grinned at him.

"Yes, I know sign language. I'm a bit rusty, but it will all come back. It's nice to know I have a mate out there, but if he doesn't like the paranormal world, I'll have to proceed with caution."

"Max is nice. He works at the local library for the moment, but he'll be leaving soon to help Dave in the coven library," Hunter told him.

"I might have to visit the library and make his acquaintance."

"I can meet you there if you want. We can grab a coffee inside, and you can meet him," Hunter offered.

"Thank you. I might take you up on that offer. We can

swap numbers in a bit," Bertrum said before looking back at Gavin. "While you're here, Gavin, you've got to tell me how to get off level eleven of Vampire Hunters."

Everyone laughed, with Gavin giving a silent chuckle.

He signed to Bert.

"Really? Then I'll go and ask him." And with that, Bert walked off.

"What did you tell him, Gav?" Sean asked.

"To ask Stefan," Hunter replied for him.

Gavin nodded and gave a silent laugh before signing.

"I don't blame you," Kayden said. "I wouldn't have told him how to do it, either."

The others laughed and Hunter dropped a kiss on Gavin's head.

"It's amazing the different types of people that play your games," Sean said to him.

Gavin signed again and Kayden translated. "I try not to pigeonhole my games, so they appeal to everyone."

"And you do it well," Seth said to him. He looked at Hunter. "How are you coping with today?"

"Surprisingly well," Hunter said. "But I might freak out later."

Gavin looked at him in concern.

Hunter put the plates he was holding on the table behind them and pulled Gavin into his arms. "I'll be fine, sweetheart," he assured, only half believing it.

"We're all here if you do have one," Seth replied.

"Thanks."

CHAPTER 38

Hunter groaned as his alarm went off. It had been a late night, the party going on long into the night and it was the early hours when they left to go home and again Hunter had slept lightly in case Gavin needed him.

Like before, Gavin was lying practically on top of him, and Hunter's arms were wrapped around him.

He managed to shut the alarm off before it woke Gavin up, his arms tightening around his vampire for a moment. He needed time with Gavin away from all the crazy, and he wondered if Gavin could take time away so they could have a weekend to themselves. He stopped that line of thinking. It wasn't fair to pull him away from helping Gabriel with his issues. Plus, he had his workroom to fix up. Taking Gavin away for a weekend would have to wait.

He felt Gavin give a silent sigh as he woke up. Gavin smiled into his chest and kissed it.

"Morning, sweetheart."

Gavin looked up and smiled at him before moving up so

he could kiss Hunter. He pulled back and smiled at Hunter before mouthing morning back.

"Did you sleep well?" Hunter asked him.

Gavin nodded and moving around, he signed to Hunter.

"I'm glad you've only had good dreams. I was hoping you would. I don't know about you, but I'm in desperate need of coffee."

Gavin frowned before signing.

Hunter didn't want to tell Gavin he'd slept lightly; instead, he smiled. "Some mornings are just desperate coffee mornings."

Gavin frowned again and touched the corners of Hunter's eyes.

"I look tired?"

Gavin nodded.

Hunter sighed and ran a hand down his face.

Gavin prodded him in the chest.

"Okay, I slept lightly. I wanted to be alert in case you had nightmares and needed me."

Gavin started signing, but Hunter caught his hands and pulled Gavin back down.

"I love you, sweetheart. I don't mind sleeping lightly in case you need me."

Gavin shook his head but lifted his face and kissed Hunter.

It was nearly an hour later when Hunter and Gavin walked into the kitchen and got a round of 'good mornings'.

Gavin smiled and looked around. Neither of his brothers were at the table, plus there were no witches, so chances were that Mathis had stayed with Gabriel, and Raz must still be with Thiago. Gavin leaned into Hunter's side.

"I'm sure your brothers are fine, sweetheart," Hunter said softly to him, picking up on Gavin's mood.

Gavin nodded and picked up the coffee pot, pouring them both drinks as the food was passed around.

"Gavin, Olly is back today. He can help Ivan if you want to go and help Hunter sort his room out," David said to him.

Gavin smiled and signed, "Thank you," before looking at Hunter.

"Sweet you can do all the heavy lifting," Hunter said with a laugh.

Gavin screwed his nose up at him.

"I'll be there, as well," Owen said.

It was then Hunter realised Taha was at the table, too. "Thanks, you two look happy."

"Could be because we are," Taha said. "I should thank you for meeting Gavin and having a killer witch after you."

Hunter laughed, as did others round the table. "Well, I'm not sending a killer witch a thank you basket."

"I'm still waiting for my thank you basket from Dave," Seth said, looking pointedly at him.

"You want me to send you a thank you basket for kidnapping me?" Dave asked, trying not to laugh.

Jack looked at Seth. "You *kidnapped* him?" he asked in shock.

"Not really. I saved him," Seth replied, grinning at him.

Dave wasn't the only one who laughed at that.

"But the thank you basket is for me helping Dave meet David. And just think, everything that's happened over the past few weeks is because I rescued you and brought you here."

"Well, I guess I could get you something. I mean, we've made a lot of new friends over the past few weeks," Dave replied.

"Thomaz, when do you pick up your puppy?" David asked the cook.

Thomaz smiled. "Today. I had a text from the breeder

yesterday saying I could collect him today. I brought a lot of things for him yesterday. I just need to put them out. Dave, I was thinking of putting Diablo's crate next to Bruno's. Is that okay?"

Dave nodded. "Yep, then Diablo — great name by the way — can learn from Bruno."

"Don't you think it's funny that the vampire who was scared of dogs is now getting one?" Cairo said laughing.

"Blame Bruno. He's too lovely to be scared of," Thomaz replied.

"Just remember for the first six months or so, they're little land sharks," Dave cautioned.

"Really?" Owen asked.

Dave nodded. "Oh yeah. With Bruno, I could time it to twenty minutes before he became a hellhound and needed a time-out. But they grow out of it. I'm sure all you'll need to do is hiss at the puppy and he'll be good."

"Diablo will be the perfect puppy," Thomaz said, full of confidence.

Dave wasn't the only one who laughed at that.

∽

"Well, this isn't too bad," Hunter said, looking at the charred remains of his sink and side.

The sink was completely destroyed, as was the worktop, and the wall had smoke damage. The air still held the scent of fire and smoke, so Hunter walked over to the windows and opened them, hoping that would help the smell leave quickly. Mind you, the whole place smelt of smoke and fire.

"How are we going to explain the smell of smoke and burning?" Taha asked him.

"It's probably easier to say it was an electrical fault," Hunter replied.

"That would work," Taha said. "Let me go and grab some gloves for everyone and we can get started on cleaning up and taking measurements. Owen, can you pop out the back door and pull the black wheelie bin in? It should be empty as the dustman came yesterday."

Owen nodded. "I can do that," he said, walking out of the room with Taha.

Hunter looked at Gavin, who was frowning, and walked over to him, pulling Gavin into his arms. "It's not that bad, sweetheart. This can all be fixed."

Gavin pulled back and signed.

"Was that, 'But you were injured?'" Hunter asked.

Gavin nodded.

"Only for a few hours, but my arm is all better now, I promise. Plus, that killer witch is no longer after me, so something like this shouldn't happen again, and I'd rather have to reorder stock and redo this room than be killed."

Gavin gave a silent sigh, stood on tiptoes, and kissed Hunter.

"Break it up, you two. We have work to do," Taha said with a laugh, walking back in with Owen, who was dragging the bin behind him.

"Ta, you have clients today," Hunter pointed out.

Taha shook his head. "Nope, I had Luke and Shell rearrange my appointments. There is no way I wouldn't help you sort this mess out."

"And Gavin and I are the muscles needed," Owen added.

"Then let's get started," Hunter said. They heard the front bell ding. "That should be Luke or Shell."

"Hunter," a man shouted out, sounding annoyed.

Before Hunter could move or reply, Matt rushed in.

Gavin moved to his side, but Matt was focused on Hunter.

"What the hell, Hunt? Someone tries to kill you and I have

to hear about it from Luke and Shelby?" he demanded, sounding hurt.

"Sorry, Matt. I was going to tell you, I promise," Hunter said, walking to him and pulling him into a bro hug.

Matt hugged him back and thumped his back before pulling away. He looked to the side and smiled at Gavin. "You must be Gavin."

"Matt, meet my Gavin. Gavin, this is Matt. We've known each other since we were three."

Gavin smiled and signed.

"It's nice to meet you, as well," Matt replied.

Gavin looked surprised.

"When Hunter told me all about you and told me he was learning sign language, I got him to send me the links so I could learn. Be patient with me as I've only just started learning."

Gavin smiled and signed, "Thank you."

Matt then looked at Owen. "You must be Owen. The boys told me all about you, as well."

"All?" Taha queried.

"About how you pounced on each other as soon as your eyes met and then how you knocked out the deranged killer. Thank you for saving our Hunter."

Owen smiled and nodded. "All in a day's work."

Matt looked around at the destroyed area. "Do you need a hand fixing this up?"

Hunter shook his head. "No, we have this covered, but thanks for the offer."

Matt nodded. "You have my number. Call me if you need me or call your dad."

"Will do. Thanks, Matt," Hunter replied.

"See you soon." And with a final wave to everyone, Matt left.

They heard the front doorbell chime and Matt speaking with someone before walking out.

"Hey, hunnies. Miss us?" Luke called out.

"Not even a little," Taha replied as Luke and Shelby walked in, standing just inside of the room.

"Charming," Shelby said, turning to look at Gavin. "I'm glad you're here. Want to come and see my room and what I do?"

Gavin smiled and nodded, so Shelby walked over to him, linked his arm with Gavin's, and drew him out of the room, chatting away like they were old friends.

"You guys good here?" Luke asked. "I've got a client in a bit."

"Yep, we've got this covered," Hunter told him.

"Okay, see you all later," Luke said, walking out.

"And then there were three," Taha said, shaking his head. He handed out gloves to Hunter and Owen, put a spare pair on the stool, and put some on.

"Let's do this," Hunter said.

CHAPTER 39

Gavin was having fun with Shelby.

Shell showed him round and then took him to look around his room. Shelby had pulled out all the different piercing tubs to show Gavin. "So these are all for different piercings," Shelby said.

Gavin pointed to one that said 'PA.'

"These are used for a Prince Albert piercing."

Gavin looked at Shelby and signed, "What?"

"A Prince Albert is a penis piercing," Shelby told him.

Gavin took a step back and crossed his legs.

Shelby chuckled. "Yeah, I don't blame you. Healing time can be anywhere from four weeks to six months." He pointed to another box. "Want to know what these ones are for?"

Gavin shook his head.

"If you ever want a piercing, come and see me," Shelby offered.

Gavin signed.

"I think that's Hunter is designing you a tattoo."

Gavin nodded.

"Nice." He glanced at the time. "I've got a client in a bit

and I need to get ready. If you're still here at lunchtime, we can go shop for lunch for everyone."

Gavin smiled, nodded, hugged Shelby, and with a quick wave, left him to get ready.

∽

Hunter was throwing damaged equipment into the black bin when Gavin walked back in. "Hey, sweetheart. Have fun?"

Gavin nodded and signed, then crossed his legs.

"Sorry, Gav. I didn't understand a lot of that." Owen said.

"I did," Hunter said. "Gavin had fun. Shelby showed Gavin some piercing jewellery, particularly, I'm guessing by Gavin's crossed legs, the Prince Albert jewellery."

Gavin nodded and grinned.

"Yeah, don't put me down for one of them," Owen said.

"Good, I would hate to have to maim or kill Shelby for touching you there," Taha said, looking at him.

Owen laughed and moved closer to Taha. "Feeling possessive, are you?"

Taha nodded, not looking the least bit repentant. "Always," he said, pulling Owen into a kiss.

Hunter shook his head, picked up the spare gloves and handed them to Gavin to put on.

It didn't take them long to throw out all the damaged items. Owen and Gavin used their super strength to pull off damaged doors, rip out the sink and destroyed worktop, and pull out the shelves. They broke everything up except for the sink and worktop, and it was all put in the bin. The sink and worktop were left leaning against the wall.

"So unfair," Hunter said, shaking his head.

"I feel jipped," Taha replied.

"Dave and I have started a support group. You automatically become a member."

"I'll take you up on that. You would think we'd get *something* though," Taha moaned.

"We did, vampire hickies," Hunter said with a laugh.

Taha nodded. "That's true."

"So, thanks to Gavin and Owen, the hard part is done. Now all we need to do is take measurements, shop, and place orders," Hunter said just as his phone pinged. He pulled it out of his pocket and clicked on his messages. "It would seem Bert wants to go to the library and asks if I have time to join him."

"I'm surprised he's lasted this long, to be honest, especially as he had his mate's scent," Owen said.

"Go and meet up with him. Owen and I can do the measuring," Taha said to him.

Hunter looked at Gavin. "Do you want to come?"

Gavin shook his head and signed.

"You and Shelby are going on a lunch run?" Hunter asked.

Gavin nodded and signed again.

"Of course not, why would I mind? I shouldn't be long, and Owen is here to protect you."

Gavin scowled at him and started quickly signing, in a clipped, pissed-off manner.

Hunter grabbed his hands. "I know you are fierce, sweetheart, and I know you can look after yourself. But until recently, you were pretty much a hermit. Owen is here in case you panic or feel overwhelmed."

"So am I," Taha added.

Gavin gave a silent sigh, leaned against Hunter and nodded.

Hunter shot a message back to Bert that he would be at the library in twenty minutes if that worked.

He got a message straight back.
B: Perfect, see you then.

CHAPTER 40

Hunter arrived at the library at the same time as Bertrum.

"Hey, Hunter, thanks for meeting me," Bert said, offering his hand.

Hunter laughed and took it, pulling Bert into a bro hug. "No problem. We were only ripping out the destroyed stuff in my studio."

"Bad business, all of this. Knowing this has been going on for so long and none of us knew… Changes are going to happen. I trust my wolf council member. He's secretly looking at things from his end and seeing what has been buried and who else in the council was involved."

"I can't even begin to imagine how something like this could stay a secret," Hunter said.

"People in high places hiding things. But now that we know about it, we can destroy the whole of this organisation. But before that, I want to see Max."

"Then follow me. We can grab a coffee and I can point him out," Hunter said, moving towards the door, Bert following. Hunter looked behind them. "Did you bring your guards?"

Bert grinned. "I might have given them the slip."

Hunter snorted. "So those two over there aren't following you?"

Bert spun round and growled. "Yes, they are mine." He turned back round. "See if I bring them a coffee." And with that, Bert stomped inside, Hunter following, shaking his head and waving to the guards.

They walked into the library and Bert looked around. "Libraries have changed since I was younger."

"Same. There didn't use to be coffee shops in the libraries I use to visit," Hunter led the way to the coffee counter. "Hey, Jamie, two coffees, please."

"Sure thing, Hunter. Does your friend want milk and sugar?"

"Just black, please," Bert replied.

Hunter paid for the drinks and waited for Jamie to make them.

"Thanks, Jamie," Hunter said, taking them both and handing one to Bert before they both walked to an empty table and sat down, putting their mugs on the table.

"So, which one is Max?" Bert asked, looking around. "Please tell me it's the sinfully handsome man walking this way with a smile."

Hunter looked around and saw Max walking towards them.

"Yep, that's Max. Hey, Max, how's your day going?"

"Hey, Hunter. It's quiet without Dave, but soon I can leave here, so I'm dealing. Hi," Max ended up looking at Bert.

"Max, this is a friend, Bertrum Mellor. Bert, Max."

"Hello Max," Bert said, holding his hand out.

Max took his hand and shook it before looking shocked and quickly dropping it taking a step back.

"Max, are you okay?" Hunter asked softly.

"Umm, of course, umm, I have work to do." And with that, Max turned and walked quickly away.

Hunter looked at Bert. "Did something happen with the handshake?"

"Not from my end. I wonder what Max felt."

"Let me message Dave. He can then check on Max for us," Hunter replied, pulling his phone out of his pocket and sending Dave a message.

H: In the library. Bert just met Max. Max shook Bert's hand and then rushed off. Can you check on him?

He then sent a quick one to Gavin.

H: Hope you're having fun. Bert met Max and Max is now in hiding x

He had just finished texting Gavin when Dave replied to his message.

D: Will message him now. I'll say you were worried about him, so contacted me.

H: Thanks

Hunter put his phone down on the table and picked up his coffee. "Dave's going to contact Max and check on him."

"From what I heard about Max yesterday, I wasn't expecting meeting him to be all flowers and sunshine," Bert said, looking into his coffee, both hands wrapped around the cup.

"It will get better. He just needs time and to probably see you more than once."

"Should I tell him I'm a king?" Bert asked him, looking up.

"I'm honestly not sure that would impress him. I mean, he knows who Stefan is but doesn't really seem impressed."

"Figures that my mate wouldn't be impressed by my title and would hate my world."

"I wouldn't say hate, just scared and unsure. He just needs time," Hunter assured him.

THE VAMPIRE AND THE TATTOOIST

~

GAVIN WAS HAVING FUN. After Shelby had finished with this client, he and Gavin went out to get lunch for everyone. As they left, Shelby shouted out that there might be some time and closed the door before anyone could answer.

Gavin gave a silent laugh as Shelby linked his arm over Gavin's and led Gavin away.

"So, before we stop off at the bakers to buy lunch, do you mind if we stop at my favourite clothes shop? It's on the way and they have a sale on."

Gavin shook his head and grinned, plucking at his top.

Shelby grinned. "Okay, so you might find something you like in there, as well. I've only seen you in dark clothes, and you do need some colour. It will take you from lovely to stunning. I'm sure as soon as Hunter sees you in colour, he'll jump your bones."

Gavin grinned.

"I know he probably does that, anyway, but you'll see."

Gavin nodded and then pointed from himself to Shelby and made pretend fangs with his hand.

Shelby snorted. "Not even the smallest bit am I scared of you or Owen. I've always read paranormal books, especially vampire books. I secretly hoped they were real, and now I know they are. It's amazing and so very awesome, and Luke feels the same way. Plus, I'm friends with two real-life vampires. My secret dream has come true."

Gavin silently laughed and patted his arm.

It didn't take them long to get to the clothes shop, and Shelby pulled Gavin inside. "This will be so much fun."

Gavin had to admit it was fun shopping with Shelby. Apart from his brothers, he'd never been clothes shopping with someone else. In truth, since he had his own money, he shopped online.

He didn't go mad, though. He brought a few shirts and polo shirts in lighter colours than normal, and Shelby talked him into buying some better-suiting jeans.

Shelby, on the other hand, went mad and bought lots, not even baulking at the cost of his shopping spree.

They walked down the streets carrying their bags. Shelby laughed. "Can you believe how much money we saved today? And your new clothes look amazing. Let's go buy lunch for everyone. They're probably hungry by now."

Gavin gave a silent laugh. The others were probably starving by now. As they were walking to the bakers, Gavin heard his phone ping. He pulled it out and saw it was a message from Hunter. He shook his head. Poor Bert. He sent a message back.

G: Oh dear. Do you both want to come back to your studio? We're just entering the bakers and can buy you both something.

He didn't have to wait long for a reply.

H: Sounds good, yes, please. We'll leave now and meet you at the studio. Love you.

Gavin smiled and sent a message back.

G: Love you x

"Did you know when you message Hunter you get a sappy look on your face?" Shelby asked.

Gavin shrugged. He didn't care; he loved Hunter. He didn't care if everyone saw.

Shelby just laughed and opened the door to the bakers.

They brought enough food to feed an army. Rolls, sausage rolls, pies, and a large selection of cakes.

They were halfway back to the tattoo studio, Shelby taking them back via a side road, when a voice called from behind, "Vampire."

Gavin turned around to see who called. There was no one

else around, apart from the three of them. Gavin felt a shiver go through him. He quickly turned to Shelby, shoved the bags into his arms and mouthed, "Run."

"No, I—"

Gavin didn't let him finish and pointed before turning back to look at the man who had called out. He could hear Shelby running away and breathed a sigh of relief that his friend would be safe.

Gavin stared at the man.

"Well, vampire, aren't you going to ask me who I am and what I want?" the man demanded, walking closer.

Gavin stood still and crossed his arms over his chest. He tried to pull off an 'I'm bored, you're an idiot' look that he hoped worked.

"Fine, don't talk. You're coming with me. You have a connection to the witches and wolves, not to mention the vampires." As he spoke, the man pulled out a wand pointed it at Gavin and started muttering.

Not being stupid, Gavin rushed out of the way and using his speed and strength, he was suddenly behind the man and grabbed his arm, pulling it back so he could get the wand away from him.

The man laughed and pulled his arm out of Gavin's hold, much to Gavin's surprise. "Silly vampire, I am so much stronger than you," he said, spinning around.

Gavin levelled a punch at the man and the man fell into a wall before righting himself. "If that was supposed to knock me out, it failed."

Gavin rushed him and knocked him into another wall.

The man stood up and shook himself, smiling. "I wasn't sure this spell would work, but look at that, it does. I should be dead now or seriously injured, and yet here I stand, ready for more."

Gavin ran for him again, but this time, the man flung his wand at Gavin, and Gavin went flying into the tree behind him.

CHAPTER 41

"Hey, folks, we're back," Hunter called out as he and Bert walked into the tattoo parlour.

"Hey," Taha said, walking out of Hunter's room, Owen following behind him.

"Gavin and Shelby shouldn't be far behind us," Hunter said.

"How did you get on with Max?" Owen asked.

"Met him, shook his hand, and he quickly dropped it before all but running away and hiding," Bert told him.

"I messaged Dave so he could check on Max," Hunter said.

Just then, Owen's phone rang. He pulled it out of his pocket and answered it.

Suddenly, the door flew open, and Shelby ran in, carrying all the bags and looking panicked. "Gavin's in trouble. He needs help."

"Where?" Owen demanded.

"The second side street on the left," Shelby panted out.

Quick as a flash, Owen vanished. Bert turned and ran after him with Hunter and Taha trying to keep up.

Owen reached the side street as a man was flinging his wand at Gavin, who was just standing up and shaking his head. Putting on a burst of speed, Owen ran at the man, throwing him into a wall.

As the man flew into the wall, he dropped his wand to the ground.

Bert arrived and saw the dropped wand, and rushing forward, picked it up, hoping it belonged to the man Owen was fighting.

The man jumped up. "You can't stop me. I've got a spell on me, making me quicker and stronger."

Bertrum stood in front of the man, holding up his wand. "I wonder what would happen if I broke this."

"I will still be strong and powerful," the man said, but something flickered in his eyes.

Bert smiled and, taking the wand in both hands, broke it in two just as Hunter and Taha came running to join them.

"See. I'm still standing," the man said, opening his arms wide like he was showing off.

"You must be really strong to survive being attacked by vampires. Just how strong are you?" Taha asked, walking towards him.

"So much stronger than all of you combined," the man boasted.

"Can I feel your chest to see how strong you are?" Taha asked, stepping closer.

The man shrugged. "Sure, why not? A handsome man wants to touch me up, so have at it."

Owen hissed and went to move, but a shake of Hunter's head stopped him.

Taha smiled at the man and touched his chest, placing his fingers in a circle and pressing, before moving them and pressing again. He took his hand away and stepped back. "Impressive."

"How long?" Hunter asked him.

"Ten seconds," Taha said, looking at Hunter and grinning.

"For what?" Bert asked just as a shocked expression passed over the man's face before his eyes closed and he crashed to the ground.

"For that to happen," Taha said.

Hunter ignored everyone and ran to Gavin's side, pulling him into his arms.

"Are you injured?"

Gavin shook his head, wishing he hadn't when his head started spinning. Pulling back, he signed.

"Let me look," Hunter said, turning Gavin around to have a look and a prod. "You have a heck of a bump, sweetheart, which is bleeding but not gushing."

"Who phoned you, Owen?" Taha asked him.

"David. He felt Gavin get hurt and phoned me as we were supposed to be together. I need to call him back," he said, pulling his phone out of his pocket.

"We need to lock this guy up," Bert said, letting out a loud whistle. His two shadows ran into the side street. "Nice of you to join us. I thought you were supposed to be protecting me?"

"We knew the vampire was with you. You're fine," one of the guards said, waving his hand dismissively.

Bertrum ignored the sniggers from those around him. "Take him to my brother's cells. They're protected against magic."

"Might be worth getting ours protected, as well," the second guard said.

"I'll talk to Gabriel. In the meantime, take him away." He looked at Taha. "How long will he be out for?"

"About an hour," Taha told him.

"Good, plenty of time then," Bert said and watched one of his guards pick the unconscious man up and carry him away.

Bert looked at the other guard who hadn't moved. "Go with Oscar just in case anything happens."

"But—" the other guard started to say.

"I will protect the Alpha King," Owen said, hanging up the phone.

"Thanks." And with a quick nod to Bert, the guard hurried off.

Owen walked over to Gavin, who was again wrapped up in Hunter's arms and touched his back. "David felt your pain. He wants you to go back to the coven."

Gavin shook his head, wincing as he did.

"Please, sweetheart? I'll come with you," Hunter said gently.

Gavin gave a silent sigh and nodded before wincing again.

"Definitely back to the coven for you, my friend," Bert said.

"How about we pack up and all head to the coven house?" Taha suggested. He looked at Bert. "Max might even be there."

"Are you sure none of you mind?" Bert asked.

"Not even a little," Owen replied.

It didn't take them long to get back to Area 51. Both Luke and Shelby were waiting for them in the reception area, Shelby pacing back and forth, nibbling on his thumbnail.

As soon as he saw Gavin, he rushed over and pulled him into a hug. "I was so worried, especially when you told me to run. I ran as fast as I could to get you help." He pulled back. "Are you injured?"

Gavin held his thumb and forefinger apart.

"Do you need a doctor?" Luke asked, coming over and touching his shoulder.

Gavin mouthed, "No."

THE VAMPIRE AND THE TATTOOIST

Luke turned and looked at Owen. "Did you stop that horrid man?"

Hunter snorted. "No. Taha, the lowly human, stopped him."

"Way to go, Ta," Shelby said, high fiving him.

"We're all taking off, though. We need to get Gavin home," Hunter told them.

"Okay, hold on a sec." Shelby dashed off towards the kitchen.

"Is anyone else hurt?" Luke asked.

"Well, the man who attacked Gavin is going to wake up to one hell of a headache, and Gavin's got one, too, and maybe a concussion, but they were the only injuries," Owen told him as Shelby came rushing back, carrying bags.

"These bags are all Gavin's new clothes, and these two bags have your lunches in them," Shelby said, handing the food bags to Taha and Gavin's shopping bags to Hunter.

Owen took them before Hunter could. "You look after our Gavin, and I'll carry the bags."

CHAPTER 42

David and Dave were standing on the front steps of the coven house waiting for Gavin and the others to arrive.

As soon as Gavin climbed out of the car, Dave ran down the steps and pulled him into a hug. "I was so worried about you. Louise and I raided Adrian's supplies, and we have things that can help you," he said, pulling back.

Gavin smiled at him.

"Come on in, everyone. Thomaz is currently out, but I can find Annie and ask her to make you all something to eat," David said.

Taha held up the food bags. "We have food covered."

As they were talking, Dave led Gavin up the steps, and they stopped in front of David.

David pulled Gavin into a hug. "I'm glad you're safe, Gavin. Come inside and sit down before you fall down."

Gavin pulled back and nodded, wincing again, realising that was a stupid thing to do. He really had to stop moving his head too much and let Hunter lead him inside.

They had just reached the kitchen when Mathis, Gabe, Sean, and Kayden ran through a portal.

"You're injured?" Mathis asked, pulling Gavin into a hug.

Gavin wrapped his arms around his brother, thankful that someone had thought to message him. He rested his cheek on his brother's chest and soaked in the brotherly love.

"You're injured?" he heard Raz say from behind him before Raz joined in the hug.

Gavin moved around and put an arm around Raz, happy that both his brothers were there. Sure, he had Hunter in his life, but it had always been him, Mathis, and Raz. He could never imagine a time that he wouldn't need them.

"We need to check your head out, little brother. I can smell the blood in your hair," Mathis said gently.

"If Gavin can sit down, I can use the healing rune on him," Gabriel said softly.

Gavin pulled away from his brothers and hugged Gabriel, Sean, Kayden, and then Thiago before Thiago pulled him to the table, pulled out a chair, and gently pushed him to sit down. "Sit."

Gavin smiled at him as he moved out of the way.

Gabriel looked at Gavin and grinned, a grin that was tinged with worry. "This shouldn't hurt a bit. I'm going to put my hands gently on your head and call on the healing, okay?"

Gavin mouthed, "Okay."

Gabe pulled out his wand and drew the healing rune on both his hands. He probably didn't need to, but this was Gavin, and he was taking no chances. He walked behind Gavin, and as soon as he placed both hands on Gavin's head, a white light surrounded his head. A moment later, the light faded, and Gabe took his hands off and walked back to stand in front of Gavin.

Gavin gave a silent sigh of relief as the pain in his head

receded. He had never had such a bad headache before. He smiled at Gabe and jumped up, pulling him into a hug before stepping back and signing his thanks.

"I will always help you when you're injured," Gabe assured him.

"So will we," Kayden said to him.

"Why don't we all sit down, and you can tell us what happened?" David suggested.

As he said this, they heard a car screeching to a stop and running footsteps as Kevin, Creed, and Ian rushed into the kitchen.

"You're injured? What happened?" Kevin enquired, pulling Gavin into a hug.

Gavin hugged him back, pulling away as Ian pulled him into a hug.

"Who do I have to kill for you?" Ian asked.

"Gavin and the others were about to explain what happened," David said. "Everyone, have a seat and we can find out."

Bert looked at his brother. "You've never come running when *I've* been injured."

Kevin shrugged. "You're not Gavin."

"I'm sure someone will come running. I mean, you do have guards," Ian pointed out.

Hunter laughed. "These would be the same guards that only came to help after they weren't needed."

Bert nodded. "We'll be having words."

"Wuss," Kevin coughed into his hand.

Chuckles were heard and everyone moved to the table to sit down as Louise and Stefan walked in. Louise walked to Gavin and touched his shoulder. "How injured are you, dear? We got healing items from Adrian's room."

Gavin smiled at her and signed.

Louise looked at Gabriel. "Thank you for healing Gavin."

Gabriel smiled. "No thanks needed. I'll help any of you that needs it."

"Mum, Dad, sit down. Gavin and the others were just about to tell us what happened," David said.

Once everyone was settled, Gavin started signing what happened, with Gabriel translating for everyone.

"Did he say what spell was used to make him stronger?" Gabe asked.

Gavin shook his head.

"He didn't tell us, either," Owen said.

"I broke his wand," Bert said, pulling the two broken pieces out of his pocket.

"You broke a witch's wand?" Sean asked in surprise.

"Is that a bad thing?" Bert asked, dropping the two pieces on the table.

Gabriel shook his head. "No, but I don't think I've ever heard of someone breaking a witch's wand before."

"Some witches think they're only magical because of their wand. If this is the case with the witch that attacked, he might think he's powerless now," Kayden said.

"I think he originally did, but then once I broke it, he realised he was still strong, so I don't know what he thinks now. He's currently in Bacon's cells," Bert replied.

"Turd," Kevin muttered.

"There was a man who came to the house we were held in," Jack said from the kitchen doorway, Bruno at his side. Bruno walked over to Gavin and rested his head on his lap, and Gavin stroked his head and played with his ears.

"What did the man say?" David asked him.

"That he was making super strong witches. He said he was going to create a witch army," Jack said, walking in.

"How did you find this out?" Gabe asked him.

"The room they met in was next to the toilets. There was a vent where you could hear what they were saying through."

"Would you know that man's voice if you heard it again?" Mathis asked.

"Maybe," Jack answered. "I mean, I heard him a couple of times. He instructed our guards to inject us with anti-shifting drugs."

"What?" practically everyone shouted.

Jack took a step back, looking scared and uncertain.

Bertram jumped up and stood in front of Jack. "No one here will hurt you. We were shocked, and if they felt anything like me, horrified that someone would inject you with something so heinous."

Jack nodded. "Sorry," he said softly.

Bert pulled him into a hug. "There is nothing to apologise for." As he said this, Gio came rushing into the kitchen.

"What's wrong?" he asked, looking from Jack and Bertrum.

Jack pulled back. "Nothing. I got scared, but I'm okay now," he said bravely, pulling back.

Gio looked at him for a moment and walked over to Jack before looking around. "What's happened?"

"It would seem someone visited the house where Jack and Spencer were held. Jack overheard a man say he was creating super witches, one of which Gavin and the others ran into today. Jack also told us that he and the other children were injected with an anti-shifting serum." Bert told him.

Gio gasped and pulled Jack into his arms. "Can you feel your fox?"

Jack hugged him back. "A little. I couldn't for ages, but I felt him inside yesterday. I still can't fully feel him, but whatever they injected me with is wearing off. I was scared I'd never feel him again, but I can."

"Can you find out what was injected into Jack?' Gio asked Gabe.

Gabe shook his head. "No, but Adrian should be able to."

"When is he back?" Dave asked David.

"I'll contact him when we've finished here and find out," David assured him.

"Once you know, can you let me know?" Gio asked.

David nodded.

"Thanks. Until then, I'm going back to training with my men." He grinned at Jack. "Wanna come and play with swords?"

Jack's face lit up. "Hell yeah. Let me run and get Spencer. He'd love to, as well." And with that, Jack dashed out of the kitchen yelling for Spencer.

David sighed loudly. "This used to be a quiet coven house."

"What? Even with Seth around?" Sean queried with a laugh.

"Did someone mention my name?" Seth asked as he walked in.

"Yes, my Seth. David said this used to be a quiet coven house. Sean asked if it could be quiet with you around."

Seth laughed. "This place was only quiet when I wasn't home. Where was Jack running off to?"

"To get Spencer. I said they could play with swords," Gio replied.

"Just keep an eye on them, and maybe start with practice swords," Louise cautioned.

"I didn't bring any with me. I'll watch them closely, though. At some point, we should talk about living arrangements, as most of the guards are sleeping in tents on the grounds."

"We can talk about that later," David replied.

"Seth, has Jack or Spencer spoken about their ordeal?" Stefan asked.

Seth shook his head. "Only little bits, and mainly Jack if

he hears us talking about them, but he hasn't really said much. Why?"

"I'll fill you in on everything later, but the men holding the children injected them with anti-shifting drugs," David told him.

Seth hissed. "We need Adrian to check them out." He looked at Gabe. "Unless you can help."

"Sorry, that's beyond me, but David said he would contact Adrian."

"Good."

CHAPTER 43

Hunter sighed as he closed the door to their bedroom. They brought their lunch bags and fresh coffee with them and sat on the floor next to each other, leaning against the sofa.

He turned to look at Gavin, touching his cheek. "Are you really all better now?"

Gavin nodded and signed, "All better."

"Good. I know you're a strong vampire, but I was so scared. When Shell ran in and told us you were in trouble, I thought my heart was going to stop."

Gavin moved and climbed onto Hunter's lap. He put both hands on Hunter's cheeks. "Sorry," he mouthed.

"Not your fault, sweetheart. I love you. My life would mean nothing if anything happened to take you away from me." He put his hand around Gavin's neck, pulled him close, and kissed him.

Gavin smiled against his lips and wrapped his arms around Hunter, returning the kiss.

After a while, they broke apart. Gavin rested his forehead

against Hunter's for a few moments before he pulled away and mouthed, 'I love you.'

Hunter smiled. "Of course you do. I mean, what's not to love?"

Gavin burst out into silent laughter, happiness shining in his eyes.

"We should eat our very late lunch. I don't know about you, but I'm starving."

Gavin nodded and pulled the food bags closer, handing one to Hunter and keeping the other.

"Are you going to stay on my lap as we eat?" Hunter asked him, making no effort to move Gavin off.

Gavin nodded and got comfy. They both ate in silence for a while, enjoying being with each other and eating.

As they ate, Gavin wondered who had called his brothers or told Kevin and Ian. He was glad his brothers had come, especially Raz. Sure, Thiago had told them that Raz would be safe, but Gavin was still worried about him.

He laughed to himself at how many people had come to check on him. He'd gone from just being him, Mathis, and Raz — Gavin didn't include his parents, as he had only seen his mother a few times when he was growing up and hadn't seen his father since the evening he tried to kill him — to having everyone here in the coven as family and pretty much hiding away from the world, to having friends who were witches and wolves, all who came running when he was injured. To having Hunter, the most amazing mate in the world.

Gavin stopped eating and kissed Hunter's cheek.

Hunter smiled, and screwing his food bag up, dropped it on the floor and pulled Gavin into another kiss.

∼

"Why go after Gavin?" Seth asked after Gio, Gavin, and Hunter left the room.

"Gavin said it was because he had a connection to the wolves, witches, and us," David told him.

"But how would this person know?" Dave asked, confused. "I've not felt or seen anybody following us."

Mathis leant forward. "Could they have bugs here, at your coven, Gabe, and the pack house, Kevin?"

"No," Kevin said "We sweep the pack house and gardens every week to make sure. In our line of work, it pays to be cautious."

"We sweep this house monthly, as well. Plus, with the new security we put in place recently, we'd know if someone broke in," David added.

"The house is swept for listening bugs on a monthly basis?" Dave asked him in surprise.

"It is."

"Cool, let me help next time. I can then play out my James Bond fantasy," Dave said happily.

"Davy, please keep your fantasies to the bedroom. No one here wants to hear about them," Willard said, walking into the kitchen and heading for the coffee pot.

"Daddd," Dave moaned as the others laughed. "It's not that kind of fantasy." He paused. "Well, it wasn't, but that might now change."

Everyone laughed again at that except Willard.

"I don't think the coven house has ever been checked for listening bugs," Gabe ran a hand down his face. "We're going to have to sweep certain rooms to make sure they are bug-free."

Mathis grabbed his hand. "I can do that for you, sweetheart."

Gabe leant into his side. "I knew if I ever got to run my

family coven, it wouldn't be easy, but never in my wildest dreams did I think it would be this hard."

"Just think, when this is all over, you can go back to a boring, quiet coven house," Seth said helpfully.

"I long for that day."

∼

Gavin was happily sat on Hunter's lap, his head resting on his shoulder when he heard a strange bark. Realising that Thomaz must be back with his new puppy, he pulled away and stood up, holding out his hand to help Hunter up.

"Sweetheart?" Hunter queried.

Gavin just silently laughed and pulled Hunter out of the bedroom and down the stairs.

"Aww, he's so cute," Hunter heard someone say, and realised Thomaz must be back with his new puppy. No wonder Gavin had pulled him downstairs to see it.

He would have to find out what kind of puppy Gavin would like. Maybe his brothers would know.

They walked into the kitchen to find Sean holding the cutest German Shepherd puppy.

Sean looked up and saw Gavin and hurried over. "Quick, Gav, take the puppy, Thomaz won't notice. I'll block the door so the two of you can run away."

Gavin gave a silent laugh and took the puppy. He turned, showing it to Hunter.

Hunter stroked his head. "Hey, little guy. Welcome to the family."

"No stealing my puppy," Thomaz said with a laugh.

"His name is Diablo. How cool is that?" Dave asked, stroking Bruno.

Gavin smiled and rubbed his cheek against Diablo's head before passing the puppy to Hunter.

Gavin walked over to Dave and Bruno and knelt down next to Bruno, giving him lots of hugs and tummy rubs. He looked at Dave and signed.

Dave nodded. "I did message your brothers. I knew they would want to know, even though you have Hunter, I knew you would need them. Plus, I messaged Ian, as well."

Gavin leaned over and hugged Dave.

Dave patted his back. "Thomaz told me there were a couple of puppies from Diablo's litter still available," Dave told him softly.

Gavin pulled back and smiled before jumping up and rushing back to Hunter.

Hunter looked at Gavin's happy face. "You want a German Shepherd puppy, as well, don't you?"

Gavin nodded.

"There were two puppies from this litter still available," Thomaz said, overhearing them.

"Will Bruno mind having two German Shepherds in the house?" Hunter asked Dave.

Dave shook his head. "Nope, Bruno won't mind."

"Gav, I've just sent you the details," Thomaz told him.

"Will you send it to me and Mathis as well, Thomaz?" Raz asked, who had just walked into the kitchen.

"Will do."

Gavin looked at Raz and smiled, walking over and hugging him. "You okay, little brother?"

Gavin nodded, hugging him back. He pulled away from his brother and pointed.

"I'm good, and Thiago's place is stunning," Raz said.

"Did you see anything of the underworld?" Dave asked him.

Raz nodded. "I did. It looks just like a normal place but is always dark. There are houses, shops, schools; you name it, they have it."

"Did Thiago get permission for us to visit?" Dave asked, sounding excited.

"He's gone back down to ask," Raz said.

Gavin looked at him and signed.

"I wanted to stay around here. Mathis wanted to stay, but he thought it would be best to go with Gabe and debug the witches' coven house." Raz explained.

"Something none of us have ever thought about," Kayden said. "I never realised what a sheltered life I've lived until all of this crap was uncovered."

"Thankfully, it's been uncovered," Kevin said. "Would one of you mind coming back to my pack so we can talk to Giles?"

"We can both come," Sean told him.

"The unbreaking potion is upstairs in Adrian's room," David said.

Dave shook his head. "No, it's just there. I wasn't sure if we needed it, so when Louise and I raided his healing supply, I grabbed it."

"Thank you, sweetheart. Seth, go with them in case you need to pull anything out of his mind."

"Will do, Bossman," Seth said cheerfully.

"Bertrum, are you staying for dinner?" Dave asked. "Max should be here soon."

"Earlier, I would have said yes. But I want to know what this Giles fellow knows, plus I want to talk to that super witch, so I'll go back with these guys."

"If you're sure," Dave said.

"I am," Bert replied.

Just then, there was a noise by the door and Max stood there, looking at Bertrum.

"Umm... hello," Max said softly.

Bert smiled but didn't move. "Hi, Max. We're all admiring Diablo," he said, hoping that would help.

"Here," Hunter said, holding Diablo out to him.

Max smiled and took the puppy. "Look at you! You're such a cutie." He looked around. "Is this a proper puppy or am I about to have a baby in my arms?" he asked, suddenly sounding panicked.

"A proper puppy," Dave assured him.

Max let out a sigh of relief. "Thank goodness."

"You don't like shifters?" Bert asked softly.

"I mean, I don't hate them, but this new world Davy has dragged me into is strange and scary. I'll get there. It's just a lot, you know?" Max said, rubbing his cheek on Diablo's head.

"But you're doing better now," Dave said, smiling at him.

"I am," he said with a smile, handing Diablo back to Hunter. He bent down and called, "Hey, Bruno."

Bruno barked and happily came over to Max and hugged him before licking his face.

"Bert, if you're ready, we're leaving now," Kevin said to him.

Bert looked at Max before nodding.

"I'm off to train. I'll call you later," Creed said, pulling Kevin into a kiss.

Kevin pulled back and touched Creed's cheek. "Have fun."

"Be safe," Creed says.

"I'll keep him safe," Ian assured him.

"I'm sure we can find a lead somewhere and keep Bacon on it," Bert said with a laugh.

"You're such a PITA. Just for that, you can make your own way back," Kevin told his brother, hitting his arm.

Max looked between Bert and Kevin. "You're brothers?" he asked.

Bert nodded. "Kevin's older brother."

Max nodded and with a final pat for Bruno stood up. "I'm

going to the library." And with that, Max turned and left the kitchen.

Everyone watched him leave.

Dave walked to Bert's side. "He didn't run screaming from the room, so that's a plus. I'll chat with him. If you send me your number, I can pass it to Max. Maybe the two of you could chat for a bit."

Bert nodded. "Thanks. Let's do that."

They swapped numbers and Dave went to join Max in the library.

CHAPTER 44

"So, how are we going to get Giles to drink this potion?" Kayden asked, standing in front of Giles' cell, with Kevin, Bert, Ian, Seth, and Sean.

Giles sat staring at them, an angry look on his face and his eyes spewing hate, his nose swollen, red, and slightly crooked.

The cell was of medium size with a single bed along one wall. A sink and a partition wall with a toilet behind and a small window high up near the ceiling completed the space. All the walls were solid brick except for the front one which were bars.

"We could hold his nose, open his mouth, and force it down his throat," Ian said, grinning like a loon.

Giles paled.

"Good idea, but he might spit it out at us," Kayden said.

"Not if we clamp his mouth shut after we've poured the potion in," Bert said.

"Let's do that then," Kevin said, using the cell key to open the door.

Seth and Ian grabbed Giles and pulled the now screaming, struggling man to his feet. Kevin held his mouth open and tipped his head back.

Kayden took the stopper out of the bottle and poured some of the potion into Giles's mouth.

Quick as anything, Kevin closed his mouth shut, holding tight so he couldn't open it, and Bert pinched his nose.

Kayden stepped back and Sean looked at his phone, ready to say the spell.

"Now," Bertrum said.

"With this potion, I break the spell put on Giles Goodsir. In this time and in this hour, I call upon my witchcraft powers. Break the spell on Giles Goodsir. I now command you to tell us everything you know about the underground network you were involved in."

Everyone loosened their hold on Giles, who flopped down on the bed, coughing as he did.

"You added different words," Seth said, looking at Sean.

"I did. It seemed appropriate," Sean replied with a shrug.

"Did it work?" Ian asked.

"Let's find out," Bert said.

Kayden pulled his phone out of his pocket and hit record, hoping to catch everything Giles said.

"Giles, tell us everything you know." And not being able to refuse Giles started talking.

∽

"So, that's all the important rooms searched," Gabe said, holding a bag. He shook it, not believing the number of listening bugs they had found.

"I was expecting maybe one or two, not this many," Mathis said, shaking his head.

"Is there a way you can trace what was listened to or recorded?" Rafe asked, standing in the doorway.

"Hopefully. I'm hoping they downloaded onto one of the devices we have from the lemmings," Mathis replied.

Rafe nodded. "Gabriel, have you used your magic to make sure you found them all? Some could be hidden by magic."

"Yes, we found a few more that way."

"Good. I have a friend who's on the staff in the Witches Council offices. It would seem Quintus and his assistant have both been arrested because of Kay and Quintus' involvement in covering up for his son. The council do not know about the investigation that you are all doing. At this point in time, I'm not sure who can be trusted in any of the council offices."

"Bertrum, the Alpha King, has faith in his council member, and Stefan hasn't said anything about not trusting his. I'm hoping Quintus was the highest-ranking person involved," Gabe said.

"It might be worth suggesting that both kings start investigations of their own into their council staff. If, as you said, this is across all paranormal groups, then vampires and shifters had to be involved, as well," Rafe cautioned.

"I'll talk to them when we've finished here," Gabe replied. He paused, looking at the Elder. "Rafe, are you okay?" he asked softly.

Rate sighed. "I honestly don't know. Everything that's happened over the last few weeks, everything Roberto and the others were into, it's a lot to take in. To know I failed in my promise to your parents breaks my heart."

Gabe looked confused. "What promise?"

"The promise to keep our coven the happy, safe place it was in your parents' day. To protect both you and Roberto and to help any way I could."

"Rafe, you couldn't have known what was going on here. None of us did," Gabe pointed out.

"But you pointed out more than once that your brother was mad, and we— I ignored you. It's only been in the last year that I realised you were right, but by then it was too late to do anything. Because of that, people have died."

Gabe walked over to the elder and touched his arm. "None of this is on you, Rafe. Roberto was the strongest witch at the time, what could any of us have done? I'm sure Sheldon is feeling the same way, if not worse. All we can do now is pick up the pieces and turn this coven back into the happy, safe place it was in my parents' day."

"We will. If I can do anything to help, let me know. Also, you need to think about who you want as your second," Rafe pointed out.

"It will be Kayden and Sean. I've just not told them yet," Gabe said, grinning.

"Good choice. Now I will leave you two to get on." And with that, Rafe left the room.

Gabe turned to look at Mathis, but before he could say anything, Mathis said, "Sean and Kayden are a good choice."

Gabe walked back to Mathis' side. "You're not mad I didn't ask you?"

Mathis shook his head and pulled Gabe into his arms. "No, little witch. I'm your mate. I'm not second-material, but your friends are. They're almost as protective of you as I am."

Gabe sighed and leaned into Mathis. "Love you, vampy."

"Just as I love you, little witch."

CHAPTER 45

"Wow," Ian said as they walked out of Giles's cell.

"Indeed. I'll need to speak to Stefan. We will both need to look into the names given. I'm only pleased that my trust in Icarus, my wolf representative, wasn't misplaced. I'll have to contact him with the names Giles gave us. We might have to go to the council offices. I hate going there," Bert complained.

Kevin snorted. "That's what you get for being the Alpha King. You could have been a normal alpha like me, but no, you had to be king."

"It wasn't like I had a choice in the matter," Bert pointed out.

Kevin shrugged. "Just saying."

"Just for that, Bacon, when I go there, you and Ian are coming with me."

Chuckles were heard from the others, except Ian who exclaimed, "How am I being drawn into this?"

"You ignore my calls and messages," Bert reminded him.

"Damn," Ian muttered.

"There, there," Sean said, patting his arm.

Bert looked at Kayden. "Do you think that potion will work on the super witch?"

Kaden nodded. "I don't see why not."

"Come on, then. Let's see what he has to say.

∼

"What do you think of this?" Dave asked Max, handing his phone over.

Max looked. "A sofa, table, and chairs? I like them. They look comfy. Are you redecorating your room?"

Dave shook his head. "No, they're for down here. I thought we could put them over there," he said, waving to an empty section.

"Nice, we could look at getting a coffee machine down here, as well."

"Oh, I like that idea. Let's make a list of everything we need, and we can place a large order." He opened the notes section on his phone and added them to it.

"Don't forget to add a scanner and a laptop," Max said.

"They're on the list. What else?"

"We probably need some gloves for the older documents, and maybe a nice display cabinet if we want to show some off, even if it's just for us. It might also be worth looking at having a room for super fragile scrolls."

"Good idea, and maybe some plants to liven this space up so it doesn't seem so dungeonie down here," Dave said, adding them to the list. That done, Dave leant against a handy table and looked at Max, who was tidying a shelf. "Talk to me," he said softly.

Max moved another book before stopping and sighing, then turning to look at Dave. "He's a wolf shifter, Davy."

Dave nodded. "He is."

THE VAMPIRE AND THE TATTOOIST

"I don't know how to deal with that," Max confessed. "This new world of yours is scary. To know all those books I've read about the paranormal world are real…. I'm not sure how I feel about that."

"You're doing better than me. I had a proper meltdown. Mind you, I had killers after me. But Max, taking out the fact that Bert is a wolf shifter, he's still a man, just with a few extras. What did you think of him when you first saw him?"

Max blushed and Dave laughed. "Well, that was a good start."

Max laughed. "He is so handsome, totally looks like my dream man. When I shook his hand, I felt something like electricity shoot up my arm. I've never had that before. That's why I practically ran away. Truthfully, I don't know what to do."

"How about I give you his phone number and you message him, then you two can chat and you can get to know him slowly."

Max let out a large breath and nodded. "That sounds like a good idea."

Dave opened his phone and sent the number to Max. "There you go. It will be fine, Max. I promise."

CHAPTER 46

The next day saw Hunter back at his studio with a notepad, making a note of everything he needed to reorder. He sighed when he realised he needed to purchase a new tattoo machine. He had several that he used, but his favourite one had been given to him by his parents on his twenty-first birthday.

That reminded him, he needed to phone his parents and let them know what had happened and that he was now practically moved in with Gavin. He would have to figure out what to do with his house.

He heard a loud knock on the studio front door, and knowing he was the only one currently in, he walked to the door expecting to see a delivery man. He was surprised when he saw his parents.

He hurried to the door, smiling as he opened it. "Mum, Dad, what a lovely surprise."

"Hello, darling," Hunter's mum said, walking in and hugging him before moving out of the way so his father could walk in. He also pulled Hunter into a hug.

"We stopped by your house, but as there was no answer,

THE VAMPIRE AND THE TATTOOIST

we thought we'd try here. If you weren't here, we were going to go and find somewhere for breakfast and call you," his father said.

"There's a cafe round the corner that does a good breakfast. Let me grab my stuff and I'll join you," Hunter said.

"Darling, why do I smell smoke?" his mum asked.

"We had a small fire in my room. I'm in the process of reordering everything that was damaged."

"Oh no," his mother said, following Hunter into his room.

"It looks more like an explosion happened in here than a fire," his father said, looking the space over.

"Some of my equipment exploded. Taha and Owen are picking up a new counter and sink for me, and some cupboards for underneath," Hunter explained as he picked up his phone and notepad.

"Have you closed the business down?" his mum asked.

Hunter shakes his head. "No, the others can carry on. I've postponed my clients and Ta has postponed some, as well." Hunter led the way back to the reception area. "The others will be here later. I should be up and running in a week at the most, depending on delivery."

"Have you ordered the worktop, sink, and cupboards?" his dad asked.

Hunter shook his head. "No, Ta and Owen have the measurements and were going shopping later."

His father looked at him. "Phone them and tell them I have it covered. Why didn't you phone me to sort this out?"

"You're busy. I didn't want you to take time away from your clients," Hunter told him.

"Son, what is the point of having a builder in the family if you don't ask for help when needed?"

Hunter one arm hugged his dad. "Thanks, if you have time."

"Always for you. I have everything you need in my workshop. I can come back tomorrow and sort it out. I also have paint that should match the rest of the walls."

"But for the moment, lead us to breakfast and coffee," his mum said.

∽

Hunter and his parents were sat in the café, Hunter nursing a coffee and his parents eating breakfast. As soon as he sat down, he messaged Taha and said his dad was going to fix everything.

T: You should have phoned him yesterday, idiot. Taha messaged back.

Hunter didn't bother to reply.

"How's your young man?" his father asked.

Hunter smiled. He couldn't help it when he thought of Gavin. "Gavin is perfect."

"He must be. I've never seen that look on your face before," his father said.

"I completely and utterly love him. I can see us getting married one day." Sure, he and Gavin were mated, but he knew his parents wouldn't understand that. A wedding they would.

His mother squealed happily and grabbed his hand. "Really? Oh, how exciting. I hope while we're here, we can meet him."

"Let me message him and arrange a time. He might be lost in work."

"I brought his vampire game. I must say, it's very good, but I'm stuck on level eleven," his father said as Hunter sent his message.

Hunter laughed. "Yeah, that seems to get everyone. I've got a friend who's stuck on that level, as well," just as he finished talking, his phone pinged with a message. Hunter smiled when he saw it was from Gavin.

G: Yes to meeting your parents. Bring them to lunch. I'll ask Annie and Thomaz to make something nice. Love you x

H: And I love you. Don't work too hard x

"Gavin said come for lunch. He's looking forward to meeting you both. You might get to meet some of Gavin's family."

"How exciting. Hopefully, we'll see Taha and meet this Owen you mentioned," his mum said.

"It's new for the both of them. They took one look at each other and *bam*, cupid's arrow struck."

His parents smiled at each other. "That can happen."

"I'll message Ta now and see if he's free."

∽

GAVIN WALKED into the kitchen and saw Thomaz on the floor with Diablo, Bruno was lying beside them.

Gavin dropped to his knees, hugged Bruno and gave him belly rubs before he looked at Thomaz and smiled.

"Hey, Gavin. You can pet Diablo if you want."

Gavin smiled at him and gently pet the puppy, who climbed onto his lap and tried to lick him. Gavin gave a silent laugh. He signed to Thomaz.

"Yes, he slept well. I worried that he might cry all night shut in his crate, but I think having Bruno with him helped keep him calm."

Gavin stroked Bruno's head before playing with the puppy's ears, then looked at Thomaz and signed.

Thomaz looked confused for a moment before he smiled. "You want me to make a nice lunch as you're meeting Hunter's... something. Oh, parents!"

Gavin nodded.

"I can do that."

Gavin moved the puppy out of the way so he could hug Thomaz.

Thomaz laughed and pulled back, looking at him. "You sleeping all right?"

Gavin nodded then signed, "I am, but Hunter isn't."

"Why isn't Hunter sleeping well?"

Gavin signed again and gave a silent sigh. "He wants to be awake in case I have bad dreams."

"It's only because he cares, Gav. He's bound to be worried about you having nightmares. Maybe tell him he doesn't have to worry, that he scares the nightmares away."

Gavin lifted the puppy and rubbed his cheek on the puppy's head before he nodded. "Thank you," he mouthed.

"I need to start thinking about lunch. Are you staying to play with the puppy, or are you working?"

Gavin handed Diablo over and signed that he was working.

"Okay, don't work too hard and remember lunch."

CHAPTER 47

Gavin was sitting in the office, still going through computers from the lemmings. The amount of information that was found on these devices was incredible. How an underground network of evil people didn't have better security on their devices or indeed, delete files properly was insane.

"Gah, it shouldn't be this hard to find who this Masters company belongs to," Ivan said in frustration.

"Do you want me to look and you can take over from me?" Olly asked.

"Sure. You'll probably find the answers straight away," he replied while standing up. "How about you, Gav?"

Gavin waved his hand in an *Okay* way and then signed to Ivan.

"There's too much to do here," Ivan replied.

Olly looked up. "What did Gavin say?"

"That I should take a break and go and see Jamie."

Olly nodded and smiled at Gavin. "And our little brother would be right. Go have a break, see Jamie, and then come back refreshed."

Ivan looked undecided.

Gavin clicked his fingers and Ivan looked at him, then laughed.

"Fine, I'll go, but only because I'm not dull. Thank you very much, Gavin," Ivan said, pretending to scowl at him.

Olly laughed. "Off you go then."

Ivan nodded. "I won't be long, but if you need me, call." And with a final wave, he left the room.

Olly looked at Gavin to see him frowning. "What?"

Gavin started to sign.

"Okay, stop right there. I do not need you to introduce me to anyone. If I have a mate out there, one day I'll find them, but that won't be today. So, no meddling in anything or telling Dave I need someone in my life," Olly told him.

Gavin gave a silent laugh.

"I mean it, Gav. You say anything to Dave, and I'll find something horrible to do to you."

Gavin laughed again, not believing that Olly would get him back. And anyway, he didn't need to mention it to Dave. He could tell Gabe, Sean, and Ian who would then tell Dave for him.

∼

BERT WALKED into the pack house kitchen and saw everyone sitting at the table eating breakfast. Sean and Kayden were there, as well as Seth, having all stayed the night.

"You look tired, Gerty Berty," Kevin said, looking at his brother. "Did you sleep last night?"

"Sit down, darling, and I'll get you coffee. Have you eaten?" Lissa asked him.

"I grabbed an apple," Bert said, flopping down at the table.

"Here," Ian said, handing him a clean plate before pushing dishes towards him while Lissa fixed him a coffee.

"Thanks," he said, taking a sip before putting food on his plate. "To answer your question, Bacon, no, I've not slept yet. I was on the phone with Icarus, going over some of the information Giles told us. Unsurprisingly, two of the named men have gone into hiding. I have guards out looking for them as we speak."

"We've not filled Gabe in on everything we found out yet," Sean said.

"It would be helpful to meet up with Stefan, David, and Gabe today to discuss what we learned," Bert said.

"Let me message them and set up a time," Kevin said, pulling his phone out of his pocket and sending them a message.

"I need to get back and check on Jack and Spencer. I also need to take them shopping for clothes and anything they want for their room," Seth said.

"I could always come back with you," Lissa offered. "Then Annie, Louise, and I can sort all that out for you."

"Lissa, I love you. That would be a big help, thank you. My idea of shopping is jumping online and ordering whatever I need."

"Leave it to us, dear. We'll make sure the boys have everything they need," Lissa assured him.

Just then, Kevin's phone beeped, and he opened his messages. "David said come to lunch and we can have the meeting afterwards. Apparently, Hunter's parents are coming for lunch to meet Gavin and his family."

Sean looked at Bert. "Maybe Max will be there."

Bert shook his head. "No, he's working all day at the library."

"Is he?" Seth asked, smiling. "How would you know that?"

"He told me when we messaged last night. Dave gave him my number and he texted me. We messaged back and forth for a while."

Ian laughed. "Now we know the real reason you're tired today."

"Oh, shut up," Bert huffed out as everyone around the table laughed.

CHAPTER 48

Gavin was nervous. It was nearly time for Hunter and his parents to arrive. His thoughts were spinning round his head. *What if they don't like me? What if they think I'm defective and not worthy of their son?*

He had so many negative thoughts going through his head.

"Whatever dark thoughts you're thinking, stop," he heard his brother say.

His eyes shot up to see Mathis standing in front of the desk, arms crossed over his chest, scowling at him.

Gavin jumped up and practically ran around the desk and threw himself into his brother's arms, hugging him, soaking up all the love he could.

"They will love you, little brother, just like everyone else does. But if, for some reason, they don't, I'll have Gabe turn them into slugs for you."

Gavin pulled back and silently laughed. "Thank you," he signed, blowing out a breath.

"There is nothing to thank me for. I'm just speaking the

truth. Now, we are all gathered in the kitchen; come and join us."

Gavin nodded but didn't move; instead, he signed again.

"You never thanked me for what?" Mathis asked, looking confused.

Gavin signed more.

Mathis pulled Gavin back into his arms. "You never have to thank me for protecting you from our father. I saw him sneaking into your room. No one with good intentions sneaks anywhere. I will *always* protect you, just as Raz, your Hunter, or anyone that knows you will. And just because you now have Hunter in your life, as I have Gabe and Raz has Thiago, nothing will ever change with us. We're brothers, now and always."

Gavin hugged him back and smiled before pulling away and signing again.

Mathis frowned for a moment. "Are you asking about the listening bugs?"

Gavin nodded.

"We found a lot of bugs at the witches' coven, more than I thought would be there. We got them all, though. Now we just have to find where they were downloading to," Mathis said as they walked to the kitchen.

"Gavin," Gabe said, coming over to hug him before pulling away and looking him over. "You've been shopping. You look amazing."

Gavin smiled and blushed. He must admit his new clothes did look good. Shelby had a good eye for clothes.

"That would be Shelby's influence. They both went shopping yesterday on their way to buy lunch," Taha said.

"In that case, I need to go shopping with Shelby," Gabe said.

"I'm sure that can be arranged," Taha said.

Just then, Kevin and the others walked into the kitchen and Dave, Gabe, and Gavin, all hugged them.

"You're back," Jack said happily, walking over to Seth.

Seth pulled him into a hug. "I am. You alright?"

Jack nodded and hugged him back, leaning into him.

Seth looked for Spencer and saw him standing by Stefan, leaning into his side. He wondered if David and Gio were about to get a little brother.

"Lissa said she would help shop for anything you and Spencer need clothes wise or for your room," Seth told him.

"I'm okay with what I have," Jack said softly.

"Too bad. You're getting more," Seth replied, laughing at him.

Just then, Gio and Creed walked in, and letting go of Jack, Seth went and said hello to his mate while Creed said hello to Kevin.

"Gav, as there are so many of us, the table has been set up in the large formal dining room. Mum and Louise have made it look really comfy and not at all stuffy," Dave said to him.

Gavin nodded and bit his lip, his nerves hitting him again.

"Here, puppy snuggles are called for," Kayden said, handing Diablo over to him.

Gavin mouthed, "thank you," took the puppy and snuggled him.

"I know you're nervous, but Hunter loves you, and you love him and make him happy. His parents will love you because of that," Taha told him, stroking a puppy ear. "Trust me. Charlotte and AJ will love you. I consider them my second parents, and I'd never lie to you." He leant forward and stage whispered, "Owen's nervous, as well."

Gavin turned and looked at Owen, who was chatting with Seth and Gio. Owen nodded at him.

"See," Taha said, grinning. "Plus, if anything *does* happen,

I'll just tell Charlotte and AJ how much Owen spends on shoes."

Gavin silently laughed, but Dave laughed loudly.

"How much does he spend?" Kayden asked.

Taha leant forward and said quietly, "Ten thousand plus."

Kayden's mouth fell open. "Seriously?"

"Oh yeah," Taha said cheerfully.

"Gav, Hunter's here," Gabe told him softly.

Gavin looked up and saw Hunter, and a smile split his face, all his nerves vanishing. He passed Diablo to Dave and walked over to Hunter.

Hunter met him halfway and wrapped his arms around Gavin, dipping his head and kissing Gavin hello. He kept it short as his parents were nearby. He pulled back, smiling at Gavin. "Missed you," he said.

Gavin smiled and mouthed, "Missed you," back.

"Come meet my parents," Hunter said, taking his hand and leading him back to his parents. "Mum, Dad, this is my Gavin. Gavin, these are my parents, Charlotte and AJ."

"Oh, Gavin, you're gorgeous. It's so nice to meet the man who looks at my son the way you do," Charlotte said, pulling Gavin into a hug.

AJ pulled him out of his wife's arms. "Don't hog my future son-in-law," he said, grinning and hugging Gavin.

Gavin gave a silent laugh, pulled back, and signed, "Thank you."

He looked at Hunter.

"Mum, Dad, let me introduce you around," Hunter said.

Introductions had been made and now they were all sat in the formal dining room, eating. Dave was right — it did look cozy and relaxed.

Everyone was laughing and joking. AJ caught Gavin's eye. "I hope while I'm here you can show me how to get off level eleven of Vampire Hunter. I've been stuck there for nearly a week."

Bert, who was seated next to AJ, laughed. "Me, too, but Gavin wouldn't tell me. I had to ask Stefan to show me."

Stefan, who was sitting nearby, laughed. "He wouldn't tell me either, it took me forever to figure out."

AJ fake scowled at Gavin. "That's just mean. What's the point of knowing the designer if you don't help?"

Gavin gave a silent laugh and signed.

"I didn't get all that, sorry. Charlotte and I only started learning sign language when Hunter told us about you."

"Gavin said he *could* tell you but isn't it better to figure it out for yourself?" Stefan translated.

"Not when you've been stuck on it for years, it's not," AJ grumbled.

"I thought you said nearly a week," Taha said, grinning at AJ.

"A week, a year, what's the difference?" AJ said.

"About 51 weeks, Dad," Hunter said with a laugh.

"Semantics," AJ said, looking back at Gavin. "You have incredible skills."

Gavin blushed and signed, "Thank you."

"Dad, Gavin is about to start designing another game, Vampires vs. Witches," Hunter told him.

"That sounds fun. I can't wait until it comes out and I can play it. Do you ever add updates to your other games?"

Gavin signed.

"Gavin said yes. If you scan the QR code that comes with the games, you can download free updates," Stefan translated. He looked at Gavin. "I didn't know that. Does it add new levels?"

Gavin silently laughed and nodded before signing.

Bert burst out laughing. "I don't think any of us have read the notes that came with the game. If AJ and Stefan are like me, we just start playing the game and ignore the notes section."

"I'll be changing that when I get home later," AJ said.

"You're welcome to stay if you want to," Stefan offered.

"Thanks, but I need to go home and get everything I need to fix Hunter's studio up. I'm a builder and have everything needed. I'll be back tomorrow with my van."

"I did tell Hunter to phone you, AJ, but he said you were too busy," Taha told him.

AJ shook his head. "Never too busy to help you boys out. You know that."

"I know, thanks, Dad," Hunter said. He looked at Gavin and leant down. "You doing okay?"

Gavin nodded and kissed his cheek.

"Gavin, Hunter, I can't tell you how happy you have both made me," Charlotte said, looking at them both and smiling. "AJ, darling, I'm coming back here tomorrow helping Louise, Annie, and Lissa shop for Jack and Spencer. The poor darlings need everything."

"If you need anything built or put together, let me know and I can do that for you."

"Thank you, Mr. Marsden," Seth said.

"Call me AJ. We're all family here," he told Seth.

"Thanks, AJ."

Bert looked at Stefan and Spencer who was sitting next to him. "Are you and Louise adopting Spencer?"

Stefan looked at Spencer and smiled before looking back at Bert. "We are."

"I said they didn't need to, but they insisted. They don't even mind that I'm not a vampire. They said it didn't matter," Spencer said.

CHAPTER 49

Suddenly, everyone stopped talking and Spencer paled. He looked at Stefan and his eyes filled with tears. "I'm very sorry," he said softly.

Stefan pulled him into a hug. "It was bound to come out at some point. Don't worry."

All eyes turned to Charlotte and AJ, who were staring at each other.

"Mum, Dad?" Hunter queried.

"You owe me a pair of Jimmy Choo's," Charlotte said, looking at her husband and grinning.

"How come?" Taha asked.

"Because before we came in here and sat down, Charlotte told me we were surrounded by vampires. I scoffed and said if she was right, I'd buy her some Jimmy Choo shoes."

"It's the all-black, isn't it?" Dave asked, laughing.

"Yes, that was a bit of a giveaway. I mean, I know you said that everyone here was in security, but somehow, the clothes seem a bit more, if you know what I mean," Charlotte replied.

"Yes, I know. But it's not just vampires. We have shifters

around the table, as well. And as you now know our secret, let me tell you that Louise and Stefan are the King and Queen of the vampires, while David and Giovanni are the princes. Bertrum is Alpha King of the wolf shifters, and Gabriel is head of the Southern witches," Dave told them.

"Wow," AJ said, looking a little stunned.

"I promise you're both safe here," David assured them.

"We didn't think for a moment we weren't. It's just a lot to take in. I mean, you're urban legends. To know that you all really exist is just... wow," Charlotte replied.

"I don't understand humans," Olly said. "Years ago, people freaked out when they found out about us. They ran away screaming and came back with torches and pitchforks. Now it's just, 'You're real cool.'"

Everyone laughed.

"It's because of all the films and books out there. I think more people nowadays are hoping you're all real, so when we find out you are, it doesn't faze many of us. Mind you, if I saw any of you in a dark alley with your fangs out coming for me, you can be sure I'd be terrified," AJ replied. He turned to look at Hunter. "Now tell me what really happened to your room. I know it wasn't an electrical fire. I know an explosion when I see one."

Hunter sighed. "Okay, but I just want to start by saying I'm safe..." and he went on to tell them what happened with the others chiming in when needed.

In the end, AJ and Charlotte found out about everything.

"We're having a meeting this afternoon to update everyone on our latest findings," David told them.

"Are there more people coming for the meeting?" AJ asked.

David shook his head. "No, everyone we need is already here."

"Then why not have it now? We've finished eating. And

THE VAMPIRE AND THE TATTOOIST

who knows? Maybe the *lowly* humans here can offer suggestions you might not think of," he said.

"We can do that," David replied. "Jack, Spencer, do you both want to leave the room?"

"If you do, we can start looking for the things that you need," Annie said.

"That's an idea. Charlotte, Lissa, do you want to join us?" Louise asked.

"I'll come with you. AJ can give me the Cliff Notes version later."

"I'll come, as well," Lissa said.

"Excellent, come along boys. Let's go and spend some of Willard's money," Annie said, standing up.

"Nonsense," Louise said, also standing. "It's been a while since I've maxed out Stefan's credit card. I'm looking forward to this."

Seth pulled his wallet out.

"Put that away, Seth. If we forget to buy anything, you can buy it. Until then, let me have fun," Louise said, grinning at him.

"Thanks, Louise."

"Yeah, thanks, Mum," Gio said. He looked at Jack and grinned. "Go forth and spend money." He looked back at Louise. "Don't buy them any weapons. I have those covered."

Jack looked at Spencer and grinned.

"Come on, then," Annie said. And with that, the mothers, Jack, and Spencer left the room.

"I'm suddenly feeling like we're being sexist," Dave muttered.

"I know what you mean, but Mum doesn't really like details, just an overview; otherwise, she'll worry," Kevin told him.

"The same for Annie. I'll tell her everything, but more gently," Willard said.

"Louise doesn't mind, but if there's a choice between listening to all this or spending money, she'll spend money," Stefan added.

"Charlotte will just want everyone safe. If she hears that you're in danger, she'll worry herself sick. Even though we have just met you all, you're family," AJ put in.

"Who wants to start?" David asked.

"I can if you want," Gabe said. "Mathis and I debugged the coven. We found lots, some hidden with magic and others not."

"Now we just have to find out where they download to," Mathis said. "I can take one apart and see what I can find."

"We can all decamp to the computer room and help," Olly said.

"Before that, we found stuff out," Kayden said. "As you know, we went back to the wolf pack to speak to Giles and the super witch."

"Super witch?" AJ asked.

"Yeah, someone has created a spell to make super-strong witches. Gavin and some of the others met one yesterday. That's how we found out about them," Gabe replied.

"Well, that can't be good," AJ said.

"No, it's not," Sean said.

"Did you get him to talk?" Gabe asked.

"We did," Bert said. "Kayden recorded everything he said and everything Giles said too."

"How bad is it?" Dave asked.

"Bad," he replied. "We have names of different shifters involved as well as the names of three vampires and more than just Cameron-Webb and his assistant for the witches."

"What are the vampire names?" Stefan hissed out.

"Antonio and Juno Garcia and Rickon Irvine," Sean read off his phone.

Gasps were heard around the table. Rickon sat forward,

looking confused. "I would *never* be involved in something like this, I swear it."

"I know," Stefan said.

"It's a good smoke screen, though, to add in the name of a king's guard, thereby calling them all into question," Kevin said.

"Rickon, we know you're not involved in any of this, but until your name is cleared, you need to stay inside the coven grounds," Gio said.

Rickon nodded. "I understand," he said, running his hand down his face. "But why pick me?"

"Because you used to be one of David's personal guards, then a king's guard and a friend of Gio's," Ian said. "By extension, they can implicate both Gio and David."

Dave grabbed David's hand and Seth took hold of Gio's.

"When I find those two vampires, I'm going to rip them to pieces," Seth ground out.

"But my Seth, remember, *everyone* turned against me. Rickon and the others were transferred out of my guards and into the King's guard. Everyone in the vampire collective would know neither David nor I had anything to do with this, as Rickon wasn't around either of us."

"But he was around me," Stefan said.

"I seriously doubt that anyone would believe you were involved," Bert said to him.

"Thank you. I'm going to need to contact my representative and talk to him," Stefan said.

"Giles also gave up the name of two wolves that work in the council offices. My representative, Icarus, sent guards out to find them, but they've gone into hiding," Bert said.

"Did the witch say who created the serum?" Mathis asked.

"No, he said he didn't know, but he said Oswald gave it to him to drink," Sean told them.

"Oswald is/was Quintus's assistant," Kayden added.

"Did he mention the shifter suppressant serum?" Gio asked.

"No, but then we didn't ask him about it," Kevin said. "That Giles chap mentioned it, though. He said Oswald gave it out, as well."

"I'll send you copies of both recordings, and you can have a listen," Kayden said.

Suddenly, shrill alarms sounded.

"That's the garden sensors," Olly said, jumping up.

"Check it out," David said, and most of the vampires and wolves rushed outside. "Dad, I need you and Mum to take the humans and children to a priest hole and keep them safe. Dave, take the dogs. Gavin, go with them since you know where all the large priest holes are."

Gavin and Dave jumped up, got the dogs, and ushered the humans out of the room, Stefan with them. They met the mothers and children in the hall, and Gavin led them to David's office and the priest hole behind the fireplace.

"I'll come and help," Gabe said, standing up. "Sean, Kayden, it's up to you if you want to go to a priest hole or come outside."

"Actually, we'll protect the inside of this house. Chances are they might be looking for their missing men, which means they might try and breach the house. Are your cells in the house?" Kayden asked David.

David nodded. "Yes, the room at the end of the hallway leads to the cells."

"We'll stop anyone that makes it inside," Sean said. "Stay safe." And with that, they took off out of the kitchen.

"Let's go and join the others," David said, rushing outside, Gabe following.

CHAPTER 50

Stefan led the way down the tunnel with Gavin going last, closing the fireplace behind him. As soon as Stefan reached the priest hole, he found the light switch and turned it on.

"Oh, it's so pretty. I wasn't expecting this," Charlotte exclaimed quietly.

"This is one of the nicer hiding spaces. There are probably others around here that are dull," Dave replied.

Gavin walked in. They could all fit, but there wasn't much space left. He looked at Stefan and signed.

"No, Gavin, we'll all stay together. We can better protect everyone if we are all in one location."

"What did Gavin say?" AJ asked.

"Gavin said there is another priest hole further down this passageway. He suggested we split up to give us more space," Stefan told him.

"Are there any weapons down here?" Dave asked.

Gavin grinned and pointed to Stefan, Louise, himself, and Taha.

"Nutter," Dave said, smiling at him. "Find a patch of floor and have a seat folks. We could be here for a while."

Once everyone was settled, Gavin closed the door.

~

David and Gabe ran outside and found a full-on battle going on.

Gabe saw spells being thrown around, and, pulling out his wand, he ran towards the fighting, throwing his magic to knock out anyone fighting against his family and friends.

He saw Creed get hit in the back with a spell and fall to the floor. Letting out a loud howl, wolf Kevin jumped the witch and ripped his throat out.

Gabe had to stop this before one of his friends died. He pulled on all his magic, and using his wand, flung it out as he turned in a circle, setting his intention to stop the attackers. He spun round twice, and as he reached the starting point, he noticed the attackers were starting to drop to the ground unconscious. A couple were left standing, but the vampires either cut their heads off or stabbed them through the hearts, killing them.

Making sure they were all down and out, Gabe rushed to Creed's side. He touched his neck and found a pulse. Calling on his healing, he pushed his healing magic into Creed, and the healing light appeared.

Unnoticed, Kevin ran to his mate's side, shifting as he did, watching Gabe.

The light faded and Gabe took his hands off Creed and sat back.

"Sweetheart?" Kevin said, touching Creed's back.

"I'm okay," Creed said, moving to sit up.

"Thank you," Kevin said to Gabe before pulling Creed into his arms.

Gabe stood up and left them together, looking around to see who else was injured and needed help. He was tired after using so much magic, but he could keep going if needed.

He ran over to a couple of vampires who were sat leaning against trees. "Do you need my help?" he asked, squatting down between them.

One of them shook their heads. "No, thank you. Blood will sort me out."

"The same for me," the other replied, "but thank you."

Gabe nodded and got to his feet, walking over to Seth and Gio.

"Thanks for your help," Seth said, pulling him into a hug. "I can see how Owen had issues stopping his super witch."

"Only death could stop some of them," Gio added.

"I'm surprised at how many super witches there are," Gabe replied, looking around. He saw Bert and David walk their way. "Are you both all right?"

"We are," Bert answered. "None of them spoke, just started fighting."

"Did any breach the house?" Gabe asked.

Just then, an explosion was heard from inside the house. Quick as a flash, David, Seth, and Gio took off at a fast run. All Gabe and Bert saw was one minute the three of them were there, and the next, they vanished.

Bert and Gabe looked at each other before running as fast as they could after them.

∼

"How do you think things are going?" Taha asked.

"Fighting is still going on but seems to be winding down," Stefan replied.

"You can hear them?" Spencer asked in surprise and sat between Louise and Stefan.

"We can," Louise answered. "As you get older, your senses will sharpen, and your hearing will heighten. It won't be as good as ours but will be better than it is now."

"Spencer, can I ask what kind of shifter you are?" Hunter asked. He was sat with his back to the wall, Gavin sitting in front of him between his legs, leaning back against him.

Spencer smiled. "I'm a Pine Marten."

"That's from the weasel family, isn't it?" AJ asked.

Spencer nodded. "Yeah. There aren't many of us around anymore, shifters or normal ones."

"It's strange. I never imagined there were other shifters out there. For some reason, I thought you would all be wolves," Taha said.

"No," Stefan replied. "There are shifters for pretty much every species."

"So much to learn," Hunter commented.

"And you will. No one expects you to learn everything in a few days," Louise replied gently.

"Do you think Seth and Gio are alright?" Jack asked quietly from between Louise and Annie.

"Of course they are," Annie said, putting her arm around him. "They might have a few war wounds but nothing serious. They can just drink blood and heal themselves right up."

Jack nodded but didn't say anything else. Willard passed him a sleeping Diablo, and Jack snuggled with him.

Charlotte looked at Hunter and Gavin and sighed. "I was so hoping you'd have a wedding, but you're already mated."

"We can still have a wedding, Mum," Hunter told her.

Gavin moved around to look at Hunter and signed, "You want a wedding?"

"Yes, sweetheart, I want a wedding. I know we're mated and that is deeper than a wedding, but I'm human. I would like us to get married."

THE VAMPIRE AND THE TATTOOIST

Gavin smiled before flinging his arms around Hunter and kissing him. He pulled back and signed.

Hunter laughed. "We can do that."

"Do what?" AJ asked.

"Get matching tattoos," Hunter replied. "Still gonna buy rings, though."

"Oh my God, did you guys just get engaged?" Dave asked happily while stroking Bruno's head.

Hunter looked at Gavin, smiling. "Did we?"

Gavin shook his head and signed.

"I didn't get all that, but pretty sure that was a no, and I need to ask properly with rings."

Gavin signed again.

"And down on one knee."

Gavin nodded and grinned.

"When you do, we can all help you plan the wedding and party. This will be epic," Dave said happily.

"I'm so happy," Charlotte said, smiling at Hunter.

"Well, hold your excitement, Mum. We're not engaged yet," Hunter reminded her.

"But you will be," she said. "Now we need to get Taha and his Owen married."

Taha laughed. "We're happy to wait. My parents don't know about Owen yet, and they're not due home for goodness knows how long."

"Where are your parents?" Lissa asked him.

"Off in Spain, walking the Camino de Santiago," Taha told her.

"Isn't that, like, five hundred miles?" Willard asked.

Taha nodded. "That's the one. It should take about a month, but they're stopping off sightseeing in different places along the way. They started four weeks ago and aren't even halfway yet, but they're having a blast." He paused and sighed.

"What's wrong?" Louise asks him.

"I'm not sure of my parents' reactions when they find out about all of you."

AJ nods. "Yeah, we might need to ensure they don't find out."

"Why's that?" Jack asks. "Because they're human and might freak out?"

"No, well, maybe? They are uber-religious, so I'm not sure how they would deal with this world. They just about tolerate me being gay, but only because I've never introduced them to a boyfriend. No matter how much I want them to meet Owen, I'm not sure of their reaction."

"Sweetheart, they just want you to be happy," Charlotte said to him. "We can be there when they meet your Owen, and they can meet Gavin at the same time. If they find out and see we're okay with everything, that might help."

Taha nodded. "Thanks, Charlotte."

Just then they heard what sounded like an explosion.

"What the hell!" Dave exclaimed, jumping to his feet, dislodging Bruno, and starting for the door.

Stefan stood up. "Dave, hold. We're safe in here."

Dave wrung his hands. "But that came from inside the house."

Stefan touched his shoulder. "It did, but my sons, their men, and friends know what they are doing."

Dave nodded. "I know, but that doesn't stop me worrying. What if we don't have enough bagged blood? Should I message the wolves and let them know what's going on? If Gabe, Sean, or Kayden get injured, do we have enough bandages to help or those sticky plaster stitches? We only have one healing room set up…" By the time Dave had finished talking, he was wringing his hands and on the verge of panicking.

Stefan grabbed his face and looked into Dave's eyes. "Calm yourself," he said gently. "Breathe with me. In... out."

Dave stared into Stefan's eyes and copied his breathing. He felt himself calming down. "Thank you, sorry."

Stefan smiled at him and let Dave's head go, touching his shoulder. "There is nothing to apologise for."

Dave nodded and flopped back onto the ground. Gavin moved next to Dave, and put his arm around him , and Jack handed the puppy over while Bruno walked over and laid his head back onto Dave's lap. "Thanks. I'm okay. Sorry, folks."

"Davy, you're so dramatic," Annie said, shaking her head at him but smiling.

"And you're just figuring this out now?" Hunter said with a laugh.

"Hey now," Dave protested.

Gavin patted his arm as the others laughed.

CHAPTER 51

Sean and Kayden were standing in the hall by the door leading to the cells, wands at the ready.

"Our lives are weird," Sean said, looking at Kayden.

"Well, they are now. Anyway, I blame you for all of this," Kayden replied, pretending to glare at him.

Sean looked confused. "How did you figure that out?"

"We were snuggled on the sofa watching that adventure film and you said you wish there was more adventure in our lives as the coven was too quiet."

Sean laughed. "I meant going on an adventure-type holiday, not dealing with kidnapped children, super witches, and everything else that we're now involved with."

Kayden smiled. "Next time, be more specific."

"Noted. Do you think one of us should go out and join Gabe?"

Kayden looked undecided before shaking his head. "No, he's surrounded by vampires, a few wolves, plus Troy. We need to protect the house."

"We can. But I'm putting it out there right now that I'm hoping the house isn't breached."

"It's mad, isn't it? There is no one in these cells, and you'd think the super witches would know that," Kayden said, looking thoughtful.

"What?" Sean asked.

"We're assuming that they think the vampires are holding their people here, but what if they are not here for them."

"Then who?" Sean asked before gasping. "Jack and Spencer."

Kayden nodded. "We know one of these rooms leads to a priest hole. Let's put a shield around all the doors protecting them as a precaution."

Sean nodded. "You do that side, I'll do this side."

It took a few moments before all the doors had shields around them. Sean was just walking to the front door when it was blown inwards, hitting Sean and flinging him backwards, the door landing on him.

Quick as a flash, Kayden threw a shield around his husband, hoping he was just knocked out, and took a fighting stance as a man and woman hurried in. He threw magic at them trying to stop them.

They both dived out of the way before they were hit; the woman recovered first and threw her magic at Kayden, who jumped out of the way just in time. As it was, the woman's magic hit the wall behind him, and the wall exploded, raining bricks and plaster down around him.

A few bits of debris hit Kayden, but he stumbled to his feet and flung more magic out. He was angry, in pain, and worried about Sean, so pulling on all of that and drawing the power rune in the air, he sent his magic out again and hit the woman full force. She went flying back out the front door landing several yards away, unconscious or dead; Kayden didn't care.

He was just aiming for the man when he saw a blur, and the next moment, the man was dead, his head now bouncing on the parquet floor and his body hitting a moment later. Gio stood there, blood dripping from his sword.

Kayden stumbled over to Sean, removing the protective shield and trying to lift the door off him. Seth bent down and pulled it off.

"Thanks," Kayden said, moving closer to Sean. "Sean, sweetheart," he said, checking for a pulse.

"He's still breathing," David said, crouching beside him.

Suddenly Gabe was there, kneeling by Sean's head. "I've got him," Gabe said, putting his hands on Sean's chest and sending healing into him. The healing light surrounded Sean before vanishing. Gabe removed his hands just as Sean sighed and opened his eyes.

"I felt your healing. Thanks, Gabe."

"You're welcome," Gabe said, patting his leg.

"Sweetheart," Kayden said, touching his arm.

Sean quickly sat up and pulled Kayden into his arms. "I'm okay," he whispered into Kayden's neck.

Kayden hugged him close for a moment before pulling back and kissing him. Kayden tapered this kiss. "I was so scared when I saw you get hurt. I didn't have time to do more than throw a shield around you."

Sean smiled and rested his forehead against Kayden's. "Thank you."

Finally, they drew apart and looked around, David and Seth helping them up.

"Sorry about your wall," Kayden said. "We realised that they might be after Jack and Spencer, so we protected all the rooms. Sean was just going to protect the front door when it was breached."

"We can fix the walls," David said.

Just then, Seth exclaimed, "They were after the children?" Turning, he ran towards David's office and the safe room. He bounced back when he got to the doorway and growled.

"I'll get it," Gabe said, sending his magic out to undo the shields from all the doors.

"Thanks," Seth said, running through it, Gio hot on his heels.

Kayden moved and leant against a wall, groaning softly. "How did you get on outside?"

"We live to fight another day," Bertram said. "But you, my friend, how injured are you?"

"You're injured?" Sean exclaimed. "How bad are you hurt?"

"Just bumps and bruises from where the wall exploded. Nothing serious," Kayden said, pulling Sean close to him.

"Want me to have a look?" Gabe offered.

Kayden shook his head. "No, I'm good."

"Kayden," Sean said, glaring at him.

"It's fine, sweetheart, I promise."

CHAPTER 52

Seth and Gio ran into David's study, Seth leading the way to the fireplace. "There are several priest holes and secret passages down here," he said, clicking the secret lock open. Once open, he rushed inside, Gio behind him, and they ran to the first large priest hole. Seth hit the secret button and the door opened.

"You're safe," Jack said happily, jumping and throwing himself against Seth and Gio. They both wrapped an arm around him.

"We're safe, just a few scratches which will soon heal," Gio told him. He looked up. "It's safe to come out now."

"What was the explosion?" Dave asked, standing up. "And how many casualties?"

"A few vampires will need blood, but that's pretty much it from our side. Sean was knocked out when the front door fell on him, and the explosion was one of the hall walls exploding," Seth answered. "Come on, let's leave here."

They all walked out of David's office and into the hall, seeing all the damage.

Dave ignored that and rushed to David's side. "Are you alright?"

David pulled Dave into his arms. "I'm fine sweetheart," he said, dropping a kiss on his head.

Gavin looked around for his brothers but didn't see them. He looked at David.

"They are both fine and still outside," David told him.

Gavin nodded and looked at Hunter.

"Let's go check on your brothers," Hunter said, holding his hand out to Gavin. "We'll be back in a bit." And with that Hunter and Gavin walked off.

AJ went and looked the wall over. "I can fix this if you want. I'll sort Hunter's room out first and then I can come back and fix your wall."

"Thank you, AJ. Your help will be much appreciated," David said.

"I'll go and make some food," Annie said. "Come on, Jack, Spencer, you can help."

"I'll come with you," Lissa said, following them.

"As will I," Charlotte said, joining them.

David stepped closer to his parents and lowered his voice. "Kayden thinks they came for the children."

Stefan hissed in anger, his eyes swirling red. "Over my dead body will they ever touch those children again," he ground out.

Louise laid her hand on Stefan's arm, calming him down. "We'll protect them," she assured him.

"We need to check on the other children that were taken back home," Bert said, looking worried. "I'll have Kev look into that."

"Look into what?" Kevin said, now dressed and walking in with Ian and Creed.

"The children the pack took home," Bert answered.

Kevin's eyes widened for a moment, realising what his

brother meant. "I'll get right on that. I just spoke to Jeff since I wondered if they'd been attacked, as well, but they weren't," he replied, pulling his phone out and walking out the front door.

"I'm going to the council offices tomorrow. We need more answers and to see what we can uncover," Stefan said.

"I'll come with you. We can show that the vampires and wolves are working together," Bert said.

"I can come, as well. I've never been there, but I can show up as the concerned leader of the Southern witches," Gabe said.

"Then we have a plan. In the meantime, Gio, call the rest of your guards here and I shall call some of mine. There is enough land that they can camp outside. Until everything is sorted, this coven house needs protecting, and David, I want no arguments from you," Stefan said, glaring at his son.

Dave sniggered, and Seth looked at him and grinned.

"I didn't say anything," David protested. "While at the council offices, are you putting in the adoption papers for Spencer?"

Stefan nodded. He looked at David and Gio. "Do either of you mind?"

"Why would we?" Gio asked. "He needs a family and couldn't have asked for better parents than you and Mum."

Stefan pulled Gio into a hug. "I'm not sure that's true but thank you."

"And I don't mind. I get another brother and nephew, well, when Seth and Gio put the paperwork in, I get another nephew," David added.

"Dad can take our paperwork with him," Gio said. "Do you want me or David to come with you to the council? I'm not sure I'm comfortable with you going alone," Gio said, quickly looking at Bert and Gabe. "This is no reflection on the two of you, but you can't be with Dad all the time you're there."

"I understand," Bert said. "I'm taking Drake with me."

"Who's Drake?" Dave asked him.

"My best friend and I guess you could call him my beta," Bert explained.

"We need to meet him," Dave said, grinning at him.

"No, you don't," Ian said. "Drake is dull and serious and boring and wouldn't know humour if it smacked him in the face."

"He's not that bad. He takes his job seriously," Bert said.

"Very seriously," Ian muttered as Kevin walked back in.

"My guys are contacting the rescued children's families to make sure they are all safe," Kevin said.

"Stefan, Gabe, and I are off to the council building tomorrow," Bert said.

"Not alone," Kevin said, looking at him.

"I'll take Drake. I was going to take you and Ian as punishment, but you two will be better off here, doing what you do best."

Kevin grinned. "So you admit we're good?"

Bert snorted. "A moment of weakness that I will deny ever saying."

"That's okay, Wolfie, we'll remember," Seth said, grinning at Bert.

Gabe looked at Sean and Kayden. Kayden looked exhausted and in pain. "Kayden, are you sure I can't help ease your pain?"

Kayden shook his head. "No, you look exhausted. I can fix myself up later."

"Do you want me to send you back home so you can sleep in your own bed?" he offered.

Sean nods. "Please, if no one minds."

Gabe snorted and opened a portal. "Rest, my friends. I'll message you tomorrow."

"We'll come to the council building with you tomorrow," Kayden told him, walking through the portal with Sean.

Gabe nodded. "Thanks. By the way, congratulations on you both becoming my seconds." And with that, he closed the portal, laughing as he did.

"Nice way to break it to them," Dave said with a laugh.

Gabe grinned. "I know. I could have told them tomorrow, but why wait?"

"I'm going back outside to check on everyone," David said as he looked at the dead body, "and get someone to remove the body."

CHAPTER 53

Gavin gave a sigh of relief when he saw his brothers were both unhurt and rushed over to them.

"You're both all right," Hunter said, looking them over.

Mathis nodded. "We are. Did we hear an explosion earlier?"

"Yeah, one of the witches tried to blow Kayden up. They missed and blew up a wall instead. Dad's going to fix it," Hunter replied.

"Handy having a builder in the family," Raz said, grinning at Hunter.

"It is. Do you know if Owen was injured?"

Mathis snorted. "If he is, it's not serious. Looks like Taha is checking his mouth out to make sure," he pointed to the side where indeed Taha and Owen were kissing.

"I still say humans are weird," Raz said.

"You could be right, but then vampires are weird," Hunter countered.

Gavin spun around and poked Hunter in the side.

Hunter grabbed his hand, laughing before kissing it. "Is every day this adventurous?"

"It has been lately," Gabe said, joining them and looking exhausted.

Mathis pulled Gabe into his arms.

Gavin signed to him. "You look tired."

"I'm exhausted, to be honest," Gabe admitted, leaning into Mathis.

"Let's go upstairs and you can rest, little witch," Mathis said to him.

"Are you sure? There are probably things I can still do."

"Gabe, go rest. Mathis, go with him," Dave ordered, having heard him.

"Okay, call me if you need me." And after a round of hugs, Mathis took Gabe off to their room.

"Is there anything you need us to do?" Taha asked, walking over with Owen.

Dave shook his head. "Nope, not for the moment. The guards are getting rid of the bodies, and Olly and Ivan are back in the computer room. David and I need to talk to AJ about additional building work we want done. You can all go off and do whatever, but Owen, keep your phone on just in case." He looked around and shook his head. "The garden's a mess."

"Royston's due back any day now. The garden is his pride and joy," Raz said.

"It can be fixed," Taha said.

"It can. Until then, David can break the news to him," Dave said grinning.

"And on that happy note, Gavin and I are off to his room. If you need us, just yell," Hunter said.

Gavin nodded and hugged everyone, and taking Hunter's hand, they walked back into the house.

Hunter saw his dad standing in the hallway with Spencer and Jack.

AJ saw them and broke off talking. "We're off in a little bit, but I'll be back tomorrow to sort your room out and then here to sort the wall. David has offered us a room to stay in, so we don't need to keep travelling back and forth."

Hunter grins. "Yes, because ten miles is so far to travel."

"Oh, hush," AJ said, pulling first him and then Gavin into hugs. "I'll see you both tomorrow."

Gavin smiled and signed.

"It was lovely meeting you, as well, Gavin. Welcome to the family."

∽

Gavin sighed as his bedroom door closed. His family was safe for the moment and that was all that mattered.

He turned and looked at Hunter and walked willingly into his arms.

Hunter dipped his head and kissed Gavin, pulling back slightly saying, "Jump up, sweetheart."

Gavin did, wrapped his legs around Hunter's waist, and leant in for another kiss.

While they kissed, Hunter stumbled to the sofa and sat down, Gavin sitting on his lap. Hunter rested his hands on Gavin's hips.

Gavin pulled back and looked at Hunter, concern showing in his eyes.

"I'm fine sweetheart. Yes, it was scary having to hide, but I knew we would be safe because you, Stefan, and Louise were there. But truthfully, I just focused on you. You kept me calm."

Gavin smiled at him and mouthed, "I love you."

"And I, you. Now, I have a few ideas for your tattoo. Do you want to see them?"

Gavin nodded enthusiastically.

Luckily next to Hunter was his sketch pad. He picked it up and opened the pad to the right page. "Here, I did a couple for you. If you don't like them, I can design something else," Hunter said nervously. He internally shook his head. He was never nervous about showing his designs, but he had never done a bespoke design for a lover before.

Gavin was stunned. He had seen some of Hunter's designs before but seeing the designs Hunter had created just for him was incredible.

After their first meeting at the library, Hunter and Gavin had sent a lot of messages back and forth, learning likes and dislikes. Gavin had revealed that he loved pretty much anything and gave Hunter free rein to design anything he wanted.

Gavin's eyes kept looking at one of them, he gently stroked over it. It was stunning. It looked like a shield which would cover his shoulder and part way down his front and back. The shield was made up of different geometric designs and was gorgeous.

"You like that one, sweetheart?" Hunter asked softly.

Gavin nodded and put the pad down signed. "It's perfect. Thank you."

"You're welcome, sweetheart. As soon as my room is back up and running, shall we do it?"

Gavin nodded and with a laugh, signed again. "Please, I can't wait. Plus, don't forget our matching tattoos."

Hunter grinned. "Yes, we can get matching tattoos, as well."

Gavin signed again. "You really want to marry me?"

"Yes, I really want to marry you, and we'll be married as soon as all this craziness has been sorted out. I need to look

THE VAMPIRE AND THE TATTOOIST

at putting my house on the market and moving fully in here with you."

Hunter didn't think Gavin's smile could have gotten wider, but it did, and he leant in and kissed Hunter, putting all his love and happiness into the kiss.

Gavin couldn't believe that Hunter was happy to move in here with him. He secretly hoped he would, but Hunter did have his own house. But then so had Dave, and he had moved in. Realising he was rambling inside his own head, Gavin pushed all thought away and continued to kiss Hunter.

Finally, they drew back. "You can help me move, you having super strength and all."

Gavin nodded and signed, "I can get my brothers to help. They're strong and wouldn't mind."

"Nice, offering your brothers up, as well. In that case, I should be moved in quickly. Would you mind if I brought my favourite chair in here?" Hunter asked.

Gavin signed, "You can move in anything you want to, and if needed, we can change this room around."

"So I think that was I can move anything I want to in here, and if needed, we can change the room around so it feels like both of ours."

Gavin nodded.

"I like the room like this, but yeah, I'll add some of my touches to it. I like this outfit, the way these jeans hug you in all the right places, and this colour top makes your already amazing eyes sparkle brightly."

Gavin blushed and signed, while laughing. "Shelby made me buy them. He said you would jump my bones as soon as you saw me in them."

Hunter laughed. "If I understood you correctly, Shell said seeing you in these clothes would make me want to make love to you."

Gavin silently laughed and signed again. "Close. Jump my bones."

Hunter looked confused. "Would make me want to jump... something,"

Gavin signed again. "Bones."

Hunter grinned. "Jump your bones?"

Gavin nodded.

"Well, now that you mention it, that sounds like the best idea."

Hunter was lying in bed, Gavin wrapped around him. After making love to Gavin on the sofa, in the shower, and finally in bed, Gavin had fallen asleep. As tired as Hunter was, he wanted to be awake in case Gavin needed him. He pulled Gavin tighter against his chest and dropped a kiss on his head.

Gavin gave a silent sigh and moved around, sleepily opening his eyes and looking at Hunter with a frown.

"Sleep, sweetheart," Hunter said softly. "I've got you."

Gavin pulled back and sat up, still frowning at Hunter. Leaning close so Hunter could see, Gavin signed to him. "You need sleep. You keep the bad dreams away, so you can rest."

Hunter looked at him. "I keep the bad dreams away, so I can sleep, as well?"

Gavin nodded, leant forward, and kissed Hunter. "Love you," he mouthed.

Hunter kissed him back. "I love you, and all right, sweetheart, we'll both sleep. But wake me if you need me. Promise me?" Hunter said, pulling Gavin down and wrapping his arms back around him.

Gavin nodded and kissed his chest. He wasn't worried. Both he and Hunter could sleep well tonight. Gavin knew he wasn't over what he did, but so much had happened since then that he could now focus on other things, specifically being in Hunter's arms.

Hunter dropped another kiss onto Gavin's head, and taking Gavin at his word, he fell asleep thinking of the happy life he and Gavin would have.

CHAPTER 54

Hunter was surprised when he and Gavin walked into the kitchen the next morning and saw his parents sat at the table eating breakfast.

"Morning, everyone," Hunter said, sitting down and pulling Gavin down next to him.

After a round of 'mornings,' he looked at his parents. "You're here bright and early."

Charlotte nodded. "Yes, your father wanted to get an early start on your room, and Annie, Louise, and I still need to do more shopping for Jack and Spencer."

"Lissa is coming over, as well," Louise adds. She looked at David. "I'm so glad you made friends with the wolves, darling."

"Me, too, Mum," David replied, smiling, before looking at his father. "Who's going with you to the council building?"

"I've asked Mowbin to meet me there," Stefan replied. "I want you to come, as well."

David groaned. "I'm busy. Take Gio."

Gio snorted. "Don't look at me. I'm overseeing the arrival of more soldiers, both mine and the King's guards."

David nodded. "I should be here for that, as well, seeing as this is my house and coven."

"You would really let your father and King go to the council building without either you or Gio, knowing there are killer people there?" Dave said, feigning shock as he looked at David.

"Yes," David replied as laughter rang around the table.

"For shame, David. No more desserts for you," Annie told him.

Stefan smiled at her. "Thank you, Annie, but I'd include Gio in the no desserts, as well."

"Me?" Gio sputtered out. "But I really am busy. I need to protect my son and little brother. No offence, Dad, but you can wipe the floor with anyone."

"You can go if you're needed," Jack said, leaning against Gio's side. "Seth will still be here."

"As will Gio. No, David shall be coming with me. It will be good practice for when I retire," Stefan said, grinning at David. "I was going to wait a few more decades, but no, I think I'll pass the crown to you sooner. It will serve you right."

"If I come without an argument, will you stay on?" David pleaded.

"Too late," Stefan said with a laugh. He stopped laughing and said, "Seriously, though, we'll be staying until we uncover all the people involved in this underground network that work at the council. While we're there, Kevin will be around doing his thing and your coven can do what they do best."

"We can," Seth said. "I'll hold down the fort until you get back, bossman."

Gavin taped the table, and when everyone looked at him, he signed.

"Yes, Mathis will be there with Gabe, Sean, and Kayden," Stefan said. "I'll keep him safe."

"Pretty sure Gabe has that covered," David added. "You realise what we are doing has never happened before? Vampires, wolves, and witches working together in the council building."

Stefan nodded. "Times are changing. If you need to pack, go and do it now. We leave in an hour."

David nodded. "We'll go and do that," he said, standing up and pulling Dave up with him. He looked at AJ. "Dave, Seth, and Gio know what needs doing here. Once you've finished Hunter's room, can you speak to them about fixing the wall and other things?"

AJ nodded. "I can. You worry about what's going on at that council of yours. We have this covered."

"Thank you," David said before dragging Dave out of the kitchen with him.

"Packing, right," Cairo said, laughing. He stopped laughing and looked at Stefan. "Do you want me and the kitty to come, as well? Having Troy with you would be an added bonus."

"I'll come if you want me to, old bean," Troy said.

Stefan nodded. "I think that would be wise. Thank you, Cairo, Troy."

"In that case, we're off to pack," Cairo said, standing up and pulling Troy up with him. "Meet you in an hour." And with that, they both left the kitchen.

"Seth, Gio, have you given Jack's adoption papers to your father?" Louise asked them.

"I put the paperwork on his desk when we came down this morning," Gio said to Louise. "I also sent copies to your phone, Dad."

"Excellent. Once both adoptions have been finalised, we shall have a celebration. Also, Louise, my love, can you contact the jewellers? We need four new crowns made," Stefan said, smiling at his wife.

"How exciting. We can play around with designs, as well."

"Four crowns?" Annie asked, looking confused.

"Yes," Louise answered. "A crown for Seth, as he is Prince Seth."

Seth gasped and looked shocked. "I am?"

Gio grabbed his hand. "Of course you are, my Seth. I'm a Prince, and as my mate, so are you."

"Wow," Seth said, still looking stunned as if he'd never considered that.

"A crown for Dave, as he is a prince, as well, for now," Stefan said.

"Our boy, a prince," Annie said happily, looking at Willard and smiling.

"Always knew he was destined for greatness," Willard added.

"I can't wait to see his face when he finds out," Hunter said with a laugh.

Chuckles were heard around the table.

"The other two crowns are for Spencer and Jack," Louise said, smiling at them both.

"Us?" they both said at the same time, looking shocked.

"Of course, you'll both have crowns. Once adopted, you'll both be princes of the vampire royal family," Stefan said.

"But we're not vampires," Spencer pointed out.

"Like we care about that. You are our son, Jack our grandson; therefore, you are both princes," Louise said, pulling him close.

"Thank you," Spencer said, leaning into Louise.

"Yes, thank you," Jack said before grinning at Spencer. "We're gonna look awesome."

"We should have a mini coronation or investiture for the four of them," Taha said. "Is that a thing?"

"That is a thing and a wonderful idea, Taha. We can start planning it today," Louise said happily. "There is so much to organise. You'll help, won't you Annie, Charlotte?"

Annie smiled. "Of course! This will be fun."

"How exciting! Of course, I'll help." Charlotte said happily. "I'm sure Lissa will, as well."

CHAPTER 55

Hunter, AJ, Taha, and Owen were hard at work fixing Hunter's room, while Gavin had stayed behind to help with computery things.

Just before they left the house, Owen walked out, saying he was coming as a bodyguard for the three of them. Taha snorted and said if he was coming, he was the muscle and could carry everything heavy.

They were happily working away when they heard the front doorbell jingle.

"Hey, honeys, are you decent?" Luke called out.

"Never," Taha called back with a laugh.

Luke and Shelby walked into Hunter's room.

"AJ, how lovely to see you," Shelby said, walking over to him.

AJ laughed, stood up, pulling first Shelby and then Luke into hugs.

"Hunter called you, then," Luke said, pulling back.

AJ shook his head. "No, Charlotte and I turned up to see Hunter yesterday, and I offered my help."

"And you roped Owen in to help with the heavy lifting, nice," Shelby said, looking at Owen. "Morning,"

"Morning, Shelby. Just to let you know, AJ and Charlotte know about us and what happened in here," Owen said.

"How amazing is all this?" Shell asked. "Did you meet Gavin? Isn't he just divine?"

"I did and he is," AJ agreed.

"I need to thank you, Shell. Gavin's new clothes are amazing. I know Gabriel was going to see if you'd go shopping with him sometime," Hunter told him.

Shelby grinned. "Gabriel is the witch, right? Tell him I will be happy to help because what is it with everyone wearing black? Just because you all belong to the paranormal world doesn't mean the only colours available are black and white."

Everyone laughed as Owen grumbled, "But we like black."

"By the way, Owen, nice shoes," Luke said, looking at Owen's footwear.

The shoes were Brogue Oxfords in black and purple.

Owen smiled. "Thanks, I had them specially made. I have them in grey and purple, as well. I'm debating black and red at the moment."

"Do you get them in specialised shoe shops?" AJ asked.

Hunter and Taha laughed.

"Owen has his shoes handmade," Taha replied.

"Nice. That's a secret dream of mine, having some shoes made especially for me. Are they expensive?" Luke asked.

"A little bit, yes," Owen replied as Taha and Hunter laughed.

"Just how expensive are they?" AJ asked, looking at the shoes.

"Very. They are handmade in Italy," Owen told them.

"And you wore them here? What if they get scuffed while we're fixing the room up?" AJ enquired.

Owen shrugged. "I'll just get them fixed. I have lots of other shoes I can wear. Mind you, I seem to be missing one."

Taha and Hunter looked at each other and grinned.

"Did you misplace it?" Shell asked him.

"I must have done, but I've no idea where. I'm sure it will turn up," Owen said.

"I'm sure it will. Now, I have to get on. I have a full day of clients," Luke told them.

"Me, too. Have fun boys," Shell said as they both walked out.

AJ looked at Owen. "I looked at getting some shoes handmade once. They ran into the thousands."

Owen nodded. "They can do, yes, but I love shoes. We had a cobbler in the village where I grew up. He made everyone's shoes. I can remember buying a standard shop pair once, but they were uncomfortable, so I went back to having them handmade. Living as long as we do, decent footwear is a must."

"I can imagine," AJ said, getting back to work.

"Hunt, have you decided if you're moving in with Gavin?" Taha asked.

"I am. Gav and I spoke about it yesterday. I was thinking of selling my house, but I might rent it out fully furnished. What about you?"

"The same. I'll rent it out for a while, as well," Taha replied.

"Now we just need to get Max and Bert sorted out," Hunter said.

"That might be tricky with Bert away, but when he's back, I'm sure we can do something to help them," Owen said.

~

E. BROOM

Gavin was hard at work. He was once again sat at Mathis' desk, working away on his computer. Well, he should have been. His thoughts, like they did at the moment, went to Hunter. Hunter had told him about everything that had been damaged, and he wanted to buy something special for him. Gavin had looked online, but there was so much that he didn't know what to buy. He grabbed his phone and sent a message to Owen, asking if he could get Taha's help with what he could get. If anyone could help him, it would be Taha. Well, he could possibly have asked Luke or Shelby, but he didn't have their numbers, either. He put his phone down and carried on his research.

"Yes!" Olly suddenly exclaimed. "I'm now in Quintus's computer. Now let's see what this bad boy can tell us."

"You're slacking, Olly. How long did that take you?" Ivan asked with a laugh.

"Least I managed to hack it. How are you getting on locating the Master's owners?" Olly shot back.

"You'd probably find that information faster than me. Chances are, it's all on that machine."

"We can hope," Olly said. He looked at Gavin. "How are you getting on with tracking those listening devices, Gavin?"

Gavin looked up and grimaced.

"That bad?" Ivan asked.

Gavin nodded and signed.

"You think I might find the recordings on this computer?" Olly said.

Gavin nodded and signed again.

Olly frowned.

"You think all the answers will be on there?" Ivan guessed.

Gavin nodded.

"You're probably right. I'll let you know what I find."

THE VAMPIRE AND THE TATTOOIST

Owen was washing a wall down when his phone pinged. He pulled it out of his pocket and saw a message from Gavin, asking for help from Taha for what he could buy for Hunter to help with the restock.

Owen smiled and showed the message to Taha. Taha forwarded the message to his phone where he had lots of links bookmarked. He then sent through links for different equipment he knew Hunter needed, all with different prices so Gavin had a choice.

"What are you smiling about?" Hunter asked him.

"Maybe I'm just happy," Taha replied with a smile.

"Or maybe you're up to something," Hunter countered.

"You'll never know," Taha said, grinning at him.

"It's something good, though," Owen added.

"Now you have to tell me," Hunter griped.

"No, we don't," Owen replied for Taha. "By the way, you've missed a bit," he said, pointing at the part of the wall Hunter was washing down.

"Fine, be like that, then. See if I buy you two any lunch today."

"You'll buy them lunch," AJ said, grinning at Taha and Owen. "I taught you better than that."

Taha and Owen laughed, and Hunter tried to scowl at his father but ended up laughing, as well.

"I might give Shell some money and ask him to go and buy lunch for us," Hunter replied.

CHAPTER 56

Stefan, David, Gabe, Mathis, Kayden, Sean, Cairo, Troy, Bertrum, and Drake met up outside the council offices. David, Mathis, and Cairo were all carrying bags with whatever they thought might be needed.

"Everyone, this is Drake, my second. Drake, this is King Stefan and Prince David D'Angelo, Gabriel Augusta and Mathis Stone. Gabriel is the head of the Southern Witches; and these are his two seconds, Kayden and Sean; and this is Cairo, who has the misfortune to be mated to the kitty," Bert introduced.

"I saw you all at Kevin's meeting," Drake said, nodding to everyone. "Kitty, still alive, I see."

"I'm more than surprised you are as well, old bean. I thought Kev would have done away with you by now, or Ian."

Bert sighed. "Children, can we try and behave?"

"Yeah, good luck with that. The only reason the kitty is still alive is because my mate won't let me kill him," David said.

"For which I am truly thankful," Cairo added.

Gabe looked at Kayden. "How are your injuries?"

"All healed now," Kayden told him. "Sean thoroughly checked me over and healed my bruises."

Sean grinned. "It was a tough job, but one that had to be done. And by the way, Gabe, seconds?"

"What, you think I would ask anyone else? I trust the two of you. Of course, I was making you both my seconds. Plus, seriously, you expected me to go through all this without the two of you?" Gabe said, grinning at them.

"I can't wait to see other witches' reactions to us," Kayden commented.

"Mowbin should be meeting us in the reception area," Stefan said, trying to bring things back to the here and now.

"I asked Icarus to meet me there, as well," Bert said. "I also got him to make sure his office is bug-free so we can go in there and talk strategies before we start."

"I didn't ask anyone to meet us because Quintus and his assistant are both in jail at the moment, and I have no idea who on the witches' council I can trust," Gabe added.

"Shall we go in and get started?" David asked.

Drake looked through the window that showed the reception area. "There seems to be an unusual number of people standing around chatting. Let's go and shock them, shall we?"

Bert laughed. "This should be fun."

"Not sure I would go right to fun, but it will be interesting," Mathis added.

Stefan and Bert walked in first with the others following.

Shocked gasps were heard when they walked in.

The inside of the paranormal council building was grand like something a high-end hotel would have. The floors were marble, the decorations were gold and yellow, and a large reception was along the far wall. Uncomfortable looking chairs were dotted around in groups, and here and there were potted plants.

Two men walked over to join them.

"Ah, Mowbin, good to see you," Stefan said, shaking his hand. "You remember my son David?"

Mowbin nodded. "I do. Hello, your Highness."

"Mowbin," David said with a regal nod.

"These are our friends. The Alpha King, Bertrum Mellor, and his second Drake; this is Gabriel Augusta, head of the Southern witches and his mate Mathis; Kayden and Sean, Gabriel's seconds; and this is Cairo and Troy," Stefan introduced.

"Gentlemen, welcome to the council building," Mowbin said.

"Your Majesty," the second man said, nodding his head at Bert.

"Hey, Icarus. Thank you for meeting us. This is King Stefan D'Angelo of the vampires, and I'm sure you heard everyone's names," Bert said.

"I did. Welcome," Icarus said, looking at the group. "Shall we go to my office? We can talk there."

"Let me sign everyone in first," Drake said, walking over to the reception desk.

"So many people are staring at us," Gabe said softly.

"Just stare back, little witch," Mathis said. "That's what I'm doing."

"Me too, old bean," Troy said. "I find it works really well." As if to prove his point, the person Troy was currently staring at turned and rushed away. Troy grinned at Gabe. "See, works every time."

"Yeah, but see, you're scary. No one will look at me and think that," Gabe pointed out.

"More fool them, then," Bert said. "Out of all of us, they should fear you the most."

Gabriel snorted.

"I'm serious, my friend. Everyone knows or has heard of

me, the same with Stefan. You are the unknown witch. All anyone here knows is that you are a strong witch, but they have no idea how strong you really are."

"He's right, little witch. You can use that to your advantage,"

Gabe looked from Bert to Mathis and grinned. "This should be fun, then," he said, echoing Bert's words from earlier.

Drake walked back and joined them. "So, gossip around the building is that the new head of the Southern Witches is sacking and arresting all the old witches that work here for laziness and gross misconduct. The vampires are looking to overthrow everybody, and the Alpha King is coming to challenge the vampire king and stop him."

Silence met Drake's statement before they all burst out laughing.

"They seriously think that?" Gabe said while still laughing.

Drake cracked a smile. "Oh, yeah. Imagine, then, the receptionist's surprise when we all walked in together and I signed everyone in."

"I need to go to the witches' offices before they all pack up, destroy evidence, or run away," Gabriel said, looking around. "That is after I find where their offices are."

"They are on the second floor," Stefan said. "The lifts are there." He pointed in their direction. "The vampires are on the fourth floor, and wolves are on the third. Other paranormal's are on all these floors, as well."

"Instead of talking strategies, let's go to our offices and see what is currently happening. Chances are, either someone at reception or someone standing around has alerted everyone to the fact we have arrived," David said.

"They probably have. Good luck one and all, and if anyone needs help, just call," Bert said.

"Same. If you need me, call," Gabe put in.
"Ditto for me," Stefan added.
"Ditto?" David asked his father, laughing.
"Exactly," Stefan said, grinning.
"Then let's get this party started," Troy said.

CHAPTER 57

Gabriel walked out of the lifts on the second floor, Mathis, Sean, and Kayden with him.

Directly in front of the lifts was another reception desk.

The woman behind it watched them walk forward, her face blank of all emotions.

"Good morning, gentlemen. How may I help you?" She looked at Mathis. "The Vampire offices are two floors up."

Mathis nodded. "I know, thank you. This is Gabriel Augusta, head of the Southern Witches and his seconds."

The woman showed surprise for a moment. "Welcome to the witches' council offices, my lord," she replied, looking at Gabriel. "I would contact Councilman Cameron-Webb for you, but he and his assistant Oswald have been arrested by the council guards."

Gabriel nodded. "I know. I need to speak to the rest of the witch council as soon as possible. Can you please make that happen? I also need directions to both Cameron-Webb and Oswald's offices."

"Certainly, my lord. I will send an emergency meeting

announcement out and have everyone meet in an hour in our boardroom. Councilman Cameron-Webb's office is literally at the end of the hall. You can't miss it. It's the biggest office. Oswald's office is next door."

"Thank you. How many witches are in today?" Kayden asked.

"All eighteen, sir," the receptionist told him.

"We need twenty-two council guards up here now, please," Mathis told her.

She looked at Gabe in shock. "Twenty-two?"

Gabriel nodded. "Now, please."

The receptionist picked up her phone and dialled a number, requesting the guards immediately. When she hung up, she said, "They will be here in a few minutes. Do you want to wait here for them?"

"We will do, thank you," Gabe replied.

"Do you have an out-of-office recording for your phone?" Sean asked her.

She nodded.

"You'd better put it on," Sean suggested.

"But—" she started to protest.

Gabriel cut her off. "The message goes on, and please put your out-of-office on your emails and the council website. After that, unless one of us contacts you, you are not to touch the computer or phone system again."

"I don't understand."

Before anyone could answer, a side door opened and council guards appeared, all wearing the council guard uniforms of black and grey.

A man walks forward. "I am General Goldbury. You requested guards?

Gabriel stepped forward. "I am Gabriel Augusta, head of the Southern witches. I need guards inside every witch member's offices. Whatever they are doing, they have to stop.

I also want a guard here in the reception area. No one in, no one out without my say-so unless they were asked to come here by the Vampire King or the Wolf Alpha King."

General Goldbury nodded. "Is this to do with Cameron-Webb and his assistant?"

Gabriel nodded. "It is."

"Then it shall be done." He turned to his guards. "You heard Lord Augusta. Denton, stay here. Everyone else, pick a room and do whatever is needed."

The guards all left the reception area.

Gabriel looked at the General.

"I'm staying with you."

"Come on, then," Gabe said before looking at the receptionist. "Don't forget the meeting in one hour, the out-of-office notices, and then no using anything."

"I remember, and the meeting announcement has been sent."

"Thank you." And with that, Gabriel and the others left the reception area, heading for Quintus Cameron-Webb's office.

∼

Bertrum, Drake, and Icarus got off on their floor.

Again a reception area was in front of the lifts, a design all floors had.

"Your majesty, Drake, Icarus," the receptionist said, smiling at them.

"Pepe," Bert said.

"Have you come to look for Caulder Drinkwater and Willy Ford? It's strange that they suddenly vanished. Well, they didn't vanish. They ran out of here as fast as they could and then vanished. They both looked panicked and angry as they rushed out. I thought at first, they had been fired as they were both carrying boxes with them, but there was no announcement of that happening. It's all very mysterious," Pepe said.

Pepe was a gossip and knew everything that was happening in the council building, not just with the wolves, but everywhere.

"Mind you, if you ask me, I think they were tied up with Quintus Cameron-Webb. It was only after he and his assistant were arrested that they did their vanishing act, so whatever they were into couldn't have been on the up and up. Rumour has it that Cameron-Webb let his son go on a murdering spree." He stopped talking and looked around before leaning closer and lowering his voice. "Rumour also has it that Cameron-Webb was the head of some big underground organisation. I'm not sure if I believe that, but I've heard rumblings for a few months now."

"Why didn't you say anything?" Drake asked him.

"I had no real proof, but I've kept a document of everything I heard."

"Can you send it to me, please? How many council members are in today?" Bert asked.

"Seventeen. Humphry Thornton is still away on his world cruise."

"I want twenty-one guards up here now, please," Bert said.

Pepe nodded and placed the call. Once he hung up, he looked at Bert. "They're on their way. Apparently, there are also guards on the way to the witches and vampires."

"Looks like you all had the same thought," Icarus said.

Bert nodded. "It just makes sense."

"It does. Better to be safe than sorry," Drake said.

Pepe looked at them all. "I'm guessing that there might be truth to that underground operation rumour."

"I need your complete silence on this Pepe. I mean it. I

THE VAMPIRE AND THE TATTOOIST

want no hint of a whisper coming from you or the consequences will be dire," Bert warned.

Pepe nodded and looked down. "It seems the witches' council has been put on lockdown. There are out-of-offices on the email and phone system and the main council website. Do you want me to do the same?"

Bert nodded. "Please."

The side door opened and again guards streamed in.

Orders were given and the guards went off.

"Let's get this started," Bert said, walking towards the offices.

~

Stefan, David, Mowbin, Cairo, and Troy walked into the vampire board room where all the vampire council members had gathered.

Like the others, guards had arrived and were guarding the council member's rooms.

Stefan stood at the foot of the table, David on one side, and Mowbin on the other.

Cairo and Troy were standing at the back of the room.

"I demand to know the meaning of this insult," one of the female council members said.

"Is it true you are taking over the whole council?" asked another, "and the Alpha King is coming to challenge you?"

Muttering was heard around the table. Stefan held his hand up for silence.

"No, that is not true. Indeed, I arrived today with the Alpha King. As of this moment, all vampire council members are under investigation," Stefan said.

Shocked gasps were heard from around the room.

"This is an outrage," the woman shouted, standing up and

leaning on the table, her eyes swirling red. "As I said before, I demand to know the meaning of this insult."

"You will calm down right now, Jessica Balding; otherwise, I will ask the guard to stun you," Stefan said calmly.

She sucked in a breath and closed her eyes. When she opened them again, they were back to normal.

"Sit down," he ordered.

She sat and glared at him.

"As you may have heard, Quintus Cameron-Webb and his assistant Oswald have been arrested. They are being charged with letting Kay Cameron-Webb go on a murder spree in the Augusta coven," Stefan explained.

"But that's the witches' problem. What does that have to do with us?" another asked.

"I have formed an alliance with Gabriel Augusta, the head of the Southern witches. Indeed, one of our vampires is mated to Gabriel. It was while we, along with the local wolf pack, were helping Gabriel that we discovered what was happening here."

Jessica Balding jumped up again. "You can't prove anything," she shouted and ran for Stefan.

Stefan rushed her and had her up against the wall, his hand around her neck before she even rounded the table. His fangs had dropped, and his nails had grown longer. He pushed them into her neck. "Your office and all your homes will be searched. All your assets will be seized. You will be held in prison until you are brought up on charges."

"You can't stop us," Jessica spat out, clawing at his hands.

"We can. We have already started." Stefan looked at the guard. "I need her put in prison."

The guard nodded. "Certainly, your Majesty," he said and walked over to them.

Stefan dropped her, stepping backwards.

The guard picked her up, and using paranormal cuffs, handcuffed her hands behind her back.

"I'll be back as soon as I can," the guard said.

"Can you ask one of your colleagues to step in while you're gone," David asked.

"Yes, Your Highness." And with that, the guard left the room, dragging Jessica behind him.

A moment later, a new guard entered the meeting room.

"Thank you," Stefan said, looking at the new guard while walking back to the front of the table.

"Sire, can you explain what's going on as I'm very confused," a council member asked.

Murmurs of agreement were heard from the others.

Stefan nodded. "Certainly. While helping the witches, we discovered the previous coven leader Roberto Augusta, Kay Cameron-Webb, and a few others were involved in a big illegal underground network. It was also discovered that other paranormal groups were involved."

"What were they into?" another asked, sounding aghast.

"Amongst the standard drugs, they were also involved in child slavery trafficking and child sex trafficking."

Outrageous gasps were heard.

"And Jessica was involved?"

"By her own admission, it looks like she was, but we haven't as yet come across her name in any of the information we found," David replied.

"What can we do to help?" someone asked.

"You will all be investigated. Your computers, your offices, your phones, your homes. If you tell us now you were involved, we will be lenient with you. If not and we discover you were, the consequences will be much worse," Stefan said. "David, Mobwin, Cairo, Troy, and I will be searching the offices. Members of David's security firm will be searching your homes, as will members of the Mellors wolf pack."

"I have nothing to hide. You can search for whatever you need to of mine. It might be worth looking at the Garcia brothers. They seem to have vanished," a council member said.

The other members agree.

"I already have guards out looking for them. For the moment, I need all of your phones and any other communication devices that you have on you handed to David. They will be checked quickly and handed back to you. You will all stay in this room for the moment, and I will arrange refreshments for you all," Stefan said.

There were a few grumbles, but all electronics were handed over to David.

"Can I ask that my phone be checked first? I know this is important, but my wife is due to give birth any day now, and I need my phone handy," one of the councilmen asked as he handed his device over.

"Congratulations and yes, we will check it straight away," David replied.

CHAPTER 58

Seth was busy. He dispatched Donny to check out Jessica Balding's main home and Neill to look into her apartment. He pulled others off various assignments and sent them where needed. There were a few assignments that weren't urgent, so Seth had no problem pulling people off them for now.

He had just walked out into the garden when he heard a crying sound. He followed the sniffs and saw Jack and Spencer sitting on the ground behind some shrubs. Spencer was leaning against Jack, crying.

He pulled out his phone and sent a quick message to Louise. Once done, he hurried over and sitting on Spencer's other side and put his hand on Spencer's back. "Hey," he said softly.

Spencer looked up and turned, throwing himself against his chest.

Seth wrapped his arms around him and looked at Jack.

"He's having nightmares and flashbacks over his time in captivity," Jack told him.

Just then, Louise came walking quickly out of the house and over to them, dropping to her knees in front of them.

"Spencer," she said gently.

Spencer pulled back from Seth and moved into Louise's arms. "I'm sorry," he said, sniffing.

"There is nothing to apologise for. Cry all you need to; shout out in anger if you must; ask Seth or Gio to help you blow something up. Whatever you need to do, you do, and we'll all be here to help you."

Spencer pulled back and looked at her in surprise. "I can blow something up?" he asked, a smile tugging at his lips.

"As long as it's not the house and an adult is supervising, I don't see why not," Louise replied.

Spencer turned and looked at Jack, who was now resting against Seth. "Wanna come and find Gio with me? You should get to blow stuff up, too."

Jack laughed. "We can. But he might be a bit busy at the moment with like the new guards coming and everything. We could raid the kitchen for cake and biscuits first."

"And after you've done that, you can search the house for more secret passages," Seth said.

"More secret passages?" Jack asked him, smiling.

"Oh yeah. Just imagine the fun you'll have looking for them and our secret library," Seth told them.

Spencer wiped his hands over his face. His eyes were red from crying, and he kept sniffing.

"Spencer, Jack, we can get a therapist in to help you sort out your emotions if you want extra help," Louise said to them. "But we will always be here if you would just rather just talk to us."

"Can we phone Stefan tonight?" Spencer asked her.

"Of course we can, darling."

"Thanks," Spencer said, giving her a quick hug and

jumping up. "Come on Jack, we have biscuits to eat, secret passageways to find and things to blow up."

∽

DAVE WAS SAT in his library. He was worried about what everyone would find in the council offices. Hopefully, a way to stop all the crap that'd been found out. He wished Max were there, but he was working all day in the library again. Deciding he was getting nothing done, he got up and left. With David gone, he really should be available to greet the new guards.

He walked into the kitchen and saw Jack and Spencer raiding the biscuit tin. "Don't eat all the biscuits, you greedy things."

"We're stocking up on biscuits and then going to search for more secret passages and the secret library before we blow things up," Jack told him, putting some into his pocket.

Dave looked at Spencer and noticed his red eyes and nose. "Let me guess, Seth said you could blow things up to make you feel better," Dave said, taking a couple of biscuits out of the tin.

"No, Louise. I'm having a bad day today. She said I could get angry and yell or find Gio and blow something up," Spencer admitted, his shoulders slumping.

"That's understandable with everything you've been through," Dave said gently. "You saw yesterday I had a mini freak out. It wasn't the first and probably won't be the last. Just know we are all here for you both for whatever you need. Just please, no blowing the house up. AJ already has a lot of work to do."

Jack and Spencer laughed.

"We've already been asked not to blow it up and to have

adult supervision when we do blow something up," Jack told him.

"That's good. Now, as for the secret library, do you want me to show you where it is, or would you rather look for it yourselves?"

Jack and Spencer looked at each other. "We'll try by ourselves first," Jack said.

Dave nodded. "Excellent. In that case, go forth and have fun."

CHAPTER 59

Gabriel sighed and rubbed his head. He was sat behind Quintus's desk, searching through the paperwork, not that he expected to find anything.

"Are you okay, little witch?" Mathis asked, looking at him in concern.

"Yeah, it's just a bit overwhelming, that's all. Do you really think Quintus would be stupid enough to have incriminating paperwork here?"

Mathis looked at him. "This is the guy that had meeting agendas sent out, used his initials, and didn't disguise his voice. Pretty sure there will be something here."

General Goldbury burst out laughing. "Seriously?"

Mathis nodded. "Oh yeah."

"You said that the wolves and vampires as well as the witches were involved. What about other paranormal's?" the General asked.

"We've not discovered any others, but that's not to say no one else was involved," Gabriel told him. "But we have no authority over them. All we can do is shut down what we know and hopefully stop those streams."

The general frowned. "That won't stop the problem. A meeting should be called for all council personnel no matter the group, so everyone knows what is going on."

"I'll contact Stefan and Bert and see what they think," Gabe said, pulling his phone out of his pocket when Kayden rushed into the room.

"What's wrong?" Gabe asked, jumping up.

"I hit the jackpot. Oswald had files upon files of this underground network in his office. I thought Leonard's secret room was full. Literally everything in his office is connected," Kayden said, grinning.

"Seriously?" Mathis asked.

"Oh yeah. Come and see."

GABE LOOKED at some of the files on Oswald's desk and shook his head. "Stefan and Bert need to see all this."

"I'll phone them," Mathis said, pulling his phone out.

∼

STEFAN WAS LOOKING through Jessica's files when Mathis phoned.

"What have you found?" Stefan asked.

"A lot, and I do mean *a lot* of files in Oswald's office. We should find all the answers we're looking for in these files. Gabe thought you should come down and see."

"I'll come now," Stefan said, hanging up. He looked at the guard who was guarding the room. "Can you stay here? I'll have David come in and carry on searching this office."

"Of course, sire."

"Thanks," Stefan said, walking out of the room and into the one David was in. "It would seem that Quintus's assistant kept files of everything regarding this underground network. I'm going down to see what's been found."

"Want me to come?" David asked him.

Stefan shook his head. "I would rather you carried on searching Jessica's room for me. This one can wait."

David stood up. "I can do that."

"Have you heard how Seth and your men are getting on?"

"They've started searching Jessica's properties as well as Oswald's and Quintus's. As soon as they find something, they'll let me know and I'll let you know. Also, Gio said that guards have started turning up, both his and yours."

Stefan nodded his head. "Good. I'll see you in a bit."

He also sent a message to Cairo and Troy asking them to come to the witches' floor since Troy and Cairo had gone off earlier to poke around the cat shifters' department.

Stefan met all of them in the lift.

"How did your vampires react?" Bert asked him.

"We discovered another vampire involved. She's currently in the cells here and her homes are being searched as we speak. You?"

"We've found no other wolves that were involved. But Pepe, our receptionist, has kept records of everything he hears. It makes for interesting reading."

"Kitty?" Bert asked.

"Nothing concrete, but a couple of the office workers look scared," Troy replied. "We should think about calling a meeting of the whole council."

"Yes, that would be wise. Let's discuss it with Gabe," Stefan said.

Just then, the lift doors opened. The receptionist jumped to her feet. "King Stefan, Alpha King Bertrum. I'm not sure..."

"Lord Augusta asked us to come," Stefan said.

"He did," Mathis said, walking into the reception area. "Come on through. You're gonna love this."

Stefan, Bert, Cairo, and Troy stared around the office.

"Seriously? Everything in here relates to the underground group?" Cairo asked in astonishment.

Gabe nodded. "Everything we've looked at so far, yes. It literally details *everything*."

"I want to say could they be any more stupid, but yes, they can," Bert commented, picking up a folder and looking into it.

"How can an organisation that's been going this long be so lackadaisy about keeping all this secure?" Sean asked.

"They got too complacent and thought they were untouchable," Troy said.

"It's gonna be a long day," Cairo said.

"General Goldbury suggested we call a full council meeting," Gabe told them.

"Troy had the same thought. But if we do that, how many more council members will go into hiding?" Stefan said.

"Pretty much all the council members are in today. I checked," Troy said.

"I can station guards at all entrances and exits, completely locking this place down, and you can call a full council meeting now," General Goldbury suggested.

Bert looked at Stefan and Gabe. "That sounds sensible." He looked at the general. "How soon can you lock this place down, quietly, so no one has time to make a run for it?"

The general pulled his phone out of his pocket. "Give me five minutes."

"You can lock a building this big down in five minutes?" Gabe asked, sounding shocked.

The general laughed. "I can lock this place down in under two minutes, but you want guards on all entrances and exits, which will take a few minutes."

"So how do we call a full council meeting?" Kayden asked.

"We use the emergency call button," Stefan said.

Gabe grinned. "Please tell me it's a red button. Also, how do we make sure everyone attends?"

"If the emergency button is used, council policy is that everyone congregates in the main meeting hall. It will fit everyone in," Stefan said.

"I can also have some guards do a sweep of each floor, making sure everyone is in attendance."

"Just how many guards does the council have?" Sean asked.

"A lot. To be honest, I'm sure everyone is enjoying today. This is the most fun we've had in years," the general said, grinning.

"Guards are so weird," Kayden said, shaking his head.

"I can't wait to see the look on everyone's faces when we all walk in together," Mathis said, grinning.

"So where is the emergency button?" Gabe asked.

"The closest will be in Quintius' room," Bert said. "All leaders have the magical red button of emergencies. Come on, Gabe, I'll show you. If you're good, I might even let you press it."

Gabe grinned and followed Bert out of the room.

CHAPTER 60

The alarm was loud. It sounded like a foghorn with three blasts.

Gabe grinned at Bert. "I should change the coven call system for this one."

"What does yours do?" Bert asked as they left the office.

"It creates a mark on the witch's wrist. It hurts until you answer the call," he replied, walking back into Oswald's office.

"But a foghorn would be awesome," Kayden said.

They heard people moving along the corridor, indicating they were on the way to the meeting room.

"We'll wait a few minutes and then go to the meeting room. I've asked David and Mowbin to meet us outside," Stefan said.

"I'll get Drake and Icarus to meet us there, as well," Bert said, pulling his phone out and sending the message.

"Troy, will you have issues with the feline representative by walking in with us?" Gabe asked in concern.

"I shouldn't think so, old bean, but I honestly don't care. They know I'm loyal to my friends."

"We love you, too, kitty," Bert said, grinning at him.

"I meant Gabe, puppy," Troy replied.

"I love you, too, Kitty," Gabe said, grinning.

"Forget it. Dave is the only one I like."

"And on that note, let's go and cause havoc," Stefan said, leading the way out.

They met the others waiting outside the main council meeting room. General Goldbury was with them.

"Everyone is inside," Drake told them. "No one has any idea who called this meeting or why."

"Then let's go in and tell them," Bert said. "Gabe, you walk in next to Stefan and I."

Gabe blew out a breath. "Okay, let's do this."

"Remember, little witch, your magic is strong. Use that to your advantage if you need to."

Gabe smiled. "Will do."

The general nodded to the door guards. They pulled the doors open and Bert, Stefan, and Gabe walked in with the others following. The general stood with them.

Gasps were heard around the room and silence descended.

The room was huge. The circular seating area had three levels, depending on your council position. The leaders and their assistants were seated in the first row.

No one quite knew how it worked, but no matter who talked, everyone could hear.

Bert, Stefan, and Gabriel moved to the centre of the room, the others forming a semi-circle around them.

"Thank you for coming to this emergency council meeting," Stefan said.

"What's the emergency and why were we not told about this meeting beforehand?" the feline representative demanded.

"If you pipe down, Donald, you'll find out," Troy growled out, glaring at him.

"It has been discovered that members of this council have been involved in illegal underground activities," Bert said.

Shocked gasps were heard.

"Quintus Cameron-Webb and his assistant Oswald are currently residing in the council prison," Gabe said, stepping forward.

"Who the hell are you?" Donald demanded.

"Donald, I swear I will knock you out in a minute," Troy shot out, coming to stand next to Gabe. "This is Lord Gabriel Augusta, Head of the Southern Witches. You will show him respect."

Gabe touched his arm and smiled at him. He turned back and looked at the other council leaders. "King Stefan, Alpha King Bertrum, and I are working together to bring this organisation down."

Mummers were heard around them.

"The three of you are working together?" a council member asked in shock. He looked at Gabriel. "I'm Stole, council leader for the flying shifters.

"Yes, Stole, we are working together," Stefan said. "For too long we have all only worked for ourselves, and looked after our own interests, and as such, this underground network has been in operation for a long time. The time for working alone is at an end," Stefan said.

"We have the files for the whole of this organisation. We have reports, meeting recordings, everything," Bert said. "We know other council members were involved with this organisation. If you come forward now, we will be lenient; if not, the punishment will be severe."

"Now hold on a minute," Donald shouted, standing up. "You have no right to tell us what to do. May I remind you, this council works on a voting system."

"All in favour of me knocking Donald out, raise your hands," Troy said.

Muttering was heard from around the room, and Donald glared at Troy.

The general stepped forward and held his hand up for silence. "Make no mistake, ladies and gentlemen, this organisation will be stopped. Every entrance and exit into and out of this building has been locked and guards posted on the doors. Guards are now standing in every office. You can either stay in here or go back to your offices. If you decide to return to your office, you will not be allowed to touch anything, and if you try, you'll be arrested.

No one in this building is above suspicion except those standing with me."

A stunned silence descended.

"You really think you can stop us?" a woman said, jumping up. "This organisation is bigger than you could possibly imagine. There is no stopping us. I can, however, stop you." And quick as anything, she threw something towards them and turned to run away.

"Bomb," Drake shouted.

Gabe flung his hand out and froze the bomb in the air, surrounding it in a bomb-proof bubble. At the same time, he caught the lady and wrapped her up in rope.

"Nice, Gabe," Bert said to him just as the bomb exploded, the bubble containing the blast.

Pandemonium broke out as two guards grabbed hold of the bound lady and dragged her away. Council members were on their feet, all talking over each other and shouting.

"So that's two bombs they've tried. Think they'll go for a third?" Kayden asked.

"Probably," Mathis replied.

"Quiet," Troy yelled out, surprising everyone.

Stole stood up and looked at them. "What can we do to help?"

CHAPTER 61

"Well, that was a good day's work, boys," AJ said, looking around Hunter's room. Everything had been fixed and repainted. "All that's left is to restock."

"It is. I'll get on to reordering things tonight," Hunter replied.

"AJ, fancy coming to the Pig and Whistle? I'm sure Matt would love to see you," Luke said from the doorway.

"Well, it would be rude not to drop in for a quick one. Are you all coming?"

Everyone said yes.

"Then let's pack up and head out. Hunter, will Gavin join us?" AJ asked.

Hunter pulled out his phone. "Let's find out."

H: We're off to the Pig and Whistle. Fancy coming?

"I've sent him a message, so hopefully he'll come. I might need to go and pick him up, though."

"That's no problem if you do," AJ said.

Just then, Hunter's phone pinged. He looked and saw a reply from Gavin.

G: Sounds good. I'll meet you there.
Perfect, Hunter sent back. **Love you x**
G: Love you, too x

"Gavin said he would meet us there," Hunter told them as he put his phone away.

"Excellent," AJ said, collecting up his tools.

∽

GAVIN WAS HARD AT WORK. He had pulled off everything he could find on one computer and was now going through another when he received Hunter's text.

Of course, he said yes to meeting up with everyone, but that meant he would have to go to the pub on his own. Sure, he was getting better at going out by himself, but— No, no buts, he could go and meet the others by himself.

"You okay there, Gav?" Ivan asked him. "You look a little stressed."

Gavin looked up and made a so-so gesture before signing.

"So Hunter's going out drinking with everyone and invited you, but because you're basically a hermit, you're nervous about going alone. And yes, I did add that hermit bit in myself," Ivan said, grinning at him.

Gavin poked his tongue out at him.

"How about if I drive? We could both do with a break."

Gavin nodded and signed, "Thank you."

"So where are we going?" Ivan asked, standing up.

Gavin stood as well and signed.

Ivan stared at him in confusion. "I'm sorry to say I have no idea what you just signed."

Gavin gave a silent laugh. He wasn't sure many people would have worked that out. He picked up a pen and his notebook and wrote *The Pig and Whistle Pub*.

He handed it to Ivan, who burst out laughing. "No way

would I have got that. I also don't think I've been there before, so Google the postcode for me and I'll let Seth know we're leaving for a bit."

It didn't take Gavin or Ivan long to get to the pub; in fact, it was surprisingly close.

Gavin paused just in front of the door and took a breath.

Ivan touched his shoulder. "Just remember you have friends in there as well as your Hunter."

Gavin nodded and signed, "Thank you."

"You're welcome, little brother. Ready?"

Gavin nodded and, pushing the door open, the two vampires walked in.

The pub was busy. All the tables were full and music was playing. Gavin looked around for Hunter and saw him and the others sitting at a large table, laughing and joking.

Hunter looked up and saw Gavin, and his face split into a massive grin as he jumped up, walking over to the two of them and pulling Gavin in for a kiss. He kept it short and sweet before pulling back and saying hello.

Gavin smiled and mouthed hello back before Hunter took his hand and led him over to their group.

Shelby and Luke jumped up and hugged Gavin hello. Shelby pulled back, looking Gavin over. "I told you, you looked good in this outfit. I can't wait to go shopping with you again."

AJ stood up and pulled Gavin into a hug. "I'm glad you could come. Have you met Matt, the owner?"

"He has," Matt said, walking over with a tray of drinks. "Hey, Gavin."

"Everyone, this is Ivan," Hunter said, waving at the vampire.

"I ordered you a whisky," Owen told him.

"Thanks," Ivan replied.

"Gavin, Hunter ordered you a coke," Matt told him.

Gavin signed, "Thank you," and then smiled at Hunter and sat down next to him.

"My mum wants to meet you sometime, Gavin. She saw you and Hunter out and wants to meet the 'handsome young man who captured our Hunter.' Her words not mine," Matt said.

Gavin blushed and nodded.

"We can do that," Hunter said, then looked at Gavin. "You'll love Rhea. She's awesome."

"I'll text you, Hunt, and we can arrange something," Matt said.

"Sounds like a plan," he replied, smiling as Matt was called away.

"How did the repairs go?" Ivan asked the group.

"We got everything done. Hunter just needs to restock now," AJ said. "I can start on the hall wall tomorrow."

"Has there been any word from David?" Owen asked.

"He's been in contact with Seth, who has sent people off to different places, but I don't know what they found. I'm hoping we'll be updated at dinner," Ivan told him.

Just then, the pub door opened, and a man came stumbling in.

Matt rushed over to help him. "Careful," he said, wrapping an arm around the man.

Gavin looked up and saw Adrian. He nudged Ivan, who looked to the door, jumped up, and ran to his side, wrapping an arm around him. He looked at Matt. "I've got him," Ivan said before he looked at the man. "What happened, Adrian?" he asked, leading him over to their table.

Adrian looked beyond tired, and his hair showed lots of white. He practically fell onto the chair. "There was a car accident. I stopped to help. A young child was badly hurt, but I fixed most of her injuries. Her father was unconscious and had a head injury. They were both lucky to be alive."

Matt stood to the side of the table, looking concerned. "Is there anything I can do? Shall I call an ambulance for your friend?"

"No thanks, Matt. We're gonna take Adrian home so he can rest," Owen said.

Matt nodded. "Phone me if you need anything."

"Will do, thanks, Matt," Hunter replied.

"Adrian, can I have your car keys and I'll drive you home? You shouldn't drive in your condition," Owen said softly.

Adrian nodded and handed them over.

"Come on, let's get you back," Ivan said, standing up.

"Let's all head off. Shell, Luke, we'll see you tomorrow," Taha added, standing up. And with that, all those who lived in the coven left, leaving a concerned-looking Matt watching Adrian go.

CHAPTER 62

Gavin sighed as their bedroom door closed. They arrived home and Louise ordered Adrian straight to bed while everyone else sat down for dinner.

Seth updated everyone on what was going on at the council offices. A full council meeting had been called and was still ongoing.

Ivan and Gavin updated everyone on their searches, and AJ told them he would start on the wall tomorrow.

Louise, Charlotte, Lissa, and Annie had all shopped for Spencer and Jack, buying clothes, bedroom things, and anything else they decided the boys needed. Jack protested it was too much, but everyone just ignored him.

But now it was just him and Hunter. He walked over to Hunter, who opened his arms and wrapped them around Gavin, before dipping his head and kissing him.

They finally pulled back and Hunter led Gavin to the sofa and sat down, Gavin sitting in his favourite place, on Hunter's lap, straddling him.

"I missed you today," Hunter told him.

Gavin smiled and mouthed, "Missed you." He then signed, "I brought you presents."

"You did?" Hunter asked in surprise.

Gavin nodded and looked at the coffee table. Dave had told him his deliveries had been taken up to his room for him. Gavin had been lucky that the items he brought had same-day delivery. He jumped up and pushed them closer to Hunter.

Hunter looked at the boxes in surprise, knowing the brands. "You replaced some of my things?"

Gavin nodded and looked a little nervous.

Hunter grabbed Gavin and pulled him into a quick kiss. "Thank you, my darling. Help me open them?"

Gavin nodded and they both opened the boxes. He'd brought Hunter new inks, a new sterilising machine, and a new tattoo machine.

Hunter looked at the machine and stroked it.

Gavin tapped his arm and waited for Hunter to look up before he signed. "Did I get the wrong one? You can change everything and get—,"

He stopped signing when Hunter grabbed his hands and pulled him into another kiss.

Hunter pulled back, smiling. "Everything you brought is perfect, my darling, and you will be the first person I use my new tattoo machine on. I'm guessing Taha helped you."

Gavin grinned. "I messaged Owen as I didn't have Taha's number. He sent me links to everything."

"I'll thank them both tomorrow. I can't believe I'll be back up and running so quickly." He pulled Gavin back onto his lap. "Thank you, sweetheart, for buying these for me. Have I told you lately how much I love you and how perfect you are?"

Gavin blushed.

"And you definitely need another shopping trip with Shelby."

Gavin gave a silent laugh and signed.

"You're going to drag Gabe along, as well?" Hunter asked.

Gavin nodded.

"That will be a fun trip. I might even come with you. We'll have to wait for him to come back, though," Hunter told him.

Gavin leant forward and kissed Hunter. How did he get so lucky? He couldn't wait for his tattoo tomorrow.

CHAPTER 63

"You really think other leaders are involved with this underground organisation?" Stole asked.

The meeting had broken up after the assassination attempt. Some delegates opted to stay in the meeting room, others returned to their office.

Stole had walked down to join them, to their surprise, Donald at his side.

"We honestly don't know. But we have all the information that we are slowly working through. We've stopped the last lot of kidnapped paranormal children from being shipped out of the country."

"Child trafficking?" Donald said with a growl. "Bad business. What can I do to help?"

Troy snorted and Donald glared at him. "Do you have something to say, Troy, don't think I haven't noticed you standing with everyone."

Troy laughed. "It's not as if you could miss me, is it Donny boy? These happen to be my friends, and I always help my friends."

"But what about family?" Donald practically demanded.

"Please, short of a DNA test, I can still believe we're not related," Troy shot out. "I refuse to have such a sourpuss in the family."

"I thought you were a loner," Sean said, grinning at him.

"I am. I have family scattered around, but..." He waved his hand in Donald's direction.

"I'm so messaging Ian and Dave later," Sean stage whispered.

Gabe snorted out a laugh. "Is there somewhere we can get food and then we can tell you both everything?"

"We can eat in the restaurant. We have two here, one just for the principal members and guests and one for the office workers." Donald said.

"Wow, elitist much?" Kayden commented.

"Maybe, but for the moment it will work in our favour as it means we have somewhere secure we can sit and talk," Bert said.

Gabe looked at the general. "Hopefully you're eating with us, as well. We would value your input."

The general nodded. "I will do, thank you."

Donald looked at the general, huffed, and walked off.

"He's an arse most of the time and more than one of us have wanted to punch him in the face, but his offer to help is genuine," Stole told them, shaking his head. He looked at Stefan. "You're right, for too long we have all worked independently and for our own good. We need to change."

"Then lead the way to food," Gabriel said.

~

Hunter, Taha, and Gavin walked into Area 51 the next morning, all carrying boxes containing the new equipment Gavin had brought him.

"Thanks for your help, Taha," Hunter said as his friend put the boxes down on his new worktop.

"No problem. I'll let you two sort all this out. I don't have any clients today, so I can catch up on everything I've been putting off."

"Good luck," Hunter said to him.

"Thanks," he replied, walking out of the room.

Gavin looked at Hunter.

"We have paperwork we need to keep up together, accounts to input onto our business spreadsheet, stock taking, deep cleaning, getting designs ready for clients, stuff like that," Hunter told him, opening a box.

They spent about twenty minutes unpacking everything, putting things away, and setting up other things.

"Perfect," Hunter said when they had finished. "Now I need to sterilise this room and get it ready so I can do your tattoo. Do you mind sitting in the kitchen for a bit?"

Gavin shook his head.

"Or you can come and see my room," Luke said from the doorway. "I have a couple of hours until my first client. Or we can go and get some cakes and then I'll show you my room when we get back."

Gavin nodded.

"Have fun, you two," Hunter said to them, pulling Gavin into his arms and kissing him.

"All right, break it up, you two," Luke said, laughing at them.

Gavin gave a silent laugh against Hunter's lips before pulling away.

Luke walked in and grabbed Gavin's arm. "Yes, I'm dragging you off before you two can start kissing again."

Hunter boomed out a laugh and Gavin gave a silent laugh and let Luke pull him out of the room.

With Gavin gone, Hunter sterilised his room and then prepared it for tattooing Gavin.

Hunter walked towards the kitchen, tying his hair up as he went.

He saw Gavin sitting with Taha and Luke, eating cake and laughing.

"I hope you brought me a cake," Hunter said.

Gavin looked up and grinned at Hunter. He gave a silent sigh. Hunter was gorgeous and all his. How had he gotten so lucky?

"Well, that's a look of love if ever I saw one," Luke commented, looking at Gavin.

Gavin nodded and made a heart with his hands.

"We love each other, what can I say?" Hunter said. "Ready for your tattoo?"

Gavin nodded and jumped up, grinning widely.

"We'll see you in a few hours," Hunter said to Luke and Taha and walked out of the kitchen with Gavin.

Gavin got settled as Hunter washed his hands and put his gloves on.

"So, I have the stencil ready. You still want this design?"

Gavin nodded, grinning.

Hunter suddenly looked uncertain. "Sweetheart, am I going to have an issue with your vampire side when I start working?"

Gavin thought for a moment and shook his head. He could keep his vampiric side under control. He loved Hunter with every fibre of his being, so there was no way his vampire side would hurt Hunter.

"Good, then let's get this party started."

THE VAMPIRE AND THE TATTOOIST

Hours later, Hunter gave a final wipe. "There, sweetheart, want to see?"

Gavin nodded.

Hunter passed the hand mirror to him, and Gavin got his first look.

He gave a silent gasp. It was even more perfect than the picture. He put the mirror down. "It's perfect," he signed.

"It really is," Hunter said. "Just like you." He rolled forward and kissed Gavin. "Love you," he said, pulling back.

"Love you," Gavin mouthed back. How lucky was he, a vampire, with his very own tattooist?

The End

ABOUT THE AUTHOR

I live in Hampshire in England, close to lots of lovely green spaces. I love coffee and can be found in coffee shops, drinking coffee and writing.

I am one of those weird people who writes their stories longhand, which is why it takes me so long to get my books out there.

When I am not writing I am keeping my lab entertained, playing ball games, or trying to teach her to count. She can now count to twenty and we're trying for twenty-five next.

I love to hear from my readers. You can find me on Facebook, Twitter and sometimes Instagram. Or drop me an email at ebroomauthor@gmail.com

Remember love is love. Be happy, and sparkle Broomies.

ALSO BY E. BROOM

The Fortuna Pack Series
The Wolves are Coming
https://mybook.to/TheWolves
The Dragons are Coming
https://mybook.to/TheDragons
The Unicorns are Coming
https://mybook.to/TheUnicorns
The Fortuna Coronations
https://mybook.to/TheCoronations
The Gods are Coming
https://mybook.to/TheGods

The Vampire and Series
The Vampire and the Librarian
https://mybook.to/VampandLib
The Vampire and the General
https://mybook.to/VampGen
The Vampire and the Witch
https://mybook.to/VampandWitch

The Paranormal Court Series
Darius
https://mybook.to/DariusTPC

The Cadenbury Town Series

The Crazy Bookshop
https://mybook.to/Crazybookshop
Where There's a Witch There's a Way
https://mybook.to/Wheretheresawitch
Double Wolf Dare You
https://mybook.to/Doublewolf
If It Ain't Broke Don't Fix It
https://mybook.to/Ifitaintbroke
You are my Sunshine
https://mybook.to/YouareMySunshine

The Fairy Brew

Clueless
https://mybook.to/Clueless

The Magic Around Us Series

The Eulogy
https://mybook.to/TheEulogy
The Haunting of Hatfield Manor

Rejection and Series

Rejection and Redemption
https://mybook.to/RejectandRedem

Contemporary

The Perfect Husband List
https://mybook.to/PerfectHusbandList

Printed in Great Britain
by Amazon